In the hall ~~women in~~ ~~past~~
them before confronting Trent.

She managed to keep her voice down. "Why did you blindside me?"

"I didn't tell you about my conversation with Judge Eaton-March because you were dealing with enough." Trent gestured toward her arm. "You'd been shot."

"You've crossed the line." Her voice shook with temper. "Why are you working so hard to have me removed from this case?"

"I'm trying to keep you safe." His words were raw with emotion.

Could she believe him? Amber searched his eyes. In their dark depths, she saw fear—for her.

Amber rubbed her forehead with three fingers of her right hand. "I'm a criminal prosecutor, Trent. Do you think this is the first time I've been threatened?"

Trent crossed his arms over his chest. "This is the first time you've been shot."

Dear Reader,

Have you ever felt as though the person you were with enjoyed being with you because of the way you made them look rather than because of your company?

That's how Trent made Amber feel. She'd given him her heart, thought he was The One. But their dates seemed more like networking opportunities than romance. After Trent proposed, Amber thought things would get better. She was wrong. She told him so when she returned his engagement ring.

It's been almost a year and a half, and now Trent's back, asking for a second chance at their happily-ever-after. But Amber's got a lot on her plate. Her sister Crystal, a homicide detective, and her sister Jade, a true-crime podcaster, are trying to solve their beloved aunt's cold-case homicide. Oh, and someone's trying to kill her.

Amber's not certain she has time to rekindle their romance—and she's not sure she wants to. Would you?

One quick note: Please excuse the liberties I took with my descriptions of the interior and exterior of the Columbus City Attorney's Office, the Franklin County Public Defenders Office, the Franklin County Common Pleas Court and the Ohio Reformatory for Women.

Thank you for taking a chance on my Justice Hunters trilogy. I hope you enjoy the stories.

Happy reading!

Patricia Sargeant

ABOVE THE LAW

PATRICIA SARGEANT

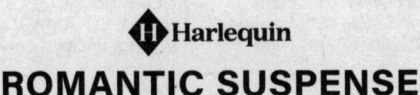

ROMANTIC SUSPENSE

MIX
Paper | Supporting responsible forestry
FSC® C021394

ROMANTIC SUSPENSE™

ISBN-13: 978-1-335-18504-4

Above the Law

Copyright © 2026 by Patricia Sargeant-Matthews

Harlequin Enterprises ULC
22 Adelaide St. West, 41st Floor
Toronto, Ontario M5H 4E3, Canada
www.Harlequin.com

HarperCollins Publishers
Macken House, 39/40 Mayor Street Upper,
Dublin 1, D01 C9W8, Ireland
www.HarperCollins.com

Printed in Lithuania

1 2 3 4 5 6 7 8 9 10 LIT 28 27 26 25

Nationally bestselling author **Patricia Sargeant** was drawn to write romance because she believes love is the greatest motivation. Her romantic suspense novels put ordinary people in extraordinary situations to have them find the Hero Inside. Her work has been reviewed in national publications such as *Publishers Weekly*, *USA TODAY*, *Kirkus Reviews*, *Suspense Magazine*, *Mystery Scene Magazine*, *Library Journal* and *RT Book Reviews*. For more information about Patricia and her work, visit patriciasargeant.com.

To my Dream Team:

* My sister, Bernadette, for giving me the dream.

* My husband, Michael, for supporting the dream.

* My brother Richard for believing in the dream.

* My brother Gideon for encouraging the dream.

And to Mom and Dad, always with love.

Chapter 1

Trent Mitchell hadn't changed. The realization was maddening—and somewhat comforting.

Right?

Wrong!

Not comforting. At all. Just maddening. Intensely maddening.

Amber Rashaad, assistant city prosecutor with the Columbus City Attorney's Office, glared at the public defender seated on the other side of the chunky rectangular maple wood table late Tuesday morning. Trent was representing the accused serial killer Maeve Rhoades, whose case Amber was prosecuting whether he liked it or not.

"I'm not recusing myself from this case, Trent." Amber gripped the ends of her black ballpoint pen with her fingertips. Her hands were stiff. Would they be frozen in this clawlike position forever?

Amber took a deep breath, drawing in the smell of commercial-grade disinfectant and a trace of Trent's cologne. The familiar sandalwood fragrance triggered an avalanche of memories she struggled to hold back.

Trent's request that they meet to discuss the case wasn't unusual. But she knew him. Their pending trial wasn't the true motive for this appointment. That's why Amber had reserved the small conference room. She didn't want Trent in her office. She didn't want him in her life. Yet here he was.

It was a miscarriage of justice that he looked even better today than he had the last time they'd seen each other one year, four months, one week and a day ago—not that she'd been counting the restless nights since he'd broken her heart.

His skin was a smooth brown with warm honey undertones. His full lips softened the effects of his sharp cheekbones and square, arrogant jaw. The intelligence in his calculating, almond-shaped ebony eyes had once excited her. She ignored her tripping pulse.

Trent sat back against the aging padded black cloth seat. "Amber, the key witness against my client is a homicide detective who happens to be your sister. Those optics are bad. The jury will hear that Columbus Division of Police Homicide Detective Crystal Rashaad apprehended the defendant who's now being prosecuted by Amber Rashaad."

"In addition to three charges of first-degree murder, your client has also been charged with assaulting and attempting to kidnap Crys." Amber was proud of how steady her hands were as she spread them above the table. Her pen didn't shake once. "You'd better believe Crys is an important witness."

Trent quirked one of his thick black arched eyebrows. A well-remembered affectation. "Will you be able to keep your personal animosity out of the courtroom? If not, I'm pretty sure your familial connection and your reaction to Maeve's alleged attack will draw the jury's sympathy. It could also be grounds for an appeal."

Was he actually using her family against her? Amber squelched a snort of disbelief. "Our case against Maeve

Rhoades is strong, but I hadn't realized you were already planning an appeal. I'm willing to consider a deal. Put one together and we'll reconvene at a later date." She stood to leave.

"Good try, Counselor." Trent called her bluff. "*You* may not think your sister being a key witness is a problem, but the jury might."

Amber sat again. She laid her pen on her unused writing tablet, resisting the urge to flex her fingers. "I'm not required to recuse myself from this matter. As you know, my office made the court aware of my familial relationship with the lead detective. The judge doesn't have an issue with it. If *you* have a problem with Crys being my key witness, then, by all means, *you* can recuse yourself."

After a two-month investigation, Amber's older sister had solved the case of serial killer Maeve Rhoades with the help of her temporary partner—now boyfriend—Ohio Bureau of Criminal Investigation Special Agent Lucas Gilchrist. Crys was a vital witness because she'd gone undercover to apprehend the suspect. She'd endangered her life to bring the former-security-guard-turned-vigilante-killer to justice. The risk her sister took was enough incentive for Amber to try the case. Trent would have to give Amber a rock-solid reason to recuse herself. She didn't think he had one.

Besides, Amber hadn't assigned herself to this matter. Her office had tapped her to prosecute Maeve in part because of Amber's reputation for being able to handle and win high-profile, complex trials. These victims were former board members of Dragon & Kelp, a life insurance company. One of the entity's principal owners, Roland Dragon, was a highly regarded, well-connected figure in the state.

Amber, Crys and their youngest sister, Jade, also believed Roland's company was connected to their aunt's
unsolved homicide.

"I'm aware Judge Eaton-March agreed with your office
assigning you to this case." Trent leaned into the table,
bringing his handsome face and hypnotic sandalwood-and-
soap scent closer to Amber. "I was copied on her response.
However, you should know this morning, I submitted a request for Judge Eaton-March to reconsider her decision."

Amber's lips parted in surprise. She told herself to count
to ten before replying. She made it to five. "You asked the
judge to reconsider her decision to allow me to stay on the
case? That was a bold move, Counselor. How did Judge
Eaton-March respond?"

"I haven't heard back from her yet." Trent watched
Amber as though trying to determine how angry he'd
made her.

Amber imagined there was smoke coming from her
ears. Would that give him a clue? "What's the real reason you don't want to face me in court?" Her wording
was deliberate.

A spark of humor brightened Trent's too-handsome
face. "It's not that I don't want to face you in court—"

"Then why are you wasting so much time, energy and
effort to have me removed from this case?" Amber leaned
back against her seat, wanting at least some distance between her and Trent's mesmerizing scent. "This meeting. Your appeal to the judge. Actions speak louder than
words, Trent."

The flash of recognition in his eyes told Amber he'd remembered her saying those same words to him one year,
four months, one week and a day ago. Her skin burned
with satisfaction.

A deep sigh raised his broad shoulders beneath his gun-metal-gray suit jacket. Amber's eyes lingered perhaps too long on the width of his chest. The man could make a worn bath towel look good, and he had. Amber briefly closed her eyes. She didn't need those images distracting her now. She forced herself to focus on Trent's words.

"As I said, I'm not afraid of facing you in court. And Maeve's not interested in a deal. She wants to go to trial."

Amber narrowed her eyes in silent warning. "Do you think my relationship with my sister will give me an unfair advantage in this case?"

Trent was shaking his head while Amber was still speaking. "No, you and Crys have too much integrity to do anything unethical."

Amber stacked her hands on top of her blank writing tablet and resisted being distracted by his flattery. "If you aren't questioning our integrity and you aren't afraid of going against me in court, what's the issue?"

Trent's dark eyes scanned her features as though refreshing his memory. "You mean besides our broken engagement?"

Amber smiled without humor. "There it is."

"Come on, Am." Trent let her hear his exasperation as they faced each other across the conference table. "Do you seriously expect me to believe our breakup isn't going to affect the way you approach this case? That you don't feel anything?"

"Oh, I feel something." Amber nodded. Her mass of wavy brown tresses swung around her diamond-shaped face and over her narrow shoulders. Her delicate cheekbones filled with an angry red blush. "Intense relief that we didn't make the spectacular mistake of getting married."

Ouch. That answered his question. She didn't seem willing to entertain his request for an appeal to her decision to end their engagement. At least not yet.

He gestured toward her. "So the sparkle in your eyes, the flush in your cheeks, the heat you're generating that's slowly burning the flesh from my bones—those things aren't residual anger from the way we ended things?"

That heat was keeping the late-spring chill in the cramped conference room at bay. Or maybe his reaction to her was the source of the warmth.

"Absolutely not." The look in her long-lidded, warm cocoa-brown eyes cooled. Her cranberry suit jacket brought out the gold undertones of her brown skin. "Those things— bright eyes, healthy color and warm blood—are the result of eight hours of sleep, regular exercise and a healthy diet."

Trent kept his grin in check. Oh, man, he'd missed her sarcasm. She hadn't usually directed it at him. The few times she had, it had been good-natured. Today, he wasn't getting those warm, fuzzy vibes. But he'd still missed her dry wit. And touching her.

Not willing to test his self-restraint, Trent folded his arms across his chest to keep from reaching for her. His eyes dropped again to her left ring finger. It was bare. Thank goodness.

Amber was even more poised and beautiful now than when she'd returned her engagement ring one year, four months, one week and a day ago. That was the last time he'd seen or spoken with her. The last time he'd felt his heart. He'd been trying to find a way back into her life ever since.

Judging by the virtual steam escaping through the crown of her head, asking her to recuse herself from the case because her sister had been the lead detective on the investigation hadn't been a smart strategy. But he didn't want their court appearance to be the first time they saw each other in more than a year. That wouldn't feel right, not when he'd ached so long to see her again. Trent swallowed the lump in his throat.

"I'm glad you're not holding on to any ill will." He tried to match her sarcasm. "Neither am I."

"I won't allow my personal feelings into the courtroom. I'll prosecute this case by the book, like any other one." Amber's eyes narrowed as she scanned his face. Trent had no idea what she was looking for. "It's strange that you should be assigned to this case."

"Luck of the draw." Trent hoped a friendly smile would mask the small lie.

Amber's expression remained cool. "I remember you once telling me you made your own luck."

Good memory. Trent's eyes swept the plain white walls that surrounded them. The conference room's harsh fluorescent lighting, thin gray carpeting and dingy, bare white walls weren't meant to encourage people to linger. Trent was sure that was one of the reasons Amber chose to meet with him here. She'd underestimated his determination to spend time with her.

Returning his attention to her, Trent revised his initial impression that Amber hadn't changed. She had. She was even more formidable now. "I could say it's a coincidence you were assigned to a case your sister investigated."

She reacted as though he hadn't spoken, but the increasing chill in her tone betrayed her. "It's understandable that, based on our past, neither of us would be comfortable facing each other in that courtroom. But if this meeting was your attempt to break the ice between us, you should have just said so."

"Be honest, Am." Trent held her eyes, trying his best to read her. "If I'd asked you to meet me for drinks after work—strictly business—would you have agreed?" He gave her a lopsided smile. The flash of interest in her eyes was brief, but enough to give him hope.

"No, I wouldn't have agreed to meet with you outside of work. But I would have taken your call. Strictly business." Her delivery was brisk, professional. It almost drained his hope. Almost.

"A phone call?" Trent waved a hand between them. "This thing between us—"

"There is nothing between us."

"Can't be addressed in a phone call. Did you really want the first time you saw me after more than a year to be in a courtroom during one of the most high-profile cases this city has ever had?"

"I wouldn't have had a problem with it." Amber managed to make a shrug look elegant and poised.

She was lying. Trent held fast to that belief with both fists.

"I would have." He caught her eyes for emphasis. "I've only been back a few months and Columbus is a large city. It's understandable we wouldn't have run into each other before this."

Not that he hadn't tried to orchestrate an opportunity for their paths to cross outside of work. But Amber seemed to have stopped attending professional association meetings and networking opportunities like the one where they'd met.

"Why *did* you return to Columbus?" Amber stiffened as though she was afraid she'd betrayed herself by asking that question.

She had. Perhaps his presence had affected her more than she wanted him to know.

"I appreciate your interest." Trent inclined his head in acknowledgment.

"No, I'm not in—"

"I came back to Columbus because this is my home."

Amber's winged eyebrow lifted. "You're from Los Angeles."

"This is my *adopted* home."

Amber folded her arms again. A slight shift in her posture indicated she'd also crossed her long, toned dancer's legs. "Is that really the reason you took a position with the public defender's office? This job seems incongruous after your glamorous careers with a prestigious law firm here and then the temporary assignment with an international nonprofit based in California." She shook her head. "I'm not buying it. What happened?"

Trent smiled. At least he had her attention. He lowered his voice to a little more than a whisper. "Why do you care?"

Her mocking smile disappeared. "I don't care. I'm just curious."

He'd take curiosity. It was close enough to "interested."

"Why do you think I applied for a position with the public defender's office?"

Amber lifted her rounded chin. "It would look good on your political résumé."

"It would." He nodded. "But so would a stint in the city prosecutor's office."

A soft rose color dusted her high cheekbones. "Then I suppose I should consider myself lucky that you applied to the public defender's office instead."

Trent cocked his head and feigned a frown. "Why, if as you say, there's nothing more between us?"

Amber's features stiffened. She rose from her seat with cool grace. "I'm not recusing myself from Maeve Rhoades's prosecution. If you don't have any additional *pertinent* arguments, then I suggest we wait for the judge's decision on your request that she reconsider my representing the city in this matter."

"Agreed." Trent stood. "Thank you for your time."

"Of course." She led him from the conference room and to the office's exit in silence. When he said goodbye, she responded without meeting his eyes.

Trent crossed to the elevator and pressed the down button. He wasn't concerned about Amber prosecuting Maeve's case. He knew the Rashaad sisters, Amber, Crys and Jade. Their integrity was unassailable. If Maeve chose to appeal her case based on Amber and Crys being sisters, he'd discuss her options with her at that time. He wasn't concerned about that now.

But he did wonder why Amber hadn't answered his question. Why did it matter to her where he worked? Despite her protests, did she still have feelings for him?

If so, how could he convince her to give him another chance?

That had been hard.

Understatement.

Amber strode back to her desk at the Columbus City Attorney's Office late Tuesday morning, straining to stay ahead of the memories that had been clamoring to escape.

Sitting across the small conference table from Trent, the man who'd broken her heart, for almost an hour had been painful. An explosion of emotions had overwhelmed her. Anger. Grief. Disappointment. And feelings she didn't want to name kept trying to make her reach for him.

She exhaled. Going against Trent in court would be easier. Right? They wouldn't be speaking to each other. They'd be addressing the judge and jury. They wouldn't even have to look at each other. Much.

Amber drew another deep breath. For now, she'd file that meeting in the back of her mind and bury herself in work. She'd dive into her cases and forget about Trent. That strategy hadn't worked the first time, though. In fact, it had had a tragic consequence, one she was still paying for and for which she'd never forgive herself.

Head down, thoughts in a dark space a million miles away, Amber stepped into her office.

"Hi, Am." Crys stood beside one of the two guest's chairs in front of her desk.

"Crys? What brings you here?" Amber wrapped her sister in a hug that lifted her spirits. "Are you all right?"

"I'm fine, but—"

Amber stepped back. "Good. I'm glad." She deposited her writing tablet, pen and case file on her desk. "You wouldn't believe who I was meeting with—"

Crys interrupted. "Am, sit down. I've got something to tell you."

Amber searched her older sister's features for some clue as to what was going on. Crys's long-lidded, coffee-colored eyes so like hers were dark and clouded with worry. Her heart-shaped lips were tight. Now that Amber was paying closer attention, she could feel Crys's tension stretching toward her, threatening to pull her in.

Her heart stopped, then leaped into her throat. "Oh, no. Is it J? Did something happen?"

Crys reached out to rub Amber's right arm. "J's fine, Am. This is about you. Have a seat."

Amber circled her desk. Her legs were weak with relief now that she knew their youngest sister was safe.

"I will if you'll have one, too." She didn't think she could handle Crys's penchant for pacing right now.

"Sure." Crys lowered her slender, five-foot-seven-inch frame into the cushioned gray-cloth-and-silver-metal chair.

Searching her sister's oval, golden-brown face, Amber sank into her padded black cloth chair. "All right. What's this about?"

Crys seemed to be struggling. Her voice was strained. "One of our confidential informants is serving time at the same prison where Maeve Rhoades is waiting for her trial. The CI got word to us that Maeve's looking for a contract killer. She's planning to put a hit out on you."

Tiny pinpricks landed all over Amber's face. A roaring sound like a building tidal wave rose in her ears. A barrage of questions exploded inside her brain. She needed a moment to collect them all.

Amber blinked. "One more time."

"I know it's a lot." Crys leaned forward, searching Amber's eyes. "According to our CI, Maeve Rhoades is trying to hire someone to kill you."

Was this really happening? Or was she in a nightmare that was getting progressively worse? First, her meeting with her ex-fiancé. Now, she was being told someone was masterminding her murder. Amber's eyes circled her office. It looked the same. When would her alarm sound to wake her?

She returned her attention to Crys. "Yes, that's quite a

bit." Her voice shook. "Who is this CI? How do we know we can trust her information?"

Crys's voice was brittle with strain. This was hard on her, too. "The detectives who've worked with her said she's given them solid information in the past. They don't think we should ignore her warning."

Ice filled Amber's chest and dropped into her gut. This had to be a nightmare. Under cover of her desk, Amber pinched her thigh just beneath the hem of her cranberry skirt. Hard. She didn't wake up.

"When did the CI tell the detectives about Maeve's plan?"

"This morning. They came to see me right after they spoke with her. The CI said she'd overheard Maeve asking another inmate for leads on anyone who'd accept a contract to...take out the prosecutor on her case." Crys watched Amber closely. It was as though her older sister was searching for cracks in her composure. Oh, those were coming.

Amber clenched her hands on her desk. She pushed past her burgeoning fear and tried to think. "Does the CI know whether Maeve has found anyone willing to...for this assignment?"

"She said Maeve hasn't found anyone yet, but she's still looking." Crys's voice was heavy with reluctance. There wasn't any doubt she didn't want to have this conversation. That made two of them.

Amber sat back against her chair. She wrapped her arms around her torso, trying in vain to get warm. "Threats against public officials have been in the news for years. I know that, but I still can't believe this is happening. I supposed it's one of those things you never think will happen to you."

"You should be shocked." Crys's words were sharp

with anger, outrage and fear. "This is shocking and threats against public officials who are simply doing their jobs are not something we should ever normalize."

"I agree." Amber looked away. She didn't want Crys to see the tears stinging her eyes as she struggled with her own anger, outrage and fear. "But Maeve's plan to have me killed doesn't make sense."

"What do you mean?"

Amber heard the frown in Crys's voice. As she stood to wander her cozy office, her eyes brushed against the framed photo of her, Crys and Jade, which stood beside her laptop. They were laughing as they posed for the picture Aunt Kendra had taken just months before her death.

Her office was a comfortable size, not too big, not too small. There was one large window to the left of her desk. The cream venetian blinds were open, welcoming the natural light from the late-spring sun.

Her framed University of Chicago law degree hung on the wall behind her desk. On the wall opposite her window, she'd displayed a sketch of her arguing a case in court. She'd gotten it from one of the local newspaper's courtroom sketch artists.

A tall, narrow dark wood bookcase faced her desk from across the room. It was crammed with law journals, the Ohio Constitution, Black's Law Dictionary and legal reference guides.

"How does killing me benefit her?" Amber paused to brush a finger over the potted African violet on her windowsill. "Even if her hired assassin gets to me, the most they'll accomplish is delaying the case. Our office would replace me."

"They obviously haven't thought that far in advance."

Crys's frustration was palpable in her tone. "I don't care if it makes sense or not. We need to keep you safe."

Amber turned to find Crys across the room, pacing the width of her office. "I appreciate that. Is there a plan in the works?" She was proud of how steady her voice sounded even as her muscles seemed to be trying to shake free of her body.

Crys gave a curt nod as she paced in front of the framed sketch. "We're assigning two officers to escort you to and from work until we're sure we've stopped Maeve and her contract killer."

Feeling another chill, Amber wrapped her arms around herself again. Someone wanted her dead because she was trying to do her job. She'd been assigned to prosecute a murderer who'd killed three people, leaving three families without fathers, mothers, sisters, brothers, wives, husbands. Nothing she could do would bring their loved ones back, but perhaps she could deliver the justice that could give them peace. And for that, someone wanted to kill her. She was having a hard time processing that.

"Thank you." She took another step forward. "I have my home security system, which alerts a service if it's activated."

Crys jerked her head toward the door behind her. "And the city attorney's office has security guards. You'll be safe, Am. I'll make sure of that."

Amber read the promise in her sister's eyes. "I know, Crys. Are there any ideas on how to stop Maeve?"

Crys crossed her arms over her chest. "We're going to have an undercover detective pose as a contract killer and make her believe he's fulfilled the assignment."

Amber stilled. "How will you do that?"

"I'm going to be your decoy."

Amber blinked. "One more time."

Chapter 2

"Trent! I missed you this morning." Barbi Howell, the newest law clerk in the Franklin County Public Defender's Office, intercepted Trent on his way to his desk late Tuesday morning. "How did the meeting with that prosecutor go?"

Barbi was about five-five with a full figure and deep red hair that framed her round, porcelain face. Her grayish-green, almond-shaped eyes spent too much time sending him inappropriate messages. At least her interruption gave him a reprieve from his thoughts.

It had been hard sitting across the conference table from the woman he'd never gotten over, the only woman he'd ever wanted to spend the rest of his life with. He hadn't given up on that wish. What did he need to do to make it a reality?

"It was productive." The lie struggled out of his dust-dry throat.

Trent circled the law clerk to continue navigating his way past the cubicles to his office. He sensed his department shadow following him.

"Is she going to recuse?" As usual, Barbi's breathy voice was too close, way too close.

Trent rounded his desk, putting the furniture between them. Her perfume made it past the barrier.

Barbi had been with the office for three weeks and had been making him uncomfortable since day one. At first, he'd thought the new employee wanted a mentor to help her learn the office culture. It hadn't taken long for Trent to realize he was being naive.

He should have put a stop to her behavior sooner. He should have made it clearer he wasn't interested in an office romance. His mistake had been in thinking that, if he ignored her overtures, Barbi would get the message and move on. Instead, she was ignoring his efforts to keep things between them professional.

Trent remained standing behind his desk. "Amber's agreed to wait for the judge's response to my request that she reconsider having the city attorney's office reassign the case."

"'Amber.' You say her name like you know her." Barbi scanned his features as though trying to read his thoughts. She continued when Trent didn't volunteer a response. "What's she like?"

Trent shoved his fists into the pockets of his black suit pants. *Caring, quirky, fascinating.* "Smart, well-prepared, capable. Amber Rashaad is an experienced prosecutor and dedicated to the law."

An ugly expression flashed over Barbi's face before she covered it. The look was so brief, Trent wondered if he'd imagined it.

"You sound like you're impressed by her." Barbi's smile was tight. "Just like everybody else. People talk about the great Amber Rashaad like she's some kind of rising star in the city attorney's office. Are the rumors true? Were the two of you a couple once?"

Her question was a reminder of how fast gossip traveled through Columbus's criminal justice system and that every member of the community was connected in some way. Case in point, the Rashaad sisters. Amber's elder sister was a homicide detective. Her younger sister was a crime beat reporter, or at least she used to be.

"I don't discuss my personal life at work." Trent spoke with a deliberate emphasis he hoped Barbi would catch on to. "What's important is focusing on doing the best possible job for our clients and in ensuring they get a fair trial."

"You make a good argument." A mocking smile hovered around Barbi's thin lips. "But will you be able to separate your personal and professional feelings when you're in the courtroom with your ex-fiancée?"

Trent felt a jolt of surprise. The criminal justice system grapevine was thorough. "Yes, I will." He looked at his watch, trying to nudge Barbi out of his office.

She ignored his hint. "I've never met her, but I've heard people describe her as being very beautiful." She cocked her head. "What do you think?"

Beautiful *is an understatement.*

Amber had a light that shined from inside. She was kind and generous, and loyal to the people she gave her heart to. The fact he'd taken her love for granted filled Trent with anger, disappointment and shame.

"I'm not objectifying opposing counsel. I'm also not interested in a workplace romance." Except when it came to Amber. If she were to give him another chance, he wouldn't just cross that line, he'd dance over it.

Barbi stepped back, spreading her arms. "You haven't said anything about my dress. It's my roommate's. She loaned it to me. She said it brings out my eyes."

The olive-green shade of the knee-length business dress

did make her eyes seem greener, but Trent wasn't going to give her conversation oxygen.

He turned his attention to his maple wood laminated desk and the piles of manila folders covering it. "You'll have to excuse me, Barbi. I need to get back to work. I have other cases to prepare in addition to Maeve Rhoades's."

"Do you think I'm as pretty as she is?" The law clerk blurted the question as though she'd gathered all her courage to ask it.

Trent's head snapped up. Her question caught him off guard. "Barbi, that's not an appropriate question. I've told you before, we're colleagues, not friends."

"Of course, Trent." Her blush clashed with her shoulder-length red hair. She gestured toward his black metal inbox on the right-hand corner of his desk. "I left those research notes you asked for. Do you want me to review them with you now?"

Trent shook his head. "No, thank you. If I have any questions, I'll put them in an email."

"Are you sure?" Barbi seemed to regroup. She ran her fingers through her bone-straight hair. "I don't mind going over it with you in person. I like spending time with you, Trent."

This was the opening he'd been waiting for—his opportunity to stop Barbi's flirtation in her tracks. He'd hoped it wouldn't get this far, but it had.

"Barbi, let me be clear. I'm not interested in an office relationship. Stop flirting with me." His tone was firm, his words unequivocal.

"Are you sure?"

"Very."

Barbi flashed a grin. "You don't know what you're missing."

Trent's temper stirred. This wasn't a joke. Not only were her advances unwelcomed, they could also damage his reputation in this office as well as later, if he pursued an elected position.

He crossed his arms over his chest and pinned her with a steely stare. "I'll make this easy for you. Stop flirting with me or I'll have you reassigned."

Barbi's smile disappeared without a trace. Her thin red eyebrows knitted. "Seriously? My flirting is just a little harmless fun."

"Not to me."

She looked confused. "Is there someone else? Is this because of Amber?"

"That doesn't matter."

Barbi's lips tightened. "All right. Fine. I want to work with you. So…no more flirting." She spun on the four-inch heels of her black pumps and marched out of his office.

Her words were reassuring. Her actions weren't. Trent had seen the glint in her eyes. He lowered himself into the gray-cloth padded seat behind his desk. He had the unsettling sense that Barbi thought his words were a challenge, as though he was playing hard to get. Trent closed his eyes briefly in frustration. He'd told her the consequences if she continued her harassment. He should clear his mind and focus on the other matters demanding his attention, like his heavy trial load and his reluctant ex-fiancée.

"I got your 911 text." Jade Rashaad crossed into Amber's home Tuesday afternoon. "What's going on?"

Amber locked the front door before leading her younger sister upstairs to her bedroom. Their steps tapped against the polished beechwood flooring. "I need your help talking sense into our sister and keeping her from making an epic mistake."

"An *epic* mistake? *Crys?*" Jade's incredulous laugh floated up the stairs behind Amber. "I don't think Crys has made *any* kind of mistake since elementary school, much less an epic one." She laughed again, seeming to enjoy her joke.

"Trust me. The possibility is imminent." Amber turned left and hurried down the hall to her bedroom where she'd left Crys. Her sister was still rifling through Amber's wardrobe, picking out an outfit for her amateur acting debut. *Urgh.*

Crys turned toward the door as Amber and Jade walked through it. Her eyes widened with pleased surprise. "Oh, good. You're here. You can help make Amber see reason."

Jade raised both hands, palms out in a stop motion. "Will someone please tell me what the—is going on?"

Amber held out her hand. The movement was a reflexive response to Jade's choice of words—or lack thereof.

Jade looked from Amber's open palm to her face. Confusion clouded her espresso-colored eyes and knitted her smooth brow. "I didn't say the actual word."

"It was implied." Amber wiggled her fingers until Jade pulled a quarter from her wallet and slapped it into her palm. "You carry actual quarters everywhere you go. That doesn't inspire confidence in your commitment to clean up your language."

Jade rolled her eyes. "You sent me a 911 text. Are you going to tell me what's happening or am I supposed to guess?"

Amber braced herself in front of her beechwood dressing table. The furniture piece sat on the edge of the sunlight streaming through the pearl-white venetian blinds covering the two large windows toward the back of her bedroom.

She swept her hand toward Crys. "Your sister wants to be an assassin's target."

"What?" The blood drained from Jade's golden-brown face. She shifted toward Crys. "Why?"

"I don't *want* to be a target." Crys dropped the hanger with Amber's caramel-colored pencil-slim skirt suit onto the queen-size bed and gestured toward Amber. "Did your sister tell you *she's* the actual alleged target?"

"What?" Jade turned back to Amber. "Enough already. What *exactly* is going on?"

"I'll tell you." Crys waved a hand toward the red-and-gold-quilt-covered mattress. "Take a seat."

Jade quirked an eyebrow. "That's rich, coming from you."

"This news isn't easy to hear." Crys waited for Jade to sit on the right-hand corner of the bed. She exhaled and spoke with care. "Luke and I received a credible tip from a confidential informant that Maeve Rhoades is trying to hire someone to kill Amber."

"No!" Jade sprang from the bed. Her tumble of ebony curves swung behind her slender shoulders as she turned her attention from Crys to Amber and back. Her eyes were wide with anger and simmered with outrage. Amber could practically see the smoke spilling from Jade's ears. "So *you're* taking Amber's place by pretending to be her, so the assassin targets *you* instead? And why should I help you talk her into this?"

Crys frowned. "Would you rather we let the assassin target her instead?"

Amber spread her arms. The lavender fragrances in the

plug-ins around her home weren't having their usual soothing effect. "I love you and want you to be safe."

Crys's eyes stretched wide with disbelief. "Ditto, but
I'm the homicide detective. It's *my* job to keep *you* safe."

Jade threw up her hands. "I agree with both of you. But
what am *I* supposed to do while you two battle for the role
of family protector?"

Amber caught her breath. All at once, she regretted
putting her little sister in the middle of her argument with
Crys. She hadn't considered that by doing so, she was putting Jade in a Sophie's Choice situation. Whose life was
she supposed to pick?

She stepped forward. "J, I'm sorry I contacted you. Crys
and I will come up with something. Don't worry about it."

Jade's eyes narrowed. Her voice was low and tense.
"You want me to leave? To act like none of this is happening?"

"Am shouldn't have texted you." Crys shot Amber an
impatient look. Amber ignored it.

Jade nodded, even as temper pulsed around her like an
invisible force field. "Okay. Sure." She took a stiff step toward the bedroom door before turning to lock eyes with
Amber. "I'm glad the two of you can figure this out because I don't think I could. I love you both very much. How
do I choose between the one who has real-world experience
with weapons and self-defense, and the one who doesn't?"

Amber stiffened, offended. "I know how to fight and
how to fire a gun."

Jade snorted. "Visiting a gun range once a month and
practicing a few self-defense moves in a gym isn't the
same as shooting at someone or taking a punch in the
real world."

Amber drew a deep breath of the lavender-scented air,

then slowly exhaled. "You're right. You've always been better at thinking things through rationally and explaining it so we can see the bigger picture."

"That's what makes her such a good investigative reporter." Crys's pride threaded through her words.

"I'm sure that's why *Capital Daily* laid me off." Jade used air quotes around the last three words. Seeming to shrug off her melancholy, she turned to Crys. "What's the plan? Are you really going to be Amber's decoy for an assassin?"

In the brief, tense silence, Amber sensed Crys gathering her thoughts.

"We have a plan." Crys strode toward them at the front of the bedroom. "One of the CI's handlers is going to pose as a hit man for hire. He'll meet with Maeve to confirm the details of the hit and accept the contract. Then we'll fake my—or rather Amber's—death, take photos of the corpse and give those photos to Maeve as proof the contract has been completed."

Amber shivered. The thought that someone in prison wanted her dead so badly they'd find a way to hire someone on the outside to kill her was sickening enough. The idea that her sister's pretending to be her corpse was the only way to ensure her safety could make her lose her mind.

Jade groaned. "Oh, my gosh. The image of you pretending to be Amber's dead body is going to keep me up for weeks, maybe months."

"Me, too." Amber searched Crys's eyes. "Is there any other way? Something else we can do to prevent Maeve from getting her way?"

Crys shook her head. "This is the quickest, safest way

we could think of. We've used this play plenty of times before and it's always worked."

Jade sent Amber a concerned look before turning back to Crys. "So how will this work?"

Crys crossed her arms under her chest. "The undercover detective will meet with Maeve tomorrow to accept the contract. Once she makes the payment, we'll add murder for hire to her other charges. Letting Maeve know people are watching her and that her situation can get a lot worse will deter her from pursuing other contract killings."

"All right." Amber hoped she appeared more confident than she felt. She scoured her mind for even a hint of danger in Crys's plan. "It doesn't sound too risky. You should be safe just posing as me for some photos."

"I'll be fine." Crys dropped her arms. "We'll need you tomorrow, though, Am. We have to take surveillance photos of you walking to the courthouse to help convince Maeve that our fake hit man has been tracking you and is serious about earning the contract."

"One more thing." Amber shared a look with Crys and Jade. "Does Trent know about this?"

"Trent Mitchell?" Crys frowned at Jade before turning back to Amber. "Why?"

Amber crossed her arms under her chest. "He's Maeve's lawyer."

Jade's winged ebony eyebrows launched themselves toward her hairline. "Trent Mitchell is your opposing counsel?"

Amber shook her head. "We have a lot to talk about."

Jade blinked. "Yeah, we do."

Amber led them out of her bedroom. "I'll make some tea."

* * *

Someone wants me dead.

"Am, I know this is hard, but act natural." Crys's voice came through the wireless earbud she'd given Amber for the surveillance photo staging Wednesday morning. "Pretend this is any other morning when your workday starts at court."

Amber guided her ruby-red four-door Toyota Camry into the Franklin County Common Pleas Court parking lot. Her hands trembled. Her palms were damp. "Except *this* particular morning, an undercover detective is taking pictures of me to convince a serial murderer to hire him to kill me."

"We're all playing a part." Crys's voice was comforting in her ear. Somewhat. "Maeve hasn't hired a gunman—"

"To our knowledge." Amber turned her sedan into a parking space toward the rear of the lot and turned off the engine.

Crys continued as though Amber hadn't spoken. "In addition to the undercover detective, Luke and I are nearby—"

Amber interrupted. "You should be careful, too. Both of you."

"And you're wearing a vest." Crys's voice was calm. Too calm. It was a tell. Her sister was more concerned about this operation than she wanted to say.

Tremendous.

Amber's sweaty, shaky right hand struggled to pull her key from the ignition before dropping it into her oversize cranberry-colored faux leather purse. Clasping her unsteady fists in her lap above her sapphire skirt, she took a moment to settle her nerves. The bulletproof vest Crys referred to felt alien and awkward beneath her suit. It also was heavier than she'd expected.

The courthouse's rear entrance was maybe fifty yards from her sedan at most. It just seemed farther. Would her quaking knees support her long enough to get inside? There was only one way to find out.

Deep breath. Her wary eyes swept the asphalt lot. Another deep breath. It wasn't yet 8:00 a.m. Still, the parking lot was congested. A couple dozen people—lawyers, detectives, police officers, court personnel and civilians—meandered, strolled or hurried toward the courthouse entrance. On the concrete sidewalk beyond the fenced-in area, a score or more pedestrians strode to their jobs in the nearby buildings.

What effect would all these people have on their plan—good, bad or none at all? Were they in danger? Were any of them the shooter? How could she be certain the confidential informant was correct about Maeve not yet hiring an assassin?

Why hadn't she raised any of these questions last night?

"By stepping out of my car, I could be putting other people in danger." Amber hadn't realized she'd spoken until Crys responded.

"There are armed guards positioned on the grounds and the roofs surrounding the courthouse. We haven't received reports of anyone nearby who shouldn't be here."

Amber nodded. "All right. I'm coming out."

"Okay, everyone, we're moving." Crys's voice was firm and commanding. "Stay alert."

That was her cue. Amber took a breath and squared her shoulders. She swung her purse strap onto her left shoulder, then pulled her hair free from under it. She grabbed her dark gray briefcase before emerging from her car.

The air felt swollen with the remnants of morning dew. Straightening her spine, Amber started forward. The heels of her two-inch sapphire pumps provided sound effects for her steady progress toward the courthouse. Amber hoped the undercover detective who'd been cast in the role of assassin-for-hire was getting good pictures. She wanted those images to show her as confident and strong.

Someone wants me dead. I won't make killing me easy for them.

"You're doing great, Am." Crys's encouragement was tinged with a hint of tension.

Amber took comfort in knowing her sister was watching out for her. She stood a little straighter and lengthened her stride. She was almost halfway to her destination. Her surveillance took in the petite, curvy woman and tall, thin man to her left, and the older woman to her right who was half jogging through the parking lot. What was her hurry? So far, so—

The first pop made her flinch. Amber wobbled as she spun toward the sound behind and to her left.

"Shots fired! Shots fired!" Crys's exclamation rang out through her earbud as a second pop sounded. Her voice grew louder. "Everybody down!"

The third pop registered before the echoes of the second had faded, yanking her attention to a white man about two yards from her. He was dressed in a gray denim jacket and dark blue jeans. It was the undercover detective, Griffin Blaze. Crys had sent her his photo that morning. His camera fell from his hands as he crumpled to his knees.

No! No! No!

A fourth pop—or was it the fifth? Someone or something pinched Amber's arm. She ignored the sting as she raced toward the fallen man. Her breath came in hitches.

She couldn't let him be trampled by the panicked crowd. Where had all these people come from?

She shoved her way through the human stampede. Anger and fear thickened her voice. "Let me pass. Move. Please."

"Am, where are you?" Crys's tone was sharp.

"I'm here!" She pushed past the handful of stragglers in the lot and finally reached the detective.

She tossed her handbag and briefcase aside and hunkered down to drag him between two parked cars and away from the mob.

"Amber?" Crys snapped.

"I'm all right." She panted as she applied pressure to the wound in Griff's shoulder. There was so much blood. Too much blood.

Now is not the time to panic.

"Who has eyes on the shooter?" That was Luke, coldly efficient.

A cacophony of negatives responded.

"Am, I need your location." Her sister was frustrated and impatient.

Frantic, Amber looked around. "Near the east gate, halfway across the lot. I'm between a blue sedan and a gray SUV. Crys, Griff's been shot. There's a lot of blood. He needs help."

"Officer down." Crys was breathless as though she was already moving. She called for emergency services, providing their location on the run.

Amber watched the detective's blood seep between her fingers. "Crys, be careful. You, too, Luke."

Luke sounded as though he was running also. "Does anyone have eyes on the sniper?" The answer again was a chorus of nos.

She was pinned down. Amber gritted her teeth.

Crys appeared on Amber's right followed closely by Luke as though the two were tethered together.

Her sister reached over and braced Amber's left arm. "Am, you're hit."

Amber inclined her head toward her bloody hands. "That's not my blood. It's—"

Crys interrupted. "Your shoulder."

Amber looked to her left. The shoulder of her sapphire jacket was stained purple with blood. That's when the pain started.

Chapter 3

"**O**fficers canvassed the area." Crys walked with Amber back to the hospital's emergency room lobby late Wednesday morning. "No one saw anything."

Amber tried to ignore her wound, throbbing beneath the sleeve of her sapphire jacket. Both her jacket and her pale blue shell blouse were stained with her blood and the undercover detective's. Amber was anxious to throw away the clothing as soon as she got home.

"That's not surprising." She took shallow breaths to minimize the sharp notes of cleaners, disinfectants and illnesses. She didn't like hospitals, not any part of them. "People were running for their lives. They weren't thinking about collecting details for police reports. I couldn't describe the people I ran past."

"I know." Crys sighed. "It's still disappointing."

"Even if they did see something, they probably aren't in any state to connect it to the shooting." Amber understood the situation from both sides. Crys needed eyewit-· ness accounts to help make an arrest. But even firsthand reports could be faulty, especially in stressful situations.

Amber had been grateful to have Crys with her in the exam room while the nurse had cleaned and stitched her wound. She'd been fortunate. The bullet had grazed her upper arm as she'd turned toward the sound of the gunshot. The nurse had speculated that she might not have a scar, at least not a noticeable one. That good news had eased Amber's anxiety. She wasn't keen on the idea of carrying a memento from this horrible day. The sooner this experience faded from her memory, the better.

The undercover detective wasn't as lucky. Griff had been struck twice, once in his arm and once in the back of his shoulder. Thankfully, neither bullet had struck a major artery. The one that caught his arm had passed through. A nurse practitioner had removed the one that had lodged in his shoulder.

Griff would have to wear a cast for a few weeks, but he'd make a full recovery. More good news, although it didn't relieve Amber's guilt. The only reason Griff had been in the courthouse parking lot earlier that morning was to help protect her. For his bravery, he got two bullets and weeks of recovery. She wore her guilt like a sodden jacket on her shoulders.

Crys's sigh was one-quarter resignation, three-quarters frustration. "Officers gave the witnesses my number to call in case they think of something later."

"I'll let you know if I remember anything, too." Amber searched her mind for any scrap of information that might help her sister find the monster who'd shot her and the detective.

Amber had turned toward the popping sounds. There'd been four or five of them. She'd seen the detective drop the camera, grab his arm and crumple to his knees. She'd smelled the warm asphalt covering the parking lot, the bitter exhaust fumes from the street and the stench of panic surrounding her, including her own. She'd felt the bodies colliding against her as she'd rushed to the detective's aid. She'd tasted her own fear as they'd waited for help.

"The shooter's smart." Crys interrupted her thoughts. Her voice was rough with irritation and impatience. "Officers checked the roofs of the nearby buildings. Nothing. Not even shell casings. They managed to get on and off the roof without being seen."

"They took the time to clean up? Isn't that risky?" Amber tightened her grip on the briefcase in her right hand.

Her purse felt awkward on her right shoulder, but her left arm was too sore from the stitches to bear its weight. Crys had offered to carry her bags, but Amber was able to manage with the minor adjustment.

"Very risky." Crys's words were tight. "It would've caused a delay and given us the chance to run into them as they were escaping. They must have picked a great hiding spot."

"Which implies they were familiar with the building. Maybe they worked there." Amber was only half paying attention to her surroundings. The hospital's walls were bright white, reflecting back the ceiling's fluorescent lights. Gray speckles dotted the shiny white floor tiles. "If we could pinpoint which of the buildings in that area they used, it could narrow down our suspects."

Crys grunted. "I know."

"Let's confront the elephant in the room." Amber stopped, turning to Crys on her left. "The CI said Maeve hasn't hired an assassin yet. Was she mistaken? Or does someone else want me dead?"

Crys laid gentle hands on Amber's shoulders. "Luke and Trent are speaking with the CI and Maeve now. We're going to get to the bottom of this."

Amber stiffened. "Trent?"

"Yeah. You know we can't speak with Maeve without her attorney." Crys gave her healthy right shoulder a comforting squeeze before continuing down the hallway. "On a positive note, we have the bullet from Griff's shoulder, which will help us identify the weapon."

"That poor man." Amber kept up with Crys. "I hope he makes a quick—and complete—recovery."

"So do I." Crys turned right out of the hallway, pushing open the door to the lobby. "In the meantime, I want to introduce you to your protective detail."

Amber followed the direction of Crys's eyes. There were dozens of people in the hospital waiting area, including police officers in standard navy-blue, button-up shirts and matching pants. Two of the officers, a man and a woman, returned her steady regard. Amber recognized one of them, Paul Ciero.

She'd worked with Paul on a couple of cases at the start of her career three years ago. She hadn't had any matters involving him in recent months, but she often saw him at the courthouse. He was tall, perhaps a little over six feet, and physically fit. He wore his thick, straight, dark brown hair very short. Almond-shaped dark brown eyes smiled at her from his blunt tan features.

She'd seen the other officer at the courthouse, too, but she'd never worked a case with her. The woman was a few inches shorter than Paul and slim. Amber stopped beside Crys and waited for her sister to make the introductions.

Crys gestured toward Paul first. "Officer Paul Ciero and Officer Tawnia Dwyer, this is Amber Rashaad. She's a prosecutor with the Columbus City Attorney's Office."

Paul offered Amber his right hand. His warm smile revealed the dimple in his left cheek. "Amber and I go way back. I was one of the arresting officers on her first case."

"How are you, Paul?" Amber released his hand.

"Good." He shrugged his broad shoulders. He'd once mentioned playing defensive tackle for the University of Cincinnati's football team. He looked like he could still suit up.

Amber shook hands with Tawnia. "Officer Dwyer, it's nice to meet you."

"Tawnia, please." The other woman gave her hand a comforting squeeze before releasing it. Her smile brightened her cornflower-blue eyes. "It might be easier if we're all on a first-name basis." She waved a pale, slender hand between Crys and Amber. "You're sisters?"

"Yes." Crys nodded.

Tawnia chuckled. "The family resemblance is really strong."

Paul's warm baritone reclaimed Amber's attention. "I'm sorry about these threats. You're one of the nicest people I know. It's hard to imagine someone wanting to hurt you."

Amber felt comforted by his words. "I'm glad you accepted this assignment. Thank you. It will help to have someone I know nearby."

"Don't worry." Paul's dark eyes brightened. "Tawnia and I will keep you safe."

Tawnia had gathered her shoulder-length, bone-straight red hair into a black scrunchy at the nape of her neck. "Paul and I go way back, too. We served in the same army unit in South Korea."

Crys's eyes widened with surprise and admiration. "Thank you both for your service. How long have you been partners?"

Tawnia glanced at Paul before answering. "We've been

assigned together since January when his previous part-ner retired. But the transition was easy since we already had history."

Amber shared a look between the two officers. "It makes me feel even more secure that the two of you know each other so well. Thank you."

"We don't want you feeling too comfortable." Crys gave her a pointed look. "We want you to be on the alert."

"I promise I will be." Amber adjusted her cranberry purse on her shoulder.

Crys turned her attention back to Paul and Tawnia. "I'm taking Amber home. Your detail starts tomorrow morning. You're picking up Amber at seven. Stay with her during the day, then take her home in the evening. You have my contact. Call if you have any questions. I appreciate your help with this."

"Sure." Paul flashed Amber another bright smile. "See you tomorrow."

"Of course." Tawnia looked from Amber to Crys and back. "We'll see you bright and early. Stay safe."

"Thank you both." Amber watched them disappear be-yond the hospital doors. "I hate the idea of putting other people at risk. Paul and Tawnia are putting themselves in danger because of me."

"Not because of you." Crys's tone was final. "Because of a stalker."

Amber drew her attention from the hospital's exit to her sister. "You mean an assassin. That's who's coming after me."

Crys flinched. "I'd rather not use that term in connec-tion with you."

"We've got to stop this person." Amber wrapped her

arms around her waist. "Even if it weren't my fault, I couldn't live with myself if anyone else was hurt."

Amber found Crys and Jade on the porch of her cottage-style home late Wednesday afternoon. Their expressions warned her that her day wasn't going to get any better.

Crys and Amber had told Jade about the shooting, Amber's treatment at the hospital's emergency room and her security detail. By now, she knew everything they did, which admittedly wasn't much.

Amber pulled her front door wider, inviting her sisters in. A warm breeze followed them, sending the scents of cut grass, new foliage and spring sunshine to join their dark cloud.

"This doesn't feel like our usual Wednesday Sisters Dinner Night. It looks like we need to talk." Amber steadied her knees and straightened her spine. She had her sisters and a security detail. She could handle this.

"We do." Crys led Jade into Amber's home. Her lips were tight. Her eyes were grim.

Jade paused in front of Amber, taking her right hand. "How're you?" Her eyes looked her over as though she didn't trust Amber to tell the truth.

She couldn't fib with Jade looking her in the eye. "I'm still a little shaken. I keep telling myself to think about something else, like the flood of cases on my calendar. But this morning's shooting keeps replaying in my head."

Crys had brought Amber straight home from the emergency room. Before leaving, she'd searched every imaginable hiding spot inside and outside the house. Between Crys's reconnaissance and Amber's state-of-the-art home alarm system, which connected to a security company with a fast response time, Amber had felt safer. She hadn't been able to concentrate, though. She'd read the opening paragraph of her legal brief on another matter over and over and over again. She still couldn't make it make sense, though.

Jade's eyes softened. "You suffered a trauma and have the wound to prove it." She glanced at her shoulder, then seemed to blink back tears. "But you're not alone, Am. Crys and I are here for you, whatever you need." She squeezed Amber's hand briefly before following Crys into the living room.

No, she wasn't alone, not as long as she had her sisters. There was a time she'd forgotten how valuable their relationship was, how necessary like air. It had taken months for her to come to her senses. She'd never make that mistake again. Never.

Amber locked her front door and straightened her shoulders before joining her family. Crys was already pacing the width of the room at the opposite end from her. Jade was seated in the near-right corner of the slim ivory faux leather sofa. Her eyes were narrowed in thought as she stared at the gray-and-tan-stone fireplace opposite her.

"What's happened?" Amber sat in the matching soft ivory armchair.

Crys turned to walk the length of the room. She strode past the fireplace, stopping in front of the collection of potted leafy plants sitting on the bay window's maple wood sill. "We had another detective pretend to be a gunman for hire. When Maeve met with him, she claimed to have no idea what he was talking about. She didn't take the bait. Said she'd never tried to contact a hit man for hire."

Amber's lips parted in shock. "The CI said she'd heard Maeve ask another inmate for a lead on a contract killer."

"Who do you believe, Maeve or the CI?" Jade's eyes were on Crys. Her question was edged with frost.

Crys hooked her hands on her slim hips above her olive-green denim pants. "I wasn't there. Luke and Trent watched the exchange on one of the security cameras. They said Maeve was surprised by the undercover detective's offer. They think she's telling the truth."

Amber felt a spark of impatience. "Of course Trent's going to say he trusts his client."

Crys spoke over her shoulder. "I trust Luke's judgment."

Amber sighed. "Me, too."

"Me, three." Jade's fingertips drummed a muted rhythm on the faux leather sofa's arm.

"Do you think the CI lied?" The possibility was chilling. Amber looked from Crys to Jade and back. "What motive would she have to cause trouble for Maeve?"

"Luke's looking into that." Crys blew a frustrated breath. "But the detectives vouched for their CI."

"Maybe her credibility can be bought." Jade spoke slowly as though the thought was forming as she spoke it.

Her words forced a chill down Amber's spine.

"Maybe." Crys's tone was grim. "More bad news— since Maeve didn't take the bait, the city attorney's office has canceled your protective detail. They said if the stalking isn't connected to the case, then it's not a work-related threat and they can't cover the cost."

Jade snorted. "Can't? Or won't? The threat is real whether it's work-related or not. Does the city know Am and one of its undercover detectives were shot?"

"Yes. They still won't budge." Crys resumed her pacing. "Am, you'll stay with me until we catch whoever's targeting you."

Amber had known Crys would say that. "I'm not leading a murderer to your door. That shooter doesn't care who they hurt. They didn't have any reservations about shooting at me through a crowded parking lot and sidewalk."

She ran a few rough budget calculations in her mind. Could she afford security on her own, at least for a little while? The short answer was no way.

Crys traveled back across the room, walking the width of the space between the living room and the entrance to Amber's formal dining room. "That's exactly why you shouldn't be alone. I'm not just your sister. I'm a detective. I can keep you safe."

"Absolutely not." Amber stood and circled her armchair. She faced Crys, gripping the chair's back to help steady her legs. "I'm not saying that I'm not scared. I'm not an idiot. I realize how dangerous this situation is. But I'm not going to use my sister as a shield. I'd lose my mind if anything happened to you." She looked at Jade. "To either of you."

"And we'd lose our minds if anything happened to you." Crys gestured from herself to Jade. She scowled at her youngest sister. "Back me up."

"Absolutely. That goes without saying. But, Crys, Am has a point." Jade pushed herself to her feet, crossing to stand in front of the fireplace. "Thanks to you, Am and I each have a gun we know how to use and one of the top home security systems. Am, I'm not worried about your safety while you're in the house. I'm worried about keeping you safe when you leave it."

Crys turned back to Amber. "That's a good point."

Amber shook her head. "I can drive myself to work. For now, we need to focus on next steps instead of arguing among ourselves regarding who gets to put themselves in danger to protect me."

Jade ignored Crys and Amber, turning her back to the room and staring into the cold fireplace. She did that when she was working through a problem. Finally, she broke her silence. "We need to minimize the amount of time you're outside and vulnerable like you were this morning in the courthouse parking lot."

Amber flinched at the reference to the site of the shooting. She didn't know how much longer she was going to have that reaction; probably quite a while.

She tightened her grip on her chair's back. "I'll be more aware in the future."

"The future starts now." Crys's voice was dry.

"I have a better idea." Jade faced her. "I'll be your chauffeur."

Amber blinked. "One more time."

"You heard me." Jade crossed her arms over her plain white long-sleeved T-shirt, which she'd coupled with faded midnight-blue denim shorts that extended halfway to her knees. "I'll pick you up to take you to work in the mornings, then bring you home at the end of the day. Door-to-door service."

"Great idea." Crys sounded as though a weight had been removed from her shoulders.

"It's a horrible idea." Amber scowled from Crys to Jade. "First, it's not necessary. Second, it will eat two hours of your day every day. You can't afford to lose that kind of time while you're building your business. Thank you for the offer, though."

"Then *I'll* drive you to and from work." Crys held her hand up, palm out, to forestall Amber's protest. "My department is close to your office. It won't be out of my way."

Amber spread her arms. "Your schedule is unpredictable. What if you get a lead in one of your other cases? Or for this case? Are you going to tell your new boss that you need to put the lead on hold while you take your sister home? I won't let you embarrass yourself like that."

Crys's eyes popped wide. "I wouldn't be——"

The chime of her front doorbell was a welcome interruption. Amber eased her nails from her armchair. "Excuse me a moment."

She turned toward her door and sensed her sisters following her. This was one of the reasons she couldn't move in with them or have either of them stay with her. Their constant shadowing of her would put a strain on their relationship. Taking a breath, Amber checked the peephole.

You've got to be kidding.

She glanced at her sisters, then shook her head. Was there no bottom to this day?

Jade's eyes were clouded with confusion. "Who's there?"

Crys tensed in alarm. "Is it a stranger?" She started to push Amber away from the entrance.

"No, no. I've got this." Amber unlocked the door and pulled it open. "Trent. How can I help you?" She ignored the muted gasps behind her.

"Are you serious?" Trent's eyes widened. His voice was strained. "I heard about the shooting. Are you all——" He seemed to finally notice her sisters standing almost on top of her. "Crys. J. It's good to see you again."

"Is it, though?" Jade's voice was cool and mocking.

She had her answer: No, there was no bottom to this day.

Swallowing a sigh, Amber stepped back. "Why don't you join us?"

Trent looked as dubious as she felt.

Whoever had coined the phrase "Hell hath no fury like a woman scorned" had never met the Rashaad sisters. The saying should be revised to "Hell hath no fury like a wronged woman and her two very protective sisters."

Trent crossed Amber's threshold and entered one of his nightmares. He'd realized long ago that he'd never regain Amber's trust without proving to her sisters he'd learned from his mistakes. He'd thought he'd have more time to prepare for this reunion, though. He'd been wrong.

He followed Crys and Jade into Amber's living room. The temperature in her home dropped five degrees with each step.

Amber's home teased him with her lavender scent, evoking memories that caused Trent's heart to ache. Love, laughter and a partner who'd inspired him to reach for his dreams. Trent clenched his fists to keep from rubbing his chest.

His eyes roamed the bright midsized room. It was a disconcerting mixture of new and familiar. She still had her small forest of potted plants on the windowsill facing the front of the house. The leafy collection seemed to revel in the pool of late-afternoon sun spilling through the half-open pearl-white venetian blinds that covered the large bay maple wood window. He remembered her ivory faux leather sofa and matching armchair, the glass-and-sterling silver rectangular coffee table. But the collection of seven black-and-red pencil sketches of cityscapes that hung on the room's three walls were new. So was the tall, wide beechwood bookcase on the edge of the room.

Trent paused beside Amber's fireplace. His hungry eyes searched the collection of framed photos on the mantel for any sign she still thought of him. He recalled the images of Amber and her sisters as they matured from mischievous girls to confident women. They were arranged with pictures of her mother, father and Aunt Kendra. But there were no photos of the two of them; no photos of him. Trent swallowed the lump of regret that threatened to choke him.

"Have a seat." Jade's words were more command than invitation. Her sharp eyes drilled holes in his head as she tried to read his thoughts.

Trent glanced at Amber before settling into the far-right corner of the sofa closest to the armchair.

"Thank you." He found and held Amber's eyes, ignoring the distance he saw in them. "I'm so sorry I didn't get here sooner. How are you?" His eyes skimmed over her dancer's figure in a loose-fitting bronze blouse and navy shorts that showcased her long, well-toned legs.

Luke had told him Amber had been shot in the upper arm. His first instinct had been to race to Grant Memorial Hospital. But Luke had reassured him Amber wasn't alone. Crys was with her. To keep her safe, they needed to take the shooter into custody—the sooner, the better.

Amber took the armchair beside him. "There's no need to apologize. I wasn't expecting to see you."

That hurt. Trent didn't want to have this conversation in front of her sisters. But if they didn't care, he wouldn't, either. "We're not together now, but I still care about you, Am. How are you? Is there anything I can get for you?"

Amber shook her head. The thick, heavy mass of wavy dark brown tresses shimmied behind her slender shoulders, seeming to call for his touch. "No, I don't need anything. I'm fine."

Liar. Trent kept the thought to himself. "Maeve denies trying to hire a someone to…hurt…you. Since we don't have proof linking the attack against you to one of your cases, the city won't provide security for you."

"Crys told me." Amber nodded toward the other end of the room where Crys was pacing.

The delicate floral pattern of Crys's pale pink blouse could make you forget she carried a gun. The intense expression in her dark eyes was a little less hostile than Jade's. Trent wondered what exactly Amber had told her sisters about their breakup. He couldn't fault either of them for their antagonism. He'd taken their sister for granted. He wanted another chance to be the man she deserved. Would they stand in his way?

Trent focused on Amber. "I believe Maeve, but I still think that attack is connected to her case. Maybe you should turn it over to someone else."

Amber was shaking her head before he'd finished his argument. "If the attack isn't connected to the case, assigning a new prosecutor won't make any difference. However, if the two *are* connected, the danger won't go away with my recusal. I'll be putting another prosecutor in jeopardy. That's not who I am. Why am I not surprised you don't realize that?"

Trent rose from the sofa and strode across the room to the fireplace. He shoved his hands into the pockets of his slate-gray slacks and stared blindly into the cold dark pit. "I don't want to put anyone in danger, either. I'm just trying to keep you safe."

"You don't have to worry about me. I've come up with a new plan to take care of myself." Amber's cool tones tried to push him away.

Trent stood firm. This time, he wasn't leaving.

"That's not true." Jade's interruption drew his attention.

He narrowed his eyes at the crime beat reporter. "What are you saying?"

Jade's eyes again tried to burrow into his mind. "We need to find a place where Am will be safe until the shooter's in custody. She doesn't want to stay with us because she's afraid she'll be putting us in danger."

Crys interrupted. "We also need a plan to get her safely to and from work."

"I can provide both." Trent didn't need to think about his offer. Amber's safety was his priority, and this was the best way for him to help her. "I bought a condo in a building downtown. It has excellent security. Key card access only to the garage and rear entrance. Two security guards on duty twenty-four hours per day every day. Security cameras in the lobby, and at all entrances and exits. I can also take you to and from work. Our offices are down the street from each other."

"Stop." Amber waved both hands. "Absolutely not."

Crys scowled at her. "This isn't a dress rehearsal, Am. It's the real thing. You have four options—me, J, Trent or a leave of absence from work. Because there's no way anyone in this room is letting you stay on your own until this hit man is caught."

"Real talk." Jade's tone was a little softer. "Someone tried to kill you today. I know you don't like to be smothered. None of us do. But are you really stubborn enough to let that get in the way of your safety?"

Trent was impressed by Jade's approach. He should take notes. Amber sent him a look. He saw the uncertainty in the cocoa depths of her eyes, as well as anger and resentment. His heart stuttered at least once while he waited for her decision.

She briefly closed her eyes. "All right. Fine. Thank you, Trent. I appreciate your offer."

Amber's response gave him his first smile of the day. It was the most grudging gratitude he'd ever received, but he'd take it. "You're welcome. I'll come back this evening after dinner to take you to my place. That should give you time to pack. Will that work?"

"Yes, thank you." Amber's nod was reluctant.

Trent sensed her looking for a way out of their arrangement before it even began.

Jade looked at Crys as she stood from the sofa. "Our work here is done." She waited for Amber to stand before hugging her. Finally, she met Trent's eyes. "Thank you for helping to keep our sister safe."

"Of course." Trent read the not-so-subtle message in her expression. If he messed this up, Jade would make sure they never found his body. No pressure.

Crys released Amber from her embrace. "This means a lot to us."

Trent inclined his head. "It means a lot to me, too. Thank you for letting me help."

He waited alone in the living room while Amber walked with her sisters to the front door. Their goodbye seemed to take a while. There were probably things Amber wanted to say to them in private. He could understand that.

"Why are you doing this?"

Trent hadn't heard her reenter the room. He glanced at her magenta slipper socks before holding her eyes. "Because I care about you. I want to help keep you safe."

"Why?" Her voice was cold as ice.

Trent expelled a nervous breath. "I want you to give me another chance, Am. Give *us* another chance." He thought he saw her tremble, or maybe it was a trick of the light.

Amber crossed her arms under her chest. "Give me one reason to want you back."

"I never stopped loving you." His throat was raw. He forced himself to hold her eyes.

The muscles in her slender throat flexed. "I don't think that word means what you think it means."

"You're wrong." He took a step toward her. "And I can prove it to you, if you'll let me."

Amber tilted her head. "It's too late. That ship has sailed." She started to turn away. "Could you pick me up at—"

Trent caught her arm. "Amber."

Her name was both a whisper and a wish on his tongue. Trent lowered his head to hers slowly, giving her time to turn away. She never did. He covered her mouth with his and ignited a firestorm.

She was intoxicating, as sweet and warm as a rare wine. His body heated, burning with need. It had been too long since he'd held her in his arms. Too long since he'd tasted her, known her. Trent stroked the tip of his tongue across the seam of her lips, and she opened for him. He swept his tongue inside her and the flames burned hotter.

The warmth wasn't just from him. Amber was reacting, too. She pressed her body against him. Trent's heart tried to punch its way out of his chest. She stroked her free hand up his torso to wrap her slender arm around his shoulder. His muscles trembled. He deepened their kiss. Amber's tongue caressed and teased his. Time didn't matter. Their surroundings faded away. She was all he needed. All he'd ever need.

In his mind, Trent knew he should leave, but his body begged him to stay. One more kiss. One more touch. One more taste. He ignored both mind and body, and listened to his heart. His campaign to convince Amber to give him another chance would not be won overnight.

He drew his lips from hers. It was one of the hardest

things he'd ever done. Almost as difficult as letting her walk out of his life.

"I think our ship is still waiting at the dock." Trent's voice was rough. He released her and turned toward the door. It seemed so far away. "I'll pick you up at eight. Lock up behind me."

He forced himself to leave. Knowing he was coming back made it easier.

Trent waited until he heard the door's bolts sliding into place before he climbed into his car. It bothered him that his opportunity to reconcile with Amber came because of the threat to her life. The sooner he found who was behind the danger, the sooner he'd know whether she wanted all of him or just his protection.

Chapter 4

"We want you to be safe." Jade braced her hips against the honey-wood dressing table at the front of Amber's bedroom Wednesday evening as she watched her pack.

Crys propped her shoulder against the pale lavender wall in front of the honey-wood vanity and matching lavender cushioned chair behind Amber. "You can change your mind and stay with me."

Amber sent her elder sister a skeptical look. "As much as I'd prefer that, we've already discussed why I won't. I'd rather move in with the devil than bring danger to your door."

She dropped her sleepwear into the large burgundy case she'd set on a stand beside her queen-size bed. They were oversize T-shirts and baggy shorts, not sexy negligee. Despite the taste of Trent that still lingered on her tongue, she wasn't trying to rekindle their past relationship. That ship was not waiting at the dock, as he'd claimed. It had sailed and wasn't coming back. If she repeated that mantra often enough, perhaps her heart would get the message. Amber straightened to continue packing.

Crys, Jade and Amber had recently finished dinner. Since no one thought it would be wise to go out the same day someone had tried to kill her, they'd eaten at Amber's

home. Crys and Jade had cooked and cleaned up, leaving
Amber free to gather her thoughts and her belongings.
She'd stacked her clothing—business suits, casual wear,
exercise outfits—on the midnight-blue blanket that covered her mattress. Amber glanced at her silver-and-tur-
quoise wristwatch. Trent would be here soon to pick her up.

What was she doing? Was it the right thing? If it was,
why did it feel so much like skydiving without a chute?
Bungee jumping without a cord?

"It's a standing invitation." Crys spoke from her position behind Amber. "In the meantime, the techs are checking the bullet we recovered from Griff's shoulder against
our database. It doesn't match the bullets from Aunt K's
or Vic's murders."

Amber selected another outfit from her bed to fold into
her suitcase. "That makes sense, considering Jasper Bright
and Martina Monaco are in prison."

She was amazed her voice was steady considering how
much her hands were shaking. Amber drew a breath to
settle her nerves, filling her senses with the soothing lavender scent from the fragrance plug-ins she'd distributed
around her cottage-style home.

Jade blew a breath. "Yeah, but it means the number of
people trying to kill us is increasing." Amber gave her a
startled look. Jade spread her arms. "Am I lying?"

Crys's sigh was long-suffering. "Two of those people
are in jail. And Am will be safe with Trent, so could you
stop trying to scare us, please?"

Hoping to change the subject, Amber slid a look at Jade.
"Cal called earlier to check on me."

Jade's expression soured. "I'm glad you've made a
friend."

"I should've known you'd react that way, J." Amber exchanged an indulgent smile with Crys. "I don't think Cal is a bad guy. I think like you, he was a pawn in Brock's efforts to curry favor with Roland Dragon."

A curtain seemed to close over Jade's dark eyes. Amber had pushed her younger sister as far as Jade was willing to go this evening. Time to retreat.

"I'm not worried about Cal." Jade's voice was cool. "We know you're staying with Trent for your safety, but how do you feel about moving in with him?"

Jade's words brought the memory of Trent's kiss to the forefront of Amber's mind again. Her body burned as her senses relived those moments: his taste, his touch, his scent. It had taken her more than a year to stop thinking about him; stop missing him. After one embrace, her cravings had returned and seemed to be making up for lost time.

Amber swallowed to ease her throat. "I'll be fine. I remember why we broke up and I doubt he's changed."

"You never told us why you broke off your engagement." Crys's reluctance to pry mingled with her concern. Amber appreciated both.

"I've wanted to ask since day one." Jade jerked her head toward her eldest sister. "Crys said we should wait until you were ready to tell us."

The sisters were close, talking with each other about anything and everything. That didn't mean they didn't respect each other's feelings. However, of the three of them, Jade had the fewest boundaries. That was one of the traits that made Jade such an effective investigative reporter.

Amber added the rest of her clothes to a second matching, smaller suitcase. She'd never explained to her sisters the reason she'd returned Trent's ring because she didn't know how. He hadn't done anything or said anything that had driven her to end their engagement. It had been more of a cumulative response to multiple little actions and unspoken words. How does one help other people understand something as nebulous as a feeling?

Her thoughts carried her backward in time as she made a halting start. "Trent had political ambitions. He probably still has them. While we were dating, he'd been passionate about building a political career."

"Did that bother you?" Jade set the larger of Amber's two suitcases beside the bedroom door in preparation for carrying it downstairs once Amber was done packing.

"No." Amber zipped closed her smaller burgundy case and chose her words with care. "We live in the state capital. Plenty of people here either want to go into politics or want the power they perceive comes with political connections. That's not why we broke up. I ended our engagement because I started to feel that Trent was using my position with the Columbus City Attorney's Office to boost his profile among the city's and state's movers and shakers."

Crys took the small matching suitcase from her. "What do you mean *using your position*?"

"It's hard to explain." Amber picked up the travel shoe bags, which contained several pairs of pumps, her running sneakers and her cross trainers, before following her sisters downstairs. "He bragged about dating *a prosecutor in the city attorney's office*. It got worse as I started winning higher-profile cases. I felt more like an accessory than a girlfriend."

"That would bother me, too." Crys spoke over her shoulder as she followed Jade into the living room.

"Did you tell him how you felt?" Jade set the larger suitcase near the front door before entering the living room.

Amber placed her shoe bags near the two suitcases, then joined her sisters. "I once asked him why he loved me. He couldn't answer." She caught her breath as she relived the pain of that discovery.

"Wow." Crys's eyebrows leaped toward her hairline.

Jade searched Amber's features as though looking for answers before asking her questions. "Why did *you* love *him*?"

"The usual reasons." Amber tossed her right hand in a dismissive manner. "He's smart, kind, hardworking, ambitious." She forced herself to stop the flood of praise. "He's everything I admire. And sexy as hell. He also made me feel as though I could succeed at anything. I loved that feeling."

"Hold on." Crys waved her hand from her to Jade. "*We* think you can succeed at anything, too."

"I know, and I appreciate that." Amber dragged her right hand over her hair, frustrated that she couldn't find better words to explain her feelings. "But it's different when someone you aren't related to by blood or marriage thinks you have potential. They aren't obligated to encourage you."

Crys shook her head and rolled her eyes. "Whatever."

Amber expelled a breath and most of her irritation. "In the end, he demonstrated his ambitions were more important to him than I was. I started feeling as though our dates were his job interviews for a political office."

"I'm sorry, Am." Jade's eyes darkened with empathy. "Do you still love him?"

Amber sensed her sisters' tension as they waited for her reply. She expelled a breath, hoping to ease her own anxiety. "I haven't asked myself that question. If I did, I'd have to answer it."

* * *

"You weren't kidding about your building's security. It's intense." Amber spoke over her shoulder as she preceded Trent into his condo Wednesday night. "Crys and J will be pleased."

Trent's security card, a thick, cream item about the size of a credit card, had let him navigate his silver SUV into the condo building's underground parking garage. It also activated the elevator that carried them to the lobby as well as the main entrance. He'd gotten a guest security card for her, nearly identical except it was gray. It gave her access to the garage, the elevators and the main entrance.

"What about you? Are you pleased?" There was a strange note in Trent's voice.

Amber turned to give him a curious look. He'd changed out of the dark blue pin-striped suit he'd worn to work. He was ruggedly handsome in khaki cargo shorts and a black T-shirt that stretched across his chest and showed off his biceps. No, Trent had not been cheating on his upper-body workouts. Or his lower-body weights, either.

She glued her eyes to his. "I'm grateful. Thank you."

"It's my pleasure." Trent rolled both of her burgundy luggage bags into his home. The wheels rumbled against the silver tiled flooring in his entryway. "We have a lot of high-profile residents who appreciate the extra security."

"Columbus's movers and shakers?" Amber tightened her hold on her shoe bag in her right hand and her briefcase in her left. Had Trent chosen this building to be his home because of its access to networking opportunities?

"You could call them that." Trent stopped beside her, close enough for her to feel his warmth. "State senators and representatives, high-profile executives."

"The type of people you'd grown up with." Amber felt

Trent's eyes on her profile. "The connections that could help with your political aspirations."

She ignored him in favor of her growing curiosity about his home. Still carrying her shoe bag and briefcase, Amber traveled farther down his hallway. Her ruby canvas shoes were almost silent as she approached his living room to her left. His condo was spacious, spotless and tastefully decorated.

"You didn't care about my money, name or social circles when we were dating." Trent spoke with certainty.

His grandparents had been biochemists. They'd founded Mitchell Tech, a successful biotechnology company outside Los Angeles. Trent's father had inherited the company, which he led with his wife. Trent was the youngest of four offspring. He had two brothers and a sister. His siblings were involved in the family business.

Trent had chosen his own path, going into law instead. However, he owned shares in the family business and was a voting member of the board of directors. That explained how a public defender could afford a condo in a building downtown that housed members of Columbus's elite.

Amber glanced up at him beside her. "I have my own money, name and social circles."

The glint of amusement in his ebony eyes trapped Amber's breath in her throat. Had she made a mistake in accepting Trent's offer of shelter? How long would she be living with him?

She straightened her shoulders. Their arrangement would be a test of her resolve. Would she be able to remain immune to Trent Mitchell's charm and attractiveness? Perhaps she could if she stopped thinking about their kiss.

Amber cautioned herself to breathe in and out as her eyes swept Trent's living room. It was decorated in classy, timeless black and cream. A long, deep, black faux leather sofa stood with its back to her. On its right was a matching armchair. Centered in front of it was a black-glass-and-bronze-metal coffee table. It claimed the space on the black-and-cream abstract area rug that lay on the warm honey-wood flooring.

Cream walls blended seamlessly with the cream drapes that hung open over tall, wide front-facing windows. During the day, the large panes would welcome plenty of natural light to feed the handful of potted plants arranged on the nearby shelving. For now, they provided an almost enchanting view of the city lights that twinkled like gems on black velvet.

Trent interrupted her thoughts. "I've known almost since the day we met that you didn't care about my money. You confirmed that when you returned your engagement ring."

Was that the reason he'd thought he'd loved her? Because she hadn't cared about his money?

Amber shook her head. Thoughts like that wouldn't help her leave the past behind. And she wanted—needed—to move forward.

She avoided his eyes even as she felt them moving over her profile. "You have a lovely home."

Amber turned her back to him and fixed her attention on his dining room to her right. The large, rectangular cherrywood dinette set gleamed under the crystal-and-bronze chandelier. It sat up to eight people.

"Thank you." Trent sounded both pleased and surprised. "I'll give you a tour—or would you like something to eat first?"

"I've eaten." Amber felt a moment of guilt. But it was their standing Sisters Dinner Night. She deserved a pass.

"I can keep you company while you eat and you can give me the tour after."

Trent's crooked smile made her heart kick against her chest. "No, let's get you settled. I can dazzle you with my cooking tomorrow night."

"Dazzle me?" Amber surprised herself with a laugh. "Are you going to thaw another frozen dinner and claim you made it from scratch?"

"That wasn't my proudest moment." His smile grew into a boyish grin. "But I've been practicing. I'm not as good as you are—yet—but I'm getting there."

Amber arched an eyebrow. "I guess we'll see tomorrow night."

"You're on." Trent gestured to his left. "The kitchen's through there."

Amber glimpsed a white-and-gray kitchen counter through the door at the far end of the dining room.

Wheeling her suitcases, Trent led her down the wide hallway. The fluorescent light overhead bounced off the cream walls and made the silver flooring gleam. The air held a trace of Trent's sandalwood-and-soap scent, making Amber feel as though she was wrapped in his embrace. She smothered a groan and forced herself to focus on their surroundings.

They passed a small half bathroom. He gave her a closer look at the kitchen with its spotless surfaces and gleaming appliances. Then they came to the bedroom.

Singular.

One.

The muscles in Amber's jaw flexed as she clenched her teeth. "Trent?" She lowered her briefcase and shoe bag to the flooring.

"Yes, Am?" Trent interrupted himself during his de-

scription of the linen closet's offerings. His dark, wary
eyes told her he'd noticed the change in her demeanor.

Amber inclined her head toward the bedroom's—the
only bedroom in the condo—wide-open doorway. "You
only have one bedroom." She tried but failed to strip the
disbelief, suspicion and anger from her voice.

Trent released her luggage. "That's right, one bedroom
and one bed. But I—"

"I don't believe this." She looked around, desperately
hoping that they'd both just... What? Overlooked a second bedroom?

Don't be ridiculous, Am.

Amber rubbed the center of her forehead with three
fingers of her right hand. "You told me I could stay here."

"I did and I—" Trent raised his hands in surrender.

Tension crawled up her shoulders and neck. "How
could you invite someone to stay with you if you only
have one—" She drew a breath, filling her senses with
his scent. It was too much. She turned her back to him.
"Do you actually think that just because you and I had a
previous relationship I'd—"

"Am, I'm sleeping on the couch." Trent's voice was
firm.

"The couch?" It had looked comfortable enough, but
Amber doubted Trent's six-foot-plus frame would fit.

"It converts into a sofa bed."

"Oh." Amber's eyes widened. Her cheeks burned with
embarrassment. "Oh, Trent. I apologize for jumping to
conclusions. I—"

"It's all right, Am." Trent massaged the back of his neck
with his right hand. "A lot has happened today. We're all
on edge and pretending that we're not."

Amber's sigh lifted her shoulders, but her tension remained. "That's very gracious of you. Thank you for understanding."

Trent dropped his hand. A deep breath lifted his broad shoulders. "We're not a couple anymore, but I care about you and want to help keep you safe."

The warmth in his eyes was melting the ice around her heart. Amber looked away. "I don't feel right taking your room. I can sleep on the sofa bed."

"Not a chance. You're my guest. Besides, I've slept on that sofa bed plenty of times when my siblings visit."

"In fairness, you know how long you'll use the bed when your family's in town." Suddenly chilled, Amber wrapped her arms around her waist. "We don't know how long I'll be imposing on you."

"You're not an imposition, Am, and I'll be fine." Trent pulled her suitcases toward the bedroom. He used his right shoulder to shove the door open wider.

"Thank you for everything you're doing, Trent." Amber followed him with her briefcase and shoe bag.

She took in the silver curtains and pale cream walls; the black-and-white abstract designs of the area rugs, and matching black-and-white coverlet on his king-size bed. Amber caught the faint trace of sandalwood and soap.

"It's my pleasure." Trent set her suitcases beside the bed and turned to her. "Am, I've been meaning to tell you. I'm so very sorry about what happened to your aunt Kendra. She was a great person, kind and warm. I really liked her."

Amber swallowed the lump in her throat. "She liked you, too."

"I hope they catch her killer soon."

"Thank you." *We will.*

* * *

Amber felt like she'd been sucker punched by a smooth-talking defense attorney with a hidden agenda.

She drew a steadying breath before turning to Trent, who sat beside her in Judge Flora Eaton-March's chambers late Thursday morning. At least this time, he had the decency to face her. Amber ignored his impressive appearance in the mahogany suit, cream shirt and burgundy tie. She sent a promise of retribution with her eyes. Trent inclined his head. Her message had been received.

Amber collected her thoughts before returning her attention to the judge. "If I could make sure I understand correctly, Mr. Mitchell called you yesterday to share additional concerns about my ability to prosecute Maeve Rhoades's case without bias?"

Judge Eaton-March sat back against her black faux leather executive chair as she studied Amber with open curiosity. Her full lips twitched, and her dark eyes twinkled. "There's no need for such formality, Counselor. Considering your past engagement, I'm sure you'd both be comfortable on a first-name basis."

The judge's reputation for gentle teasing and harmless jokes had slipped Amber's mind. Her face heated with a blush, part embarrassment and part anger. Another thing to blame Trent for.

Flora Eaton-March was one of Amber's unofficial mentors. The fifty-something-year-old judge commanded respect but remained approachable. She'd studied the other woman's career and tried to adopt her demeanor. In addition to her disarming sense of humor, she had a sharp intellect. She could communicate complex legal issues in a way that made them relatable to juries. She was unapologetically ambitious, but the array of framed personal photos assembled around her office attested to the importance she placed on family and friendships.

Amber took another breath, drawing in the faint scent of peppermint that lingered in the judge's chambers year-round. That and the slight chill in the room could lead an unwise attorney to mistakenly compare the stern-but-fair judge to Mrs. Claus.

She forced herself to ease her grip on the cool wooden arms of the black-cushioned chair. "I'm sorry, Judge Eaton-March. I wasn't aware of the meeting's agenda. I must have missed that email."

"It was a phone call." Flora gave Trent a disapproving frown. "Trent?"

"I'm afraid the confusion is my fault." Trent straightened in his visitor's chair. "I was so focused on Amber's safety, I forgot to brief her on our discussion. To be candid, Judge Eaton-March, I hadn't expected you to be able to meet with us so quickly."

His charming smile dispelled the judge's displeasure. Amber dropped her eyes to the thin dark gray carpet to keep from rolling them. She didn't buy his weak excuse for a millisecond.

Trent had had plenty of opportunities to tell her about this meeting: last night during the tour of his condo or while she'd kept him company during his dinner; this morning over breakfast or as they drove to work. How much time did he need to say, *Amber, I've found a new way to try to get you thrown off this case*?

He'd chosen not to tell her about the meeting. Why? Had he wanted to catch her unprepared? Why was it so important for him to have her removed from Maeve Rhoades's case?

Flora's arched brown eyebrows traveled up her smooth

forehead. Thick honey-brown finger-coiled curls crowned her round head. "When I'm told someone shot one of the attorneys with a matter before my court and that the attack may be connected to the trial, I make the time." She turned her attention to Amber. "How are you, Amber?"

"I'm fine, Judge. Thank you." Amber shrugged her shoulders, ignoring the slight twinge in her left upper arm from the healing bullet wound. "I don't understand why opposing counsel felt the need to call you yesterday or for this meeting. If he's so discomforted by events outside of this case, perhaps *he* should recuse."

"It's good to see that the unfortunate attack hasn't thrown you off your stride." The admiration in Flora's words soothed some of Amber's aggravation with Trent. "All right, why don't you start us off, Trent, since you asked for this reconsideration."

Trent gestured toward Amber. "I originally asked the court to request Amber be recused from this case because of her personal connection to the prosecution's key witness, Detective Crystal Rashaad."

Flora waved a dismissive hand. "Which prosecution brought to my attention. I still don't see a bias or a conflict of interest. You'll have the opportunity to interview the witness on cross."

Yes! Amber restricted herself to a mental fist pump and resisted the urge to give Trent the gloating look he so deserved.

Trent nodded. "I'll accept the court's decision."

"I appreciate that." There was a hint of amusement in Flora's response. "Now, to your other concern."

"Detective Rashaad and Special Agent Luke Gilchrist received what they consider to be a credible tip that my client is involved in a murder-for-hire." Trent's voice quavered. He paused as though to compose himself. "Amber is the intended target. Maeve denies these allegations, but I'm concerned the damage has already been done and this threat will bias Amber against my client."

You know that's not true. Amber pressed her lips together to keep the words from bursting free.

Flora frowned as she processed Trent's concern. The well-manicured, black-polished nail of her right index finger tapped a steady beat on the surface of her desk. Amber's nerves tensed as she waited her turn to speak.

The judge shifted her laser-sharp attention to Amber. "What's your rebuttal, Counselor?"

Once again, Amber's grip choked the arms of her chair. "This amounts to prosecution shopping. The suspect doesn't like the prosecutor assigned to their case, so they try to scare them into stepping down, hoping to get a more favorable opposing counsel. Not on my watch. This case was assigned to me, and I will see it through."

The glint of approval in Flora's eyes was almost satisfying enough to make this meeting worth it. Almost.

Trent's response burst Amber's bubble. "Maeve has denied any connection to this threat, and I believe her."

Amber shifted on her seat to face him. "Regardless of who's behind the attacks and threats, I won't give up this case. I don't know what else to say to make that clear to you."

Flora interrupted. "I agree with Amber, and I admire her courage in sticking with this case. I don't see any reason for her to recuse." She pinned Trent with a look. "You also explained to me that you're helping the police to protect Amber. Have you both discussed keeping a firewall in place for the duration of the trial?"

"Yes, Your Honor." Amber's response echoed Trent's.

"Good. Then I think we're done here." Flora looked at each of them in turn. "Be careful. Be safe. Godspeed to both of you."

Amber sensed Trent following her from the judge's chambers. Her muscles were so tight with anger, she felt like a mechanical toy as she marched toward the exit to the judicial suite. Crossing the reception area, her attention was drawn to the collection of chairs. Trent's law clerk, Barbi Hamlin, glared as their eyes met. Amber gave a mental shrug. Either the younger woman always looked like that or she thought she couldn't be civil to opposing counsel. The younger woman would grow out of it.

She spoke over her shoulder to Trent. "Could we speak in the hallway?"

Amber pushed open the heavy wooden door. She didn't wait for a response lest he thought it was a request.

"Of course." Trent sounded cautious.

In the hallway, Amber waited for three women in dark business suits to walk past them before confronting Trent. She managed to keep her voice down. "Why did you blindside me?"

"I didn't tell you about my conversation with Judge Eaton-March because you were dealing with enough." Trent gestured toward her arm. "You'd been shot."

"You've crossed the line." Her voice shook with temper. "Why are you working so hard to have me removed from this case?"

"I'm trying to keep you safe." His words were raw with emotion.

Could she believe him? She searched his beautiful eyes. In their dark depths, she saw fear—for her.

Amber's knees trembled. She took a unsteady step

back from Trent and the inexorable force, tugging her toward him.

Resist. Don't let him break your heart again.

She rubbed her forehead with three fingers of her right hand. "I'm a criminal prosecutor, Trent. Do you think this is the first time I've been threatened?"

Trent stepped closer. His sandalwood scent was weakening her defenses. "This is the first time you've been shot."

She'd give him that.

Amber squared her shoulders. "You're keeping me safe by letting me stay with you. For that, I'm beyond grateful. I truly am. But you need to back off and let me do my job or you and I are going to have problems."

She turned, hoping her legs had the strength to carry her away from him. Amber trusted his heart was in the right place even as his actions begged her to take a closer look at his motives.

Chapter 5

Trent's heart sank as Amber preceded him into his condo after work Thursday evening. The cold shoulder she'd been giving him since he'd picked her up from her office an hour ago could give him frostbite.

"I take it you haven't forgiven me for the meeting with Judge Eaton-March this morning." He followed her across the threshold and secured his front door.

"What?" She shook her head, seeming confused. "We dealt with that earlier. There isn't anything more to say."

"You were angry, and I understand why." Trent stored his briefcase in his coat closet before following Amber down the hall to his bedroom. Or should he think of it as hers, temporarily? The idea warmed him despite Amber's chilly demeanor. "I apologize for the way I handled that—"

"You didn't handle it. That was the problem."

Fair. "You have the right to be angry—"

"Thank you?" She scowled at him over her shoulder.

Trent loosened his burgundy tie. "Taking my concerns about your safety to the judge without giving you advance notice was a mistake."

"An epic one."

"I also remember you don't hold grudges." Or at least she hadn't before they'd broken up. Now he wondered if he'd ever be able to convince her to give him another chance.

"Holding a grudge is a waste of energy." Amber entered the bedroom. She set her briefcase beside the bed and placed her sensible-though-still-sexy black pumps in the closet. "But I do wonder why you're doing this."

It was Trent's turn to frown in confusion. He unfastened the top two buttons of his crisp cream shirt. "We've been through this. I want you to be safe. Don't you believe me?"

Amber returned to stand between Trent and the foot of the bed. Her eyes roamed over his features in a way that brought Trent back to a time when he enjoyed a much warmer relationship with her. His body whispered to him that they could have that close connection again.

She'd responded to your kiss yesterday. Her taste had turned your mind to mush. Maybe she'd respond to you again. It was worth a try. Wasn't it?

Trent gritted his teeth and stepped back, increasing the distance between them. He sucked in air like a drowning man. Amber frowned as though she'd noticed a change in him. He turned away, clearing his mind before facing her again.

Now was the time to talk. There were things that needed to be said and things they each had to hear before they could decide whether they could ever be together again.

Amber held his eyes as though she wanted to see into his soul. "It's more than that. What's your agenda this time? The last time we spent this much time together, you were parading me around like your community service appendage, the corporate lawyer's criminal prosecutor. You don't need me for that now. You're providing your own community service as a public defender. So what purpose would I serve for your career? Why do you need me?"

Why? Trent's eyebrows leaped up his forehead. *Because you inspire me to be the best version of myself. You help me to see solutions where I normally see problems. You make me feel like I can handle anything. Why* wouldn't *I want you in my life?*

Now wasn't the time to admit any of that, though. For one thing, she wouldn't believe him, not after he'd frozen when she'd asked why he loved her one year, four months, one week and two days ago.

Trent pinched the bridge of his nose, trying to bring his thoughts into focus. "Am, it was never my intent to make you feel that way. I wish you'd told me."

"I tried." She threw her arms up. "We weren't talking anymore. Not really. Then you stopped listening. It was as though you were prioritizing your political ambitions over our relationship."

Trent felt her frustration. It was like an electric current between them. He was frustrated, too. "You never told me you felt like an appendage. I think I would have heard that."

She turned from him, wrapping her arms around her lithe waist. "I didn't think of that description until after I gave you back your ring."

Trent scrubbed his face with both palms. It was hard hearing Amber's grievances. Would it have been easier to deal with if she'd told him all this when she'd returned her ring? He was honest enough with himself to give that a "hell, no."

He dropped his hands. Trent considered Amber's stiff back and tense shoulders. "Did you end our engagement because of my political ambitions, as you call them?"

She faced him. Her frown was a perfect blend of irritation and surprise. "No, of course not. I knew you wanted to be a public servant. I think you'd be a wonderful representative for any community you worked for. But I didn't want to be a politician's sidepiece. I have my own identity separate from yours."

Trent hooked his hands on his hips. "You told me you didn't enjoy the social events, but I thought the connections you could make would benefit your career, too."

"I don't find networking romantic." Amber's sigh lifted her shoulders. "The only connection I wanted to make was with you."

Trent swallowed the lump in his throat. He'd really messed up. How did he fix this? "We did things you enjoyed, too, like hiking the Scioto Trail. I did that for you, and I thought you went to those mixers for me. I thought that's what relationships were, a give-and-take. Were you looking for something else?"

"I understand the give-and-take of relationships." Amber paced across the room. "I know spending time in each other's world creates shared experiences and helps us understand each other better. But our dates started feeling more like networking opportunities. You were more concerned about impressing the city's movers and shakers than spending time with me. I started to feel as though we were always working."

She was describing an alternate reality. Trent shook his head, part vehement denial and part utter confusion. "That's not the way I remember our past at all. I remember weekend mornings spent hiking park trails, and one or two nights a week at community or professional events."

Amber's smile was crooked. "And the other one or two nights, having dinner with your colleagues from the mayor's office or going to hockey games with old college friends who work at the state Capitol."

Trent fought against a sense of defensiveness. How could they have viewed the situation so differently? It was as though they'd lived through two different pasts. "Why didn't you tell me you felt this way? I can't fix a problem I don't know exists."

"I. Tried." She repeated the statement with more passion. "Then when you proposed, I thought things would change. That we'd start talking about us again, instead of our careers. Where we'd live. How many children we'd have. But none of that happened."

Trent turned away this time. Images of raising children with Amber burned into his mind. A stolen paradise. "You usually express yourself so well. You draw pictures with your words. It's one of your best qualities and what makes you so successful in court." He pivoted to face her. "If you'd told me how you felt, I would've understood."

Amber's eyes broke from his. "Opening and closing arguments in court are easier for me than talking about my feelings."

And there it was. At least that was one thing they shared. "I'm sorry, Am. I wish I'd realized how my actions were making you feel."

Her eyes filled with relief—and remorse? "I'm sorry, too, Trent. I wish I'd tried harder to make you understand."

Trent hadn't realized how heavy a burden his confusion and regret had been until he heard her words. He could breathe again. "I understand now. And I appreciate your caring enough to explain it to me." His features relaxed into a smile. "Want to help me make dinner? I'm hungry enough to eat one of your Hawaiian pizzas."

Amber's eyes lit up like stars in the night just as he'd hoped they would. Her laughter was contagious. "That's a code red emergency. You must be on the verge of fainting from lack of sustenance. Let me change out of my suit. I'll meet you in the kitchen."

"All right." Trent's eyes lingered on her delicate features—long-lidded, cocoa eyes, slim nose, heart-shaped lips and stubborn chin. Was it too soon to ask that they start over? Try again?

Yes, it was. Trent absently grabbed casual slacks and a long-sleeved T-shirt from his closet, then wandered into the bathroom to change. Amber had given him a lot of food for thought. He'd have to digest it one course at a time to figure out the best way to reclaim her heart.

"I didn't mean for you to clean the kitchen by yourself." Trent scanned the table, counters and sink. No one would know they'd cooked dinner, much less eaten in this room. "I'd forgotten how quickly you work."

Amber straightened from the dishwasher and turned toward him. "It's the least I can do. Remember, I'm not a guest. I'm more of a roommate who's been forced on you."

"No. Not forced." Trent closed the space between them, catching her lavender perfume over the lingering aromas of tomatoes, cheese, oregano and pasta. "I'm happy to have you here."

"And I'm grateful for your hospitality." Amber stepped back as though she welcomed the space between them. "Thank you."

"Of course." Trent wandered back toward his kitchen table, resisting the urge to massage the muscles knotting at the back of his neck. "That was CeCe on the phone, by the way. She says hi."

Amber's face lit with pleasure and the muscles in his neck and shoulders relaxed. "Your sister is hilarious."

Trent grinned. "She misses you, too. She was thrilled

when I told her you and I were having dinner." His expression sobered. "I didn't tell her you were in danger, though. I don't think either of us could handle having my sister stay with us indefinitely."

Amber threw back her head with a laugh. Trent knew she understood what he meant. From the moment they'd met, Amber and Cicely had connected as though they'd known each other all their lives. It saddened him that after he and Amber broke up, two of the most important people in his life had lost touch.

"How is CeCe?" Amber braced her hips against the kitchen counter beside the dishwasher. She'd changed into a turquoise blouse and bronze shorts that revealed her long, toned dancer's legs.

"Power hungry and happy." Trent crossed his arms, bracing his shoulder against the threshold between his kitchen and dining room.

"I'm glad. She deserves to be happy. And so do you." Amber scanned the kitchen as though making sure she hadn't missed anything. "I'm going to get some work done before going to bed so I'll wish you good-night now."

Did she seem nervous or was he projecting his discomfort onto her? "Good night. Sleep well."

Trent watched Amber leave the kitchen. He wanted the happiness she said he deserved. How would she respond if he told her that happiness wouldn't be possible without her by his side?

Maeve didn't look happy to see him. Trent wasn't surprised. This was their fifth in-person meeting at the Ohio Reformatory for Women, not counting the one with Luke after someone had shot at Amber and the undercover detective.

She gave him the sense she didn't care about the trial's outcome, which was frustrating. He wanted to give her his best effort. That would be easier with her cooperation. Everyone—even those who were guilty—deserved a fair trial. It was only by giving the defendant a voice that society could understand what drove them to commit their criminal acts and how such tragedies could be avoided in the future.

"Have you found the person who tried to kill the prosecutor?" Maeve's drawl tagged her southern Ohio roots. Her small, angry gray eyes bored into his late Friday afternoon. Her graying red hair had grown a little longer in the month since she'd been in prison. She'd scraped the thin strands into a ponytail that hung almost to her thick shoulders.

Trent searched her expressionless face. The red buttoned shirt and pants seemed to drain the color from her pale skin. "No. Are you sure you don't know anything about the attack?"

Maeve's eyes brightened with rare and brief humor. "Like I told you last time when you were here with that good-looking special agent, I don't have any interest in killing a prosecutor. I wouldn't even threaten one."

Trent laid down his black ink pen and folded his hands on his notepad's blue-lined white paper. "Maeve, we need to be honest with each other. I'm always going to tell you the truth, no matter how hard it is to say or hear. I need you to give me the same courtesy. You have to be honest with me. Otherwise I won't be able to do my job."

"I am being honest with you." Maeve spoke without inflection. "Look here. I want my day in court. The sooner, the better." She paused as if to give emphasis to her claim. "So why would I hire someone to shoot Amber Rashaad or ask someone to get a shooter for me? If I were going to hire a hit man, it would be to kill someone who's wronged me. Crys Rashaad's little sister hasn't done anything to me."

Trent forced himself not to react to Maeve's chilling words. "As your legal counsel, I have to remind you comments like that won't help your case."

Maeve cocked her head to the left. "You're the one who wanted complete honesty. That's what I'm giving you." She shook her head, causing loose wisps of red and gray hair to wiggle against her round cheeks. "I'm not the one looking to harm the prosecutor. That would only delay my plan."

Trent's eyes narrowed as alarm bells clanged in his head. "What are you planning, Maeve?"

Her eyes were steady as they remained locked onto his. "I know Amber Rashaad has a strong case against me. When the police searched my apartment, they found the knife and fishing lures used in the murders, as well as notes on the targets."

Trent interrupted. "If you're willing to admit to the murders, why won't you take the plea deal Amber offered and save the taxpayers money?"

"I haven't admitted anything." Maeve's round cheeks turned pink, and her dark eyes burned with temper. "Compared to what Rita Gomez, Alfred Murphy and Sally Stead did to my family and to hundreds of other families, I don't consider what happened to them to be a crime. I consider it justice."

Maeve had been forced to sell her brother's home to pay his outstanding medical bills, funeral costs and other expenses. She'd brought his three children—the eldest now only twenty—to live with her. Although Trent understood the source of her pain, murder was never the solution.

"Maeve, the jury won't agree." Trent strained to get

her to understand. "As you said, the evidence against you is strong. They'll see you don't have any remorse for the victims or their families. There's a very strong possibility they'll convict you of murder based on the evidence and your demeanor. If you won't help me defend you, you should take the plea deal for a lesser sentence."

"No." Maeve snapped the word. Her body shook with anger.

In his peripheral vision, Trent saw several people flinch and turn their heads to stare at her. He lowered his voice. "Maeve, you—"

She spoke over him, jabbing a finger in his direction. "I want my day in court. I have the *right* to my day in court. I want to expose the truth about Dragon & Kelp or whatever name they're using now, and if I have to rot in jail for that to happen, so be it. Those greedy, soulless thieves have profited in the shadows for long enough. It's time their criminality was brought into the light." She took a breath, and her temper seemed to ease. "So you see, I don't have any motive to kill Amber Rashaad. Her prosecuting me will help me expose Dragon & Kelp."

Trent pushed harder. "Not even in retaliation for her sister arresting you?"

"Is that all you've got?" Maeve's pale eyes gleamed with sarcasm. "That my motive for wanting Prosecutor Amber Rashaad dead is that her sister, Detective Crystal Rashaad, caught me? Give me a break. That's just stupid."

"People have killed for reasons you might consider stupid."

Maeve's features tightened with fury. "I wouldn't have had any reason to kill anyone at all—if Dragon & Kelp had treated my brother's kids with fairness and common decency. Instead, they betrayed my family's trust. They lured my brother into giving them tens of thousands of dollars, money that was meant to help his kids—teenagers—settle his debts after he died. Then they stabbed his kids in the back. Left them with nothing. And why?" Her eyes filled with angry tears. "Because Dragon & Kelp said they were too late filing their claim. *Too late?* No, sir. You're not supposed to treat people like that. It doesn't feel good when people use you. When they betray you. And now they know that. Or at least, some of them do."

Maeve had never expressed her feelings to him before. In that brief statement, she'd poured all her emotions out to him: anger, sorrow, shame. Those emotions were the impetus to her alleged serial attacks. She'd just described what had been done to those victims and why. She'd been accused of kidnapping former members of the Dragon & Kelp board of directors. She'd supposedly stabbed them in the back, twisted the knife, then planted fishing lures in their mouths. A first-year law student would be able to get a conviction from what Maeve had just said. His client didn't care about that. She wanted a jury of her peers to know what Dragon & Kelp had put her family through. Trent may be able to empathize, but murder was something he'd never condone.

He returned his writing tablet and pen to his briefcase in preparation for leaving. "In full disclosure, Maeve, I want you to know I was once engaged to Amber Rashaad. I promise that won't affect the way I represent you. I'll give you my best work. However, I'll understand if you'd rather have someone else defend you in court."

Maeve's smile was slight but genuine. "I've seen Amber's photo on the internet. She's beautiful. Why did you two break up?"

Trent hadn't expected the question from the usually standoffish Maeve. "We wanted different things."

Maeve hummed. She didn't appear to believe his explanation. "Well, if it'll help you patch things up with Amber, maybe my trial is a good thing for you, too."

Trent frowned. Maeve's enthusiasm seemed odd. "That's one way of looking at it."

He ended his meeting with Maeve and waited for the guard to take her back to her cell.

Trent was glad his client wasn't behind the threat against Amber. But he wished he had a lead—any lead—on the person who was. Other than Maeve's trial, they didn't even have a motive. He hoped Crys and Luke were having better luck tracking the threat to Amber's life.

"You're a trial lawyer. Make your case." Cicely Mitchell Dyson's command rang through the satellite connection of Trent's personal cell phone early Wednesday evening, almost drowning out the soft notes of the John Coltrane jazz song playing in the background.

Whose bright idea had it been for him to confide to his sister his insecurities about his future with Amber?

Oh, right. His.

Cicely was two years older than Trent and thought she knew everything. In fairness, the chief financial officer for their family's biotechnology company knew a lot.

"That's easy for you to say, CeCe. It's a lot harder for me to do." Trent sat behind his aged maple wood desk, staring blindly across his office toward his dark faux-wood bookcase. "I fumble my words when I'm around her. I always have. Besides, I'm not good at expressing my feelings."

Amber had admitted to having trouble talking about her feelings as well. Trent had been surprised. She was such a good communicator. It helped to know he wasn't the only one struggling to put his thoughts, hopes and fears into words.

"Speak from your heart." Cicely's order brought him back to their conversation. "Tell Amber you want the two of you to start over, learning from the mistakes you both made in—" She stopped abruptly.

Just above the soft notes of the jazz piece, Trent heard the strident calls of his six-year-old twin nephews, "Mom! Mom! Mom!"

Trent frowned. He usually took his cues on whether to continue their conversation from Cicely. But his nephews kept screaming for her and she was ignoring them. "Um, Ce, should I wait while you check to see if my nephews need something?"

"Oh, no. It's fine." Her voice was thick with amusement. "Nic's got them. They're having a guys' night out in the kitchen."

Dominic Dyson was Cicely's husband of eight years. He was a great guy, and the chief financial officer of a large investment company headquartered in Los Angeles, which meant they had a lot in common. It was excruciating listening to the two of them geek out over new tax laws or amortization tables. He sometimes worried for his nephews.

Trent could see Nic doing something like a guys' night out with his still very young twin boys. He smiled at the image. His brother-in-law was the stereotypical proud father. Part of him envied that.

The guys' night out reminded Trent of Amber, Crys and Jade's Sisters Dinner Night. In fact, they were scheduled to have one tonight. Neither he, nor Crys or Jade thought it would be a good idea for Amber to go out on the town until the stalker was caught. The fact that someone had already taken a shot at her was proof the threat was real. But Trent didn't want their weekly get-together to be put on hold. He knew the situation was enough of a strain on Amber without adding another disruption to her routine. That's why he'd offered for them to meet at his condo. He'd already made plans to meet a colleague for drinks after work, so they'd have the place to themselves for a couple of hours.

Trent's thoughts returned to his nephews and their doting dad. "A guys' night sounds fun, but why are the twins calling for you?"

Cicely lowered her voice. "He's been doing this for a few weeks now, but I don't think they understand the concept yet." She raised her voice to a normal volume again. "But back to you, little brother. Your love life is so much better than any rom-com."

Trent shook his head, despite his sister being unable to see him. "Then why am I not laughing? I'm worried, CeCe. What if she doesn't want to give me another chance? What if she's moved on?"

Cicely sighed. "Look, Trent, you won't know if she's willing to give you another chance if you don't ask her. See how that works?"

Trent pinched the bridge of his nose. "Isn't it too soon? We only reconnected a week ago." Eight days; he'd been counting.

"No, it's not." Her voice was firm. "Besides, there's no better time than the present to ask for what you want."

Trent wished he could bottle some of his sister's enthusiasm to pull out when he needed it. "I still don't know what I could say that would convince her to take another chance on me, on us."

"Remind her of all the ways the two of you were so

good together in the first place." Cicely paused as though she was remembering the past, too. "I always thought you made a great couple. I never understood why you broke up."

Neither had he, until recently. It bothered him to think the key to the end of their relationship was poor communication. What if Amber agreed to try again and they still weren't able to talk with each other?

Trent clenched his teeth. He couldn't let that happen.

He *wouldn't* let that happen.

His thoughts went back to the first time he'd seen Amber. It had been at a holiday party hosted by a Columbus-based lawyers' association during the second Saturday in December three years earlier. Attorneys, judges, law clerks, paralegals from every industry—corporate, government, nonprofit—had been invited. The association had rented a ballroom at the Greater Columbus Convention Center. It had been packed, yet Trent had noticed Amber from the first moment she'd entered the room. She'd hypnotized him.

He'd been certain she'd arrived with a friend—or with a romantic partner. Or perhaps she was meeting a companion at the event. Someone that alluring couldn't possibly be alone. Trent had waited, watching as she circulated the room. She'd exchanged smiles and quick comments with various groups of judges, lawyers, clerks and paralegals. But she never lingered long. His curiosity—and impatience—grew as the minutes ticked by. Was anyone coming? Was she really here alone?

Other men approached her. Trent waited in a bubble of anxiety, watching to see if the two were together. The guy would say a few words. Amber would smile—then wander away and Trent would give himself a mental high five.

He'd waited a total of twenty-seven minutes. He'd meant to wait thirty, but he couldn't hold out that long.

When no one arrived who managed to stay for more than five minutes, he approached her. Keeping her in his sights, he discarded line after line he'd wanted to use or considered using. When he finally reached her, all he could think to say was, "Hi, I'm Trent." They'd spent the rest of the event together, then made plans to meet again the following Saturday. He wished he could go back in time.

Trent shook himself out of his mental fog. "CeCe, thanks for the talk. I'd better get going. I'm meeting a colleague from my former firm."

"Have a good time." There was a smile in her voice. "I'm getting back to my book and savoring my me time."

How she thought she'd be able to do that with her sons periodically shouting for her was anyone's guess. "Enjoy."

Trent checked his watch as he collected his coat and briefcase. The restaurant where he was meeting his colleague was a short distance from the public defender's office. He'd leave his car parked and walk over. In a couple of hours, he'd be home with Amber. Trent stilled at the pleasure-pain that image evoked. His greatest wish was to make their temporary arrangement last forever.

Chapter 6

The downtown restaurant and bar smelled of overpaid white-collar career professionals. That description fit the patrons who filled its·tables and sat at its bar. Trent stepped away from the entrance early Wednesday evening and scanned the crowd for his former law firm colleague, Alan Ma. Alan had chosen this overpriced, chichi establishment where diners were more interested in being seen than being fed. Diners like Alan.

The scents of savory sauces, seasoned meats and grilled vegetables wafted up from the circular tables, dressed in snow-white cloths and decorated with crystal vases of evergreen sprigs. Muted lighting cast a warm glow over the dark-wood-and-white-tiled interior. Scarlet accents against the sparsely covered silver walls gave the space an upscale appearance.

Trent had been surprised to get Alan's email invitation for drinks after work. They'd met seven years ago at Pearce Teller Abbott, the Columbus-based international law firm that had recruited them. Trent had graduated from Stanford Law School. Alan had attended the University of Chicago Law School.

Trent and Alan hadn't been friends at the firm. They hadn't had much interaction at all. They'd worked for different partners in different divisions. And now their paths had diverged. Alan was on the partner track at Pearce Teller Abbott. After his assignment with the international nonprofit based in California, Trent had reassessed his professional goals and returned to Columbus to be a public defender. But he was always open to networking opportunities.

This restaurant wasn't on a normal public defender's budget. But Trent wasn't a typical public defender. His savings from his Pearce Teller Abbott days and quarterly stock dividends from his family's biotech company supplemented his income. He could cover tonight's meal—once he found Alan in this crowd.

"Table for one?" The wiry maître d' could be a second- or third-year student at a local college. His pale, weary features pointed to more late nights at the library than afternoons on the student oval.

"Actually, I see my friend." Trent pointed toward a table in a dimly lit section of the restaurant. But Alan wasn't alone.

Trent hesitated, trying to place Alan's companion. The sixty-something gentleman had a shock of well-coiffed auburn hair and craggy features. Despite his expensive dark gray, pinstripe business suit that tagged him as a corporate executive, he reminded Trent of a lumberjack: tall, broad and rough around the edges. Then it came to him. Alan was sitting with Roland Dragon, the named partner of Dragon & Kelp, the life insurance company at the center of Maeve Rhoades's case. Trent had seen the older man's photo in the local papers, mostly the business section.

Why would Alan have invited him? The answer couldn't be good.

Trent continued to the table, cautioning himself against

jumping to conclusions. "Alan. Mr. Dragon." He pitched his voice just above the sounds of silverware clinking against porcelain dishes, and the low murmurs of nearby conversations. "Sorry to keep you waiting."

Slender and average height, Alan wore a slim silver double-breasted suit, snow-white linen shirt and wide black tie. His straight, dark brown hair was longer than Trent remembered. The other man also carried himself with more authority.

Alan stood to shake Trent's hand. "Don't worry about it. Roland and I were early."

Roland stood, giving Trent a polished smile. "You know who I am?"

"Of course, Mr. Dragon. I read the news." Trent released the older man's hand and took the chair between the two of them. "Alan hadn't mentioned you'd be joining us." He glanced at Alan.

"Roland, please." Polished smile still in place, Roland reclaimed his seat. "Alan was right about you. You're intelligent, well-informed and confident. I like that. In fact, I like everything I've heard and read about you."

Trent didn't allow Roland's compliment to distract him. Between his career and his relationship with Amber, there was too much at stake. "Have you been researching me because I'm representing Maeve Rhoades?"

"No, of course not." Roland's stiff smile cooled. "I've taken an interest in you, Trent, because of your political ambitions."

Alan leaned into the table, drawing Trent's attention to him. "Roland wanted to meet you, Trent. He's here to discuss your political future and contributing money and resources to your campaign."

Warning bells rang in his head. "Alan, I'm representing

Maeve Rhoades in the trial that accuses her of killing multiple people who worked for Roland's company. It would be a conflict of interest for me to accept any support—financial or otherwise—from someone connected to the case. In fact, I shouldn't be here with Roland at all." He stood to leave. "Have a good evening, gentlemen."

Alan and Roland stood with him.

Alan caught his arm. "Trent, wait. This isn't about the case. Roland wants to hear about your political views and policy proposals. It's a completely different topic."

"Al's right." Roland's smile was almost self-deprecating. "Of course, I have no interest in putting my thumbs on the scales of justice. I'll leave those matters to the lawyers and courts. My only concern is to ensure we have smart people, good people, people with your high measure of integrity in charge of this great country of ours."

That brief statement was inspiring. How many people had fallen for it? Had Alan?

His former colleague regarded the insurance executive with adoration. That answered Trent's question. "Roland would be a great supporter for you to have, Trent. You should listen to him."

The older man gave Trent a critical look. "I think you would be an asset to this country in the U.S. Congress."

Congress? It was time for him to leave.

Trent pushed his chair under the table. "And my only intent is to provide Ms. Rhoades with a strong defense and ensure she receives fair representation. I don't want anyone to question my ethics because I've been seen with you. That's one of the reasons I'm declining this meeting."

Roland's eyes narrowed to a calculating stare. "And the other reason?"

Trent wished he could read the thoughts behind the older man's cool gray eyes. "I don't trust you, Mr. Dragon."

Roland cocked his head. "You don't know me, Mr. Mitchell."

He knew enough. Trent inclined his head. As he turned to leave, he sensed Alan behind him.

"Trent, what are you doing?" His former colleague hissed the question. "Roland Dragon is one of the wealthiest, most well-connected men in the region. Did I mention he's loaded?"

"What are *you* doing, Alan?" Trent faced his former associate. He stepped to the side of the restaurant's entrance to avoid blocking other patrons. "You knew you were putting me in a compromising position by inviting me here."

Alan's dark eyes widened. "No, I—"

Trent spoke over him, struggling to keep his voice down. "Why didn't you tell me Roland would be here? Is it some kind of test?"

"Trent." Alan extended his hand. "I was trying to help you, buddy."

"When did we become buddies?" Trent felt like he was being gaslighted.

Alan feigned surprise. "I've always considered us friends. Look, you've wanted to get into politics for forever. Roland can make that happen."

"I'm not interested." Ignoring Alan's entreaties to reconsider, Trent left the restaurant.

He was furious. Alan wasn't a stupid person. Trent would never believe his former associate didn't realize the ramifications of arranging for Trent to meet with Roland while he was preparing for Maeve's trial.

Setting that aside, meeting with Roland could also jeopardize his efforts to reconcile with Amber. That was a risk he would never take.

"Hi! Are you on your way?" Amber's warm greeting through their cell phone connection Wednesday night eased some of Trent's restless tension.

Her sisters' laughter sounded in the background. It made him smile. "Yes, but you don't have to break up your party. I can hang out in my home office until your sisters are ready to leave."

Amber hesitated. She lowered her voice almost to a whisper. "Is something wrong? You don't sound like yourself."

"Everything's fine." Trent should've known Amber would have heard the strain in his voice. She'd always been able to tell when something was troubling him just by listening to him. He tried to inject more enthusiasm into his tone. "I just wanted you to know I was on my way. I promise not to interrupt you and your sisters."

"This is your home, Trent." She didn't sound like she bought his response. "But Crys and J are getting ready to leave. They're waiting to see you first."

"All right. I'll see you soon, then." Trent wondered if Amber had heard his discomfort. Her overprotective sisters were waiting for him. That didn't bode well. Could this night get any worse?

He walked into his condo less than fifteen minutes later. A chorus of "Hi, Trent!" greeted him as he entered the living room. Trent was confused. Considering their frigid reactions to him last week, he hadn't expected this warm welcome.

"Good evening, ladies." He sent an uncertain smile to

Crys and Jade before his eyes came to rest on Amber. "How was your visit?"

"It was great." Crys stood away from the fireplace and closed the distance between them. "Thanks for letting us meet here."

"Of course." Trent set his briefcase beside him. "I understand how important these nights are for you. At the same time, we need to keep Amber safe."

"You have a nice place." Jade stood beside Crys. Gone were her nonverbal threats, which he'd decoded last night. In their place was a fragile acceptance. It offered him hope.

"Thank you." Trent jerked his head behind him in the general direction of his home office. "You don't have to leave. I'm going to get some work done in my office. Stay as long as you like."

Jade quirked a winged eyebrow. Her dark eyes were suspicious. "All night?"

"Sure." He gestured toward the couch. "We could pull out the sofa bed."

Amber shook her head as she led her sisters from the room. The gesture set her wavy, dark brown tresses in motion. "Please don't encourage J."

"You should know better." Crys's tone was dry. "Thanks for your hospitality, Trent, and for looking out for Am. Let us know if there's anything you need."

"Yes, thank you for keeping her safe. She's very important to us." The intensity in Jade's eyes underscored the urgency of her message.

She's important to me, too.

Trent didn't think Amber or her sisters were ready to hear his words. Not yet. He held them back.

"Of course." He addressed Crys. "Do you have any leads in the shooting?"

Crys's eyes darkened with temper. "The CI's sticking to her story. We can't find anyone to corroborate it, though. And, as you know, Maeve insists she has nothing to do with it. We're coming up empty comparing the bullet from Griff's shoulder to other shootings." She looked to Amber. "But Luke and I are doing everything we can to identify the attacker."

"I know." Amber's tone was flat. She seemed to be masking her fear.

Jade frowned at Crys. "What reason would the CI have to make up a story about Maeve?"

Trent moved to stand closer to Amber. "That's a good question."

Jade shrugged. "I'm a reporter. I've got a million of them."

"And we can talk about them in the car." Crys turned toward the door. "It's getting late."

Trent wished the sisters good night before locking the door. He straightened his shoulders, then faced Amber. "There's something I want you to be aware of regarding the Maeve Rhoades case."

"I sensed something was wrong. I could hear it in your voice when you called." Amber led him back to the living room. She crossed to the faux leather sofa, sinking into it with a dancer's grace. "What's happened?"

"As I told you earlier, I was supposed to meet Alan Ma for drinks after work." Trent had followed the trace of Amber's lavender scent into the room. He took the armchair on the other end of the sofa. He leaned toward her, balancing his forearm on his knees.

Amber watched him, patiently listening to his update. "I remember. Your former colleague at Pearce Teller Abbott, which seemed odd. I don't remember the two of you being friends."

Good memory. "We weren't. But Alan had a different agenda for our meeting. He didn't tell me he'd invited Roland Dragon to join us."

Amber pressed back against the sofa. "One more time."

"Roland Dragon was with Alan when I met him tonight."

Amber's winged eyebrows soared up her forehead. "I don't understand. What possible reason would Alan have for inviting Roland Dragon to have drinks with you?"

The statement sounded even stranger when Amber said it. "I wish I knew. They claimed Roland is interested in contributing to my political campaign."

"I beg your pardon." Amber's brow creased in confusion. "I wasn't aware you were running for public office."

"I'm not. But supposedly, Alan has been singing my praises to Roland, talking up my commitment to the community. They encouraged me to consider a run for the U.S. Congress."

"Congress?" Amber's eyes widened, then her features hardened. It was an unsubtle sign of the coming storm. "I'm impressed. And what would Roland and Alan want in exchange for Roland's support?"

Trent felt a cold breeze roll across the space between them. He tasted bitter disappointment. Did Amber believe he'd entertain Roland's offer, even for one second? The thought stung.

"I don't know, Am." Trent heard the coolness in his voice. It almost matched the look in her dark eyes. Almost. "I didn't ask. As you know, any connection with Roland Dragon during this case would be a conflict of interest. Maeve would be within her rights to file a complaint against me on the grounds she didn't think I provided her with fair representation because Roland promised to bankroll my alleged political ambitions."

Amber's eyes were steady on his. "Except they aren't alleged, are they?"

Trent didn't flinch. "No, they're not."

Amber broke the short, tense silence. "Did Alan know you were representing Maeve Rhoades *before* he asked you to meet him tonight?"

"Yes, he did." Trent pinched the bridge of his nose with the first two fingers and thumb of his right hand. "He brought it up when he called. He congratulated me on getting such a high-profile case. I didn't think anything of it at the time."

"Why would you have reason to?" Amber shrugged her narrow shoulders. She seemed restless. "And why would Alan invite Roland to meet with you? He had to have known the ethical optics wouldn't be good. You're representing the person accused of killing former members of Dragon & Kelp's board of directors."

"I believe he did know, but he didn't care." Trent stared at his honey-wood flooring as the image of Alan's urgent, almost desperate expression returned to his mind.

"Why not?" Outrage lifted Amber's voice several octaves.

"When I asked, he wouldn't answer. But I believe he's trying to gain favor with Roland."

"Are you going to recuse yourself from the trial?"

Trent raised his eyes to meet Amber's. "No. I want to defend this case. I'm going to finish what I've started."

"So will I." Amber inclined her head. Trent thought he saw admiration brighten her dark eyes. "Why are you telling me about Alan's efforts to set you up with Roland?"

Because I want you to trust me again. I want you to give us another chance.

Trent straightened, sitting back against his chair. "You know gossip is currency in this town. I wanted you to hear about this situation with Roland from me, not from someone else."

Amber's sigh was restless frustration. "I think you're right. Alan probably arranged for Roland to meet you as a way to get into his good graces. And I don't believe Roland wanted to discuss your political ambitions. I think he had a different agenda, but what?"

Trent felt as confused and aggravated as Amber sounded. "It must have something to do with Maeve's case. We need to figure it out fast. I wouldn't put it past him to try to tamper with the trial."

"Remember, everything we discuss in connection to the investigation of Aunt Kendra's homicide cold case is not to be shared outside of the six of us. Understood?" Amber sat between Caleb Brunson and Jade on Trent's sofa Sunday afternoon. "We have to be able to trust the information we share here will not become public."

She sent a do-not-cross-me look to everyone in Trent's living room. That included Crys, Jade, Luke, Caleb and, of course, Trent.

Trent had been dubious about the Cold Case Team, which had been formed to investigate Kendra Chapel's unsolved homicide. He'd argued law enforcement should be allowed to do their job. Laypeople like her, Jade and Caleb shouldn't get involved. But then Amber had told him Crys's deceased partner, Detective Victor Hansen, had been murdered after accepting a bribe to destroy Kendra's case file. Trent had been furious. That's when he'd asked to join the team.

He'd also agreed to let the team meet in his condo while Amber was using it as an unofficial safe house. The concern was, if someone were monitoring Crys's or Jade's homes and saw Amber visiting them, they could follow her and discover where she was staying. Of course, they also could follow Amber from work. It was a good thing Trent's condo building had such vigilant security.

Amber's order regarding the team's strict confidentiality was met with a chorus of agreements. She hadn't expected anything else. However, she, Crys and Luke felt compelled to give that same speech at the beginning of each meeting. Technically, they shouldn't be discussing their aunt's cases with people who weren't involved in the investigation. They certainly shouldn't be sharing information with Caleb and Jade since they were members of the media. But everyone on the team was driven by their desire to get justice for Kendra Chapel. For that purpose, they'd bend a few rules.

Jade rolled up the sleeves of her pale blue T-shirt. "I still feel that you're directing that comment to me. I understand it makes you feel better to say it, but you know you can trust me."

"You can trust me, too." Caleb, executive editor of the *Capital Daily*, raised both hands in surrender. He wore an olive-green shirt with khaki pants. "I promise not to discuss anything about our investigation without unanimous permission from the team."

Jade snorted. "It's a relief that at least some people can trust you."

Crys interrupted their exchange. "Is there an update on

Jasper's or Martina's case? Have they accepted the plea deal?"

Crys's former supervisor, Lieutenant Jasper Bright of the City of Columbus, Division of Police, and Luke's former supervisor, Special Agent in Charge Martina Monaco of the Bureau of Criminal Investigation, were in prison. They were awaiting separate trials on serial murder charges of Kendra Chapel, Victor Hansen and Brock Mann, the late *Capital Daily* editor and Jade and Caleb's former boss. The city attorney's office had offered both defendants plea deals if they would provide the name or names of the person or people who'd hired them to commit the murders.

Amber shook her head, crossing her right leg over her left. She smoothed her cranberry mid-calf skirt over her knee. "Jasper and Martina haven't rejected it, but they haven't shown any signs of accepting it, either. It's as though they're more afraid of whoever hired them for the murders than of going to prison."

Trent frowned. "That doesn't make sense." He sat in the armchair to the right of the sofa. Like Jade, he'd rolled up the sleeves of his deep gold jersey, which he wore with black slacks. "Prison's not a good place for former members of law enforcement."

"Especially corrupt ones." Jade sat on the right corner of the sofa, closest to Trent's armchair. "Revenge is a whole thing."

From the opposite corner of the sofa, Caleb shifted his attention between Amber beside him and Jade. "Maybe they think they can beat the charges?"

Crys rose from her chair, one of two Trent and Luke had carried in from the dining room, and paced to the gray-and-tan-stone fireplace across the room. "They can't. Jasper's on tape, admitting he and Martina were paid to kill Aunt K, Vic and Brock."

"It's not enough that only Jasper and Martina would be convicted for Aunt Kenny's murder." Jade looked from Amber to Crys. "The person who paid them has to be brought to justice, too. We need the mastermind."

Amber squeezed Jade's shoulder beside her. "I agree."

Seated in the other dining room chair, Luke ended his pensive silence. His dark eyes tracked Crys's journey around Trent's living room. "Martina opened an investigation against Crys to discredit her and distract her from investigating your aunt's murder."

Caleb picked up the backstory. "It also looks like Brock was involved in the cover-up." He gestured toward Jade. "He laid off Jade when she wouldn't stop investigating Dragon & Kelp for allegations of unethical practices."

Trent stirred in his seat. Amber wondered what he was thinking as he looked around the room at the members of the Cold Case Team. "And Roland Dragon arranged to meet with me and a colleague Wednesday night."

Amber had wondered if Trent was going to bring up his close encounter with Roland. She was glad he had. If he hadn't, she would have. Trent waited until the exclamations of outrage and surprise—mainly from Jade—died down before giving details of the encounter.

"This is an interesting development." Jade gave Trent a considering look. "He's probably hoping during your defense of Maeve Rhoades, you'll suppress any allegations of Dragon & Kelp's corruption."

Amber was impressed as always by her younger sister's sharp mind. "You raise a good point, J. That could be what Roland's after." She looked at Trent. "He's probably planning to donate to your campaign, if you do him the favor of keeping allegations of his company's wrongdoings out of the court's records."

"It makes sense." Trent nodded as he seemed to consider the possibility. "But Maeve wants her day in court. She's determined to use the platform to expose Dragon & Kelp's alleged unethical practices."

Luke balanced his right ankle on his left knee. "And that's what has Roland Dragon scared." His emerald polo shirt and worn blue jeans were the most casual clothing Amber could remember the special agent wearing.

"How scared?" Amber held Trent's coal-black eyes. "Frightened enough to delay the trial by killing the prosecutor?"

Crys's words were sharp with anger. "Let's ask him."

"I want to know, too." Trent's voice was rough with emotion.

Amber shivered as a chill tumbled down her spine. Could Roland Dragon be the one who'd hired a killer to get rid of her?

Chapter 7

"Dang, Ciero. And I've been telling everyone chivalry's dead. You've made me a liar."

Amber turned her head toward the sound of Officer Tawnia Dwyer's voice. Dressed in her navy-blue uniform, the tall, fit public servant sauntered down the Franklin County Common Pleas Court hallway early Monday morning.

She stopped beside her partner, who stood with Amber outside one of the courtrooms. Paul happened to appear just in time to help her into her turquoise-blue trench coat. Tawnia gave him a mocking smile.

"What do you mean?" Officer Paul Ciero's tan cheeks darkened with a faint blush. He removed his hands from Amber's shoulders and let them drop to his sides. "My mother taught me manners."

"Really?" Tawnia's police cap was tucked under her left arm. Her bone-straight red hair was pulled back into a messy, stubby ponytail that emphasized her small, bright blue eyes. "You've never helped me with my coat."

Amber smiled, waiting for Paul's response. She turned toward the bench beneath the tall, wide window to collect her belongings. Sunlight struggled through the threatening clouds and rolled into the courthouse hallway. She settled her cranberry purse onto her left shoulder, collected her briefcase with her left hand and carried her umbrella in her right.

The tall, muscular patrolman gave his partner a comically uncertain look. He wore the short-sleeved version of the police uniform's shirt. "You're my partner. Why would I help you with your coat? We're equals."

Tawnia pounced on Paul's statement, arching a thin red eyebrow. "If we're equals, does that mean Ms. Rashaad is above us—or beneath us?"

Amber rested her hand on Paul's thick bicep in a light touch, drawing his attention back to her. It was time she gave her chivalrous knight an assist.

"Thank you for helping me, Paul. It was very kind of you." She turned her smile to Tawnia. In her black tactical shoes, the other woman was as tall as Amber in her three-inch heels. "Officer Dwyer, it's good to see you again. Please call me Amber."

"Good to see you, too." Tawnia inclined her head. "And I'm Tawnia."

"Thank you. I hope you both have a good day." Amber turned to leave.

"Do you want me to escort you back to your office?" Paul fell into step on Amber's right as she walked down the hallway toward the courthouse's exit onto High Street. His steps were silent in contrast to the rhythmic tapping of Amber's heels.

Tawnia's singsong commentary carried from behind Amber. "More chivalry."

The teasing drew a grin from Amber and more blushes from Paul.

He sent his partner a sour look over his shoulder. "I'm

concerned for her safety. She was shot in the courthouse parking lot two weeks ago. Remember?"

"Thank you for your concern." Amber looked up at Paul beside her. "I appreciate it, but I'll be fine. The prosecutor's office is only a couple of blocks away."

Paul lowered his voice to almost a whisper. "How's the investigation going? Any ideas on who's threatening you?"

"Unfortunately, no. They haven't uncovered anything promising yet. But as you know, these investigations take time." Arriving at the end of the interior hallway, Amber turned right, leading the trio toward the courthouse's front entrance.

The glass facade allowed more natural light, making the dour courthouse appear bright and almost welcoming despite the proceedings occurring behind the closed courtroom doors.

Paul gave her his crooked smile. "I don't know about you, but it makes me feel better that your sister's in charge of the investigation."

"I agree." The hallway widened, giving Tawnia room to move to Amber's left. "I mean, everyone on the force takes their cases seriously, but I'm sure it helps to know family's looking out for you. Relatives are the most important people in our lives."

"I agree." Amber shared a look between Tawnia and Paul. "And you're right. Whoever was tapped to lead the investigation would work diligently to arrest the gunman. Attacks against public servants for doing their job hurt our whole community."

"That's the truth." Paul hooked his thumbs on his utility belt.

Tawnia nodded. "Absolutely."

Amber sighed. "I hope the assailant is caught soon."

"So do we." Tawnia glanced at her partner.

"Of course." Paul rested his hand on Amber's shoulder. "You're one of the good ones, Amber."

Amber's smile returned. "Thank you, Paul. So are you."

Tawnia squeezed Amber's right shoulder, claiming her attention. "In the meantime, you be careful. It's a short walk back to your office, but make sure you stay aware of your surroundings."

"I will, Tawnia. Thank you for your concern." Amber gave them a quick wave goodbye before heading down the stairs to the exit.

It was comforting knowing so many people were looking out for her: her sisters, Trent, Luke, Caleb, Paul and Tawnia. It also was discomforting because it was a constant reminder an unknown assailant intent on causing her harm was still running loose. Amber glanced over her shoulder, wondering if she was being paranoid or if someone was even now watching her.

"I'll need those findings in the morning." Trent looked up from his notes Monday morning to find Barbi staring fixedly at him. His eyes dropped to the notepad on her lap. From his seat behind his desk, he couldn't tell whether she'd taken any notes from their meeting. He felt his brow tighten in frustration and confusion. "Did you get all that?"

Barbi straightened on the gray-cloth-and-silver-metal visitor's chair in front of his desk. The generous cinnamon note of her perfume bridged the space between them. "Yes, you want the findings for the Rhoades case by tomorrow morning." She scribbled something in her tablet.

Trent counted to five. "Not the Rhoades case. The Allen case, the defendant charged with killing an auto mechanic."

"Oh. That's right." Barbi's pale cheeks filled with a deep

blush. She drew her blue-ink ballpoint pen across the sheet of paper and wrote something else. "You have so many cases. It's difficult to keep them all straight."

Trent felt the first tingling of irritation. "I need you to try harder. These are complicated defenses. We have to provide our clients with our best, most competent representation. To do that, we have to be well prepared. We can't slap information together. We can't make mistakes."

Barbi's grayish-green eyes pinned his. Her thin pink lips curved in a suggestive smile. "It would be easier if you weren't so darn distracting."

Trent's temper frayed a fraction more. "I've told you before, Barbi, we're not here to flirt. Focus on the work."

Barbi arched a curved red eyebrow. "I'm trying but I'm only human."

She wasn't listening. Trent clenched his teeth in annoyance. As Barbi had noted, he had too many cases to spend time and energy repeating himself.

"Stop. Flirting." His voice was hard. His impatience was clear. "If you can't work with me in a professional manner, you'll be reassigned."

He didn't think it was necessary to tell Barbi he'd already spoken with the director of human resources regarding his concerns with her behavior. Reassigning her would be his last option. As he'd explained to the director, Maeve Rhoades's and Chad Allen's cases were coming up fast. He didn't want to take the risk of changing law clerks at this late stage. But if Barbi continued to act unprofessionally and created a hostile workplace, he'd have no choice but to have her replaced on his cases. The human resources director was supportive of his decision. Cold comfort when he felt crushed between his caseload and a law clerk who acted like the Franklin County Public Defender's Office was a reality dating show.

"You'd reassign me?" Her wide eyes swept his office as though looking for hidden cameras. "Just because I like you? Because I'm attracted to you? I don't understand."

Trent pinched the bridge of his nose. "I've been telling you this for weeks. What isn't clear to you?"

Barbi spread her arms. She still gripped her notepad in her left hand. "Why are you taking this so seriously? I'm paying you a compliment."

Trent struggled to control his impatience. "Compliment me by staying focused on our cases and doing good work. Help me provide strong, competent representation to our clients."

Barbi scowled. Angry color filled her round cheeks. "Why do you make such a big deal about our not going out? You're not in a relationship. You're not even dating anyone. Why are you so against having dinner with me?"

An image of Amber inserted itself into the space between Trent and Barbi. In his mind, the image's delicate, golden-brown features went through a series of expressions: frowning in concentration, smiling in seduction and laughing with full-throated hilarity. The last memory made him smile.

"What are you thinking?" There was hope in Barbi's voice. "Are you reconsidering our relationship?"

Trent's smile vanished. "No, I'm not." He rubbed his forehead, trying in vain to ease the muscles tightening across his brow. What would it take for her to stop treating the public defender's office like a singles bar? "It doesn't matter whether I'm in a romantic relationship. The fact is I'm not interested in a personal relationship with you—"

"Why not?" Barbi scowled, angry and confused.

Trent ignored her interruption. "Your refusal to accept my decision is creating a hostile work environment." He felt odd making that statement, but he'd seen Idris Elba in the movie *Obsessed*. He wasn't going out that way. "If you continue to ignore my wishes, you'll leave me no choice but to have you reassigned."

Barbi glowered at him for several silent moments. Trent held her gaze. He sensed her searching her mind as though she was looking for a way to change his. He hoped she could see from his expression that wasn't going to happen.

His law clerk's solid shoulders rose and fell with a deep sigh. Barbi pushed herself to her feet. In reflex, Trent stood as well. It was an innate courtesy his parents had drilled into him nearly from the cradle.

"Fine, Trent. If you want to keep our relationship strictly professional, then I will." Barbi's eyes moved over him almost with regret. "Let me know if you change your mind at any time."

"I won't. I've made my decision." Her last lingering look made it clear to Trent that her lips were saying the words he needed to hear but her mind was set and he seemed to be her goal. "This is your final warning, Barbi. If we can't work together, you'll be sent elsewhere."

She looked at him over her shoulder. "Oh, I understand, Trent."

He frowned. He didn't think she did, but his mind was made up. This was one problem he'd be happy to remove from his plate.

"Let me help you." Trent's voice sounded so close behind Amber.

She hadn't heard him enter her office Monday evening. She gasped, part surprise, part desire. She could admit it at least to herself. His baritone reverberated through her body from her torso to her knees, just as it had while they'd been dating and he'd whispered something to her: a question, a comment, a sexy request, a grocery list.

"You scared me." *And aroused me.* She slipped her arms into the sleeves of her trench coat, then turned to face him, putting more space between them. "Thank you. That makes two acts of chivalry in one day."

"Excuse me?" He gave her a crooked, quizzical smile that trapped her breath in her throat.

The lights in his ebony eyes dazzled her, but they didn't mask the fatigue and stress tightening the skin across his brow. He'd had a hard day. Amber wanted to ease his tension, but that would be courting danger. She couldn't allow these softer feelings to take root, not if she wanted to walk away from their temporary arrangement with her heart intact.

Amber collected her cranberry bag and navy briefcase from one of her visitor's chairs, then led him from her office. "A police officer was helping me with my coat at the courthouse this morning. His partner teased him that chivalry wasn't dead."

Trent kept pace beside her as they made their way out of the office suite to the bank of elevators. "I helped you with your coat when we were dating, too."

Amber heard the amusement in his voice. "I remember." Was it wrong that she missed their closeness?

Memories kept her preoccupied as they rode the elevator to the lobby. Perhaps similar memories had silenced Trent, too. The doors opened and Amber felt those moments and emotions follow her from the conveyance. Their shoes tapped in almost perfect sync as they crossed the gray-and-white-tiled lobby to the building's front entrance.

Trent held the door open for Amber to precede him. A warm breeze swept over her as she waited to step into the evening rush-hour pedestrian traffic. Trent paused beside her, watching for an opening to merge with the crowd. He scanned the group as he escorted her across the street to the public garage where he'd parked his car. His hand was protective—possessive?—against the small of her back. His silence was increasingly concerning.

"How was your day?" Amber touched Trent's arm to lead him away from the garage's elevator toward the stairs.

His voice sounded behind her as they mounted the steps. "I thought you'd be more comfortable taking the elevator because of your heels."

"That's very thoughtful of you." Amber sent a smile over her shoulder. "But I have a desk job. The stairs help restart my blood flow. Now, don't avoid my questions, counselor. How was your day?"

The stench of garbage, gasoline and motor oil was strong in the public parking facility. The sour mixture tried to nest at the base of her throat. Amber took cautious breaths.

Trent's throaty laughter was a distraction. "It was fine. How was yours?"

He touched her arm, directing her away from the staircase and onto the structure's second level. His car was parked in a nearby space.

Amber rolled her eyes behind his back. She drew a breath to ease her tension, which was a mistake. She breathed in more of the garage's mixture of gas, oil and trash.

Trent's response was less than satisfying. It stirred another half-forgotten memory. He had a tendency not to share his burdens. It had frustrated her more often than she wanted to recall. She had the sense he thought an admission of his concerns was a sign of weakness. Amber rolled her eyes again thinking about it.

His manner was the exact opposite of the way she was brought up. Her parents had insisted a problem shared was a problem halved. Or between her, Crys and Jade, it was more like a problem divided into thirds. She couldn't imagine not talking about her worries with her sisters.

"My day was fine as well. Thank you." And it had been. It also was stressful and busy, but that was par for the course.

Trent put their briefcases in the back as Amber settled into the front passenger seat. He remained preoccupied on their drive back to his condo building. He responded to her questions and asked a few of his own. From the outside looking in, it probably seemed as though they were having a normal conversation. But Amber knew Trent. He was distracted and he wasn't letting her in. Her frustration built.

After the interminable drive back to his place, Trent pulled into his assigned parking space. Amber stood beside him as they rode the elevator to the lobby. She greeted the guard on duty with a nod and a polite smile. The other woman responded in kind. Amber wondered what the guard thought about her staying with Trent. What had he told building management in order to get security key cards and identification for her?

Amber let the silence linger between them as they rode the elevator to the eleventh floor and later as he let her into his condo. In his bedroom, Amber changed into more comfortable clothes while trying to reel in her impatience and devise a strategy to get Trent to admit something was wrong.

Minutes later, she found him in the kitchen starting dinner. She took his hand and led him into the dining room.

"What are you doing?" His tone was amused and slightly confused.

Amber shoved him onto the chair at the head of the table, then sat in his lap.

Trent's eyebrows jumped up his forehead. "Uh, do you want to tell me what's on your mind?"

Amber angled herself to face him. "I want *you* to tell *me* what's on yours or I'm not moving."

He quirked a thick, black eyebrow at her. "You *do* realize that's not really an incentive? Who says I want you off my lap?"

Amber's eyes dropped to Trent's arms hanging at his sides. His fists were clenched. She frowned. Perhaps sitting in his lap was rude, despite their past relationship. Her intent was to keep him from walking out as he'd done when they were dating, but if she wanted him to respect her boundaries, she first had to respect his.

"I apologize." Amber started to stand.

Trent's right arm shot up and curved around her waist. "No, this is fine. In fact, it might make it easier for me to talk about this."

"What's on your mind, Trent?" Amber held his eyes. She sensed him struggling. "We're not in a romantic relationship anymore, but I'd like to think we can at least be friends. My parents always said—"

"A problem shared is a problem halved." He finished her sentence.

"So you *had* been listening." Amber's lips curved in her first genuine smile since the morning, during Paul and Tawnia's banter.

"Yes, I was listening, Am. You repeated it often enough.

It's something I've tried to work on. I just haven't had much success."

"Take your time. It helps to talk about a problem. It's always helped me and my sisters. Who knows? Maybe I can brainstorm solutions with you." She was keenly aware of Trent's large hand on her waist. She felt his warmth through her amethyst cotton blouse. His sandalwood-and-soap scent surrounded her.

Trent searched her eyes through several heartbeats. "There's a situation with my law clerk."

Amber waited. When Trent didn't continue, she prompted him. "What type of a situation?"

Trent looked away. "She's been flirting with me, and she refuses to stop. I know this sounds ridiculous since I'm her supervisor, but—"

"It doesn't sound ridiculous. Your assistant is creating a hostile work environment for you. The hierarchy doesn't matter." Amber's temper strained as Trent went on to summarize some of their encounters. "Have you spoken with HR?"

Trent let his hand drop from her waist. "Yes, I told Barbi today that if she crosses the line one more time, I'll have her replaced. HR is on board with that."

Amber realized she was gritting her teeth. She stopped. "I'm so sorry this is happening to you. You don't deserve this harassment and disrespect. But you should be proud of yourself for the way you handled it. You acted quickly and professionally."

"Quickly." Trent exhaled. The sound was pure self-disgust. "I let her behavior go on way too long. No wonder she doesn't believe me when I tell her I'm not interested. I think I was in denial. I couldn't believe I was being harassed."

"But you did correctly identify the situation, and you confronted it. Good for you. I guess you don't need me after all."

Her temper was starting to cool. So was her waist where his touch had been. Part of her wished he'd put his hand back, another part knew she shouldn't want that. She'd ended their engagement and had finally started to move on. This threat to her safety was undoing all the hard work she'd completed toward that goal.

Trent met her eyes. "You're wrong. Your support has lifted the weight from my shoulders. At least a bit." He smiled when she chuckled. "My main concern was getting her to focus on our cases. Her distraction could compromise my clients' defense."

"That's a risk you can't afford to take. It's too important to ensure everyone receives fair and competent representation."

Trent nodded. "That's exactly what I told her. She still didn't get it."

Amber frowned at memories of her only encounter with Trent's law clerk. "I wonder whether Barbi's attraction to you could be the reason she glared at me the last time we met in Judge Eaton-March's chambers." Beneath her thighs, Amber felt Trent's muscles tighten in surprise.

"She glared at you?" He shook his head. "She's heard through the justice system grapevine that we were once a couple."

"The officers I mentioned to you earlier, Paul Ciero and Tawnia Dwyer, asked if it was true that we'd dated."

"What did you tell them?"

Amber heard the surprise in Trent's voice. She hesitated. "I told them that was a long time ago."

She felt herself sinking into his ebony eyes. His scent

and his warmth wrapped around her. The months they'd been apart drifted away like wisps of smoke in the wind.

"Yes. A long time ago." Trent's voice was gruff. The sound broke the spell they'd fallen under.

Amber stood. "If you're feeling better, I'll help you with dinner."

She stepped away, putting physical if not emotional distance between them. Staying here was protecting her life, but she hadn't realized how much harm it would do to her heart.

Chapter 8

"We're here to see Maeve Rhoades." Trent spoke through the security glass separating Amber and him from the officer behind the security counter at the Ohio Reformatory for Women Tuesday morning. The name badge pinned to the middle-aged Black woman's blue uniform shirt read Worthy.

The reformatory was in Marysville, about a thirty-minute drive from his condo in downtown Columbus, forty minutes during rush hour. Trent placed his professional identification card on the counter beside Amber's. Standing next to her, Trent drew in Amber's faint lavender scent. It helped keep the sharp smells of cheap disinfectants and burnt coffee at bay.

Officer Worthy compared their identification photos against their appearance. After that, she seemed to tune them out while she completed the visitor paperwork. Trent and Amber signed the visitor's log and handed over their cell phones as they waited for Officer Worthy to acknowledge their existence again.

Amber leaned into the counter. Her trim, bronze skirt suit was a bold wash of color against the beige laminate counter. "Excuse me, Officer Worthy, could we see the visitor logs for the previous three weeks?"

The brown-skinned woman gave Amber a bland stare as she reached for a well-worn manila folder barely visible from their side of the security glass. She slid it through the opening toward Amber. "You can look at it right here."

"Thank you." Amber was already skimming through the stack of papers.

"What are you looking for?" Trent shifted closer. Another cloud of lavender wafted toward him.

Amber flipped to the next page. "I want to see who'd visited Maeve in the days before I was shot. So far, it seems that you were her only visitor."

Trent glanced at her delicate profile. "I trust you know I wouldn't have anything to do with an attack against you."

"Of course I—hold on." She tapped the top sheet with a well-manicured, clear-coat fingernail, drawing Trent's attention to the name on the list: Barbi Hamlin, his law clerk. She kept her voice low. "Have you asked Barbi to meet with Maeve without you?"

"No, I haven't." Why would he? "I didn't know she had. Why wouldn't she tell me?"

Amber glanced up at him. "I'd like the answer to that question, too."

"I don't recognize the names near hers." He read them again and searched his memory. He came up with nothing. "The date is last Monday. Based on the times of the entries around hers, it seems she came alone. Why would she have met with Maeve?"

"We'll have to ask them. Starting with Maeve." Amber returned the folder to Officer Worthy. In exchange, the officer gave her and Trent their visitor badges. "Thank you."

Trent followed Amber through the security check. "Once we've spoken with Maeve, would you have time to join me in my office? I'd like to speak with Barbi about this as soon as possible."

Amber adjusted her cranberry purse on her shoulder. The color suited her. "Of course. And thank you for dropping everything to come with me here this morning. I wanted to speak with Maeve myself about these threats. I want to hear her voice, see her reactions, ask my own follow-up questions. And since I can't speak with her without you…"

"Of course. I didn't have any meetings this morning, so it wasn't a problem to schedule the visit for today. Besides, I'd feel the same way, if this were happening to me." Trent walked beside her.

Amber's long legs strode assertively down the hallway toward the visiting room. He remembered that stride. Like everything else about her, it enthralled him.

Amber tossed him a laughing look. "I know you would. That's one of the things I admire about you. You always roll up your sleeves and get involved in the action."

Her smile winked off as though she'd said something she shouldn't have. Trent's heart clenched. It hurt to think she didn't want to acknowledge their shared memories, not even the happy ones.

Focus on Amber's safety and on this case.

Yes, he agreed Amber should be able to confront Maeve herself. Yes, he'd want to do the same thing if he were the one being threatened. None of that changed the fact that from the minute she'd asked him to schedule this meeting, he'd had the image of her seated at a table with someone who'd tried to kill her sister, someone who was credibly accused of trying to have her killed. That vision turned his blood cold.

Trent pulled his eyes from Amber's profile and glued

them to the wide, white-and-beige hallway. "As you know, Maeve's denied trying to hire a hit man to kill you." It hurt to think of those three words in connection with Amber— *to kill you*—much less say them out loud.

From his peripheral vision, he caught Amber's dubious look. She shook her head, making her wavy dark brown tresses swing behind her narrow shoulders. "I hope you'll forgive me if I have a hard time believing an accused *serial killer* wouldn't try to have the prosecutor assigned to her case *murdered*. Am I supposed to believe she's suddenly squeamish?"

Halfway down the hallway, Trent paused to face her. "You said yourself, if something like that happened, it wouldn't stop the trial. And you're right."

Amber stood less than an arm's length from him. "I didn't say the plan wasn't stupid. What I'm saying is I couldn't believe a serial killer wouldn't consider having the prosecutor murdered."

"Fair enough." Trent looked away, resisting the draw of her cocoa eyes. "I haven't forgotten Maeve has been charged with serial murders, but you should know I believe her."

"Then she must be very convincing because you're not easily persuaded." Amber turned to continue down the hall. "I'll keep that in mind when I'm questioning her."

Trent hesitated before joining Amber. "I'm committed to providing Maeve with the best legal defense possible. Everyone is entitled to competent representation in court—"

Amber interrupted him. "Of course."

He continued as though he hadn't heard her. "But if we determine Maeve's involved in threats against you, I'm going to recuse myself. Your safety is the priority for me."

Amber froze, blinking at him. "I—I—"

"I wanted you to know." Trent hadn't meant to make her uncomfortable.

He could tell he'd surprised her. She didn't know how to respond. It was as though she didn't want to say anything that could be construed as her wanting to give them another chance. She didn't have anything to worry about. He wasn't operating under the burden of that assumption.

Trent stepped back so she could precede him into the inmate visiting room. Like the rest of the facility, the area smelled of disinfectants and burned coffee. The familiarity of the odors was reassuring. The room itself was large and bright. The battered walls, aged tables and stained tiled flooring were pale beige. The hard plastic chairs were orange.

He spotted Maeve at a seat toward the back of the crowded room. "There she is."

Trent rested his hand against the small of her back. Her warmth seeped into his skin. Under his palm, he felt her muscles tense. His heart sank. He dropped his hand. Whatever ground he may have gained over the past few days seemed to have disappeared with his ill-timed admission of her safety being his main concern.

Focus on Amber's safety and on this case.

Trent turned his attention to Maeve. She sat handcuffed to the simple silver metal table as she tracked their progress toward her. Trent stopped in front of the tabletop beside Amber.

"It's good you two finally showed up." Maeve shared a look between them. "I was beginning to feel like a wallflower."

Amber couldn't tell whether Maeve was joking. It didn't matter. This wasn't a social call.

Trent pulled one of the chairs for Amber before taking the seat beside her. "Maeve, you remember Assistant City Prosecutor Amber Rashaad."

"Of course I do." Maeve turned her attention to Amber. "How have you been, Counselor?"

Amber frowned. Was the other woman being sarcastic? She couldn't tell. Maeve's small, dark gray eyes were hard to read.

"Let's not waste our time with small talk. You know why I'm here." Of her and her sisters, Amber considered herself the best at chitchat, which set the bar pretty low. They all preferred to get to the point. In contrast, their aunt Kendra had been a master of social conversations.

The handcuffs clanked when Maeve spread her hands. Legally, Maeve couldn't be referred to as a serial killer because she hadn't yet been convicted.

"And you know why I'm here." Maeve cast her eyes around the stuffy visiting room before bringing her attention back to Amber. "You and your sister are practically twins. I bet you hear that a lot."

Amber considered Maeve with narrowed eyes. Why wasn't the suspected serial killer taking this meeting seriously?

She looked at Trent beside her. He was distractingly handsome in a gray-and-white pin-striped suit, black shirt and black tie. He shrugged one broad shoulder as though to say, "Feel my pain."

Amber turned back to Maeve and started over. "I'm here to ask you myself whether you're planning to contract a hit man to kill me."

Maeve's thin red eyebrow knitted. She frowned from Amber to Trent and back. "Didn't Trent tell you? I don't have anything to do with any threats against you, Counselor. I already told Trent and that good-looking Special Agent Gilchrist." She turned her attention to Trent. Her voice was solemn. "I think you're very handsome, too. In fact, you and Amber here make an attractive couple."

Amber froze. Maeve's words had turned her to stone. Her face was on fire. What was Trent's reaction? Did she even want to know? What was he thinking? She couldn't bring herself to look at him. She was too embarrassed.

"You should see your faces." Maeve's boisterous laughter broke the spell. "I'm sorry. I couldn't resist teasing you. Trent told me the two of you had been engaged."

"I had to disclose that information to Maeve since we're opposing counsel for her trial." Trent's voice was stiff. He wasn't amused by Maeve's joke. Neither was Amber.

"I'm aware you had to tell her." Amber looked at him from the corner of her eyes. "It's protocol. Were you hoping I'd recuse myself so you *wouldn't* have to tell her?"

Trent's lips curved in a crooked smile, but he remained silent.

Amber met Maeve's curious gaze. She probably should have kept her question about Trent's motives to have her recused to herself. Her blush wasn't going away.

"How would you explain a witness's claim that she'd overheard you asking multiple other inmates about getting you in contact with a contract killer?"

"I wouldn't." Maeve shrugged her solid shoulders beneath her inmate's uniform. "I'd expect you to ask this anonymous witness to explain herself."

Good point, but Amber didn't like being stymied.

"My law clerk, Barbi Hamlin, came to see you last week." Trent's voice was businesslike. "Why?"

Maeve sent Amber a confused look before addressing Trent. "She told me you asked her to meet with me."

It was Trent's turn to look confused. "I hadn't and she didn't tell me about the meeting. What did you talk about?"

"Nothing really." Maeve shrugged both shoulders. The handcuff clanged again with the movement. "It was kind of annoying. It was as though she didn't really have a reason to be here. I kept asking her what she wanted."

Amber exchanged a look with Trent before turning back to Maeve. "How long was Barbi here?"

"About thirty minutes, which was about twenty-nine and a half minutes too long." Maeve leaned into the table and lowered her voice. "Seriously, if you didn't tell her to come here and she didn't have anything to say to me, why was she here?"

Amber exchanged a look with Trent. She could tell what he was thinking by the look in his eyes. Like her, Trent was compiling all the questions he wanted to ask Barbi once they arrived at his office.

"Ah, the silent communication between the two of you." Maeve's tone was mocking. "Classic sign that there's still a there, there."

Amber unclenched her teeth. She wasn't comfortable with a matchmaking inmate. "Why should we believe you when you say you're not trying to have me killed?"

"We're back to that?" Maeve rolled her eyes. "Listen, I don't know how to make myself more easily understood. If I were to hire a hit man—and I'm not saying I would— it wouldn't be to kill you. I don't have a problem with you, other than you and your sister allegedly interrupted my operations. I'd hire a hit man to finish what I'd started, whatever that might have been. Although I prefer to handle my business myself, whatever that may be."

Amber studied the inmate. "You're making a good point."

"Yeah? Am I finally getting through? Then here's something else to consider." Maeve gave her a narrow-eyed stare. "If you think the motive for getting rid of you is to delay my trial, who would be the biggest beneficiary of that happening?"

Amber felt as though someone had rubbed ice over her skin. In the chair beside her, she sensed Trent's tension.

He spoke without inflection. "Why don't you tell us who you think would benefit from your trial being delayed."

"Dragon & Kelp, of course." Maeve turned her scowl to Amber. "I've been listening to your sister's podcast. She's really good. She hasn't come right out and said it, but from her reporting, it sounds to me like we both have reason to go after Dragon & Kelp. Have you considered Roland Dragon or someone who reports to him is trying to kill you?"

Amber took time to process Maeve's words. Her premise seemed both unfathomable and undeniable. She, Crys and Jade were determined to discover the person who'd ordered their aunt's murder—and all evidence led to Dragon & Kelp.

Trent's voice was taut with emotions he seemed to be struggling to contain, just as Amber was. "Why would Dragon & Kelp want to kill the prosecutor who's trying the person charged with murdering their current and former directors?"

"Are you really asking me that?" Maeve gaped at Trent. "Haven't you realized how corrupt Dragon & Kelp are? What do you know about their having people killed? They killed Carter Wainscott and tried to pin that on me." She shifted her eyes to Amber. "If they'd try to frame me for Carter's murder, why wouldn't they try to blame me for yours?"

Amber was chilled in the stuffy room. She exchanged another silent communication with Trent. Maeve had a solid theory regarding her deceased aunt's former employer. Amber and her sisters were going after Dragon & Kelp. Wasn't it at least possible that the company would go after them?

Trent leaned against the faded and battered beige wall in the Ohio Reformatory for Women late Tuesday morning as he watched Amber pace the width of the narrow waiting area. He watched her long legs make quick work of the short space. She'd stepped away to call Crys right after their meeting with Maeve. Trent respected her need for privacy but kept watch over her from a comfortable distance. As comfortable as he could be. He briefly considered the practicality of handcuffing her to him for his peace of mind until they took whoever was targeting her into custody.

Maeve's theory of who was behind the threats against Amber had flooded his system with boiling anger and chilling fear. He'd wanted to hurl the table across the room, punch a hole in the wall. It had also filled him with an almost crippling protectiveness. What more could he do to ensure her safety? Should he take her somewhere out of the city? Out of the state?

As he imagined them racing down some winding, isolated one-lane road, Amber ended her call with Crys and rejoined him. "Thank you for your patience." She dropped her cell phone into her handbag and paced beside him to the rear exit into the parking lot. "Crys thinks Maeve's theory's worth looking into. She's going to discuss it with Luke."

"Good." Trent pushed the glass-and-dark-gray-metal

door open, letting in a strong blast of warm late-spring air. "Especially since Roland Dragon is trying to meet with me. He must know you're my opposing counsel for Maeve's trial."

Amber shivered as though she was walking into a snowstorm. "It's impossible to believe he wouldn't know. This is a high-profile trial and our names—along with Crys's and Luke's—have been included in the news coverage."

Trent's eyes swept the parking lot for potential danger: drivers sitting alone in their cars, pedestrians lingering aimlessly near their vehicles, signs someone had tampered with his SUV. The cars were empty. The lot was vacant, and his car appeared untouched.

Careful not to put his hand on the small of her back, Trent walked with Amber to his car. He tried to position his body to block her from the open soft-target areas between the reformatory and his vehicle.

"Trent." Her voice sounded just above the chirping of his car as he unlocked the door remotely. "Could you give me a little more space, please? Otherwise, I'll have to climb over these cars to get to yours."

Embarrassed, Trent stepped to the side to give her room. "I'm sorry. I hadn't—"

"Don't apologize. I'm rattled, too. And I'm really glad you're here." She smiled into his eyes and his tension eased just a bit. "Now let's go speak with Barbi."

The post-morning-rush-hour traffic was much calmer, which was a relief. Trent didn't need his temper to be further frayed by daredevil drivers. He needed a clear mind and calm nerves during their meeting with Barbi.

The law clerk was seated at her desk when Trent and Amber entered the office suite. Barbi's welcoming smile morphed into a hostile expression when she saw Trent with Amber. It was another indication that his warning to her hadn't worked.

Trent stopped in front of Barbi's desk. "Could you join Amber and me in my office now, please?"

"Of course, Trent." Barbi's voice was sweet, but her expression soured again when she looked at Amber.

The vibes she was sending signaled the coming confrontation would be ten times worse than he'd even imagined. Great.

Trent stood to the side, allowing Amber and Barbi to precede him into his office. He invited them to join him at the small circular blond-wood conference table in the front-left corner of his office.

He positioned himself closer to Amber, making it clear whom he was supporting. "Did you get my email, explaining I was meeting with Maeve this morning?"

Barbi had crossed her arms over her chest. Her bright yellow dress made her red bob seem darker. Her almond-shaped gray-green eyes were clouded with hate. "Yes, but I didn't know you were going with *her.*"

Her voice was thick with disrespect and disdain. Incredibly, Amber smiled. Her eyes sparkled with amusement. Her reaction eased some of Trent's strain. He should be the one comforting her.

Trent unclenched his teeth. "Barbi, there's no reason for you to address Amber with disrespect. We need to show her courtesy. She's here as a guest of our department."

Barbi narrowed her eyes at Trent. "She's not *my* guest."

Trent's face heated with anger. Under cover of the conference table, he felt Amber kick his left shoe, signaling for him to move on. The gesture brought back past memories, further easing the tight muscles in his back and shoulders.

A deep breath carried Amber's soft lavender scent to

him, though it was almost lost under Barbi's cinnamon perfume. "Why didn't you tell me you'd met with Maeve at the reformatory last Monday?"

Barbi jerked upright in her seat. "What are you talking about?" Her eyes, dark with confusion and temper, ricocheted between Trent and Amber before settling on him. "I didn't go to the reformatory. I haven't seen Maeve since the last time I went with you." She stabbed her short, stubby right index finger at Amber. "If *she* says I have, she's *lying*."

Trent frowned. Barbi sounded as though she believed what she was saying.

Amber appeared unaffected by Barbi's accusation against her veracity. "We saw your signature on the visitor's log, dated last Monday. And we confirmed with Maeve that you met with her that day. You stayed for half an hour."

Barbi leaned into the table, her arms still crossed over her chest. "That's a lie. Why would I meet with Maeve without Trent?" She waved a stiff hand toward him. Her greedy eyes lingered on him until she noticed his scowl.

Amber drew the photocopy of the visitor's log page that Officer Worthy had made for them from her purse. "Is this your signature?" She slid the sheet to Barbi seated across the table.

Barbi scanned the sheet until she came to her name. An expression of vicious satisfaction formed on her face. "That's my name, but it's not my signature." She held out her hand. "Do you have a pen?"

Amber gave her a pen from her purse. Trent watched as Barbi flipped the sheet over and scrawled her full name across its back three times. She gave him a smug look as she shoved the paper toward him. Trent positioned the sheet closer to Amber so they could assess the signature samples together.

Barbi was right. The handwriting was markedly different. The signature from the log was modest, sharp and precise with several letters disconnected. Barbi's signature was looped in multiple spots and flowed together continuously. Trent didn't think Barbi was masking her handwriting. She'd provided it without hesitation and written it with confidence each time.

He looked up at the law clerk. "These signatures are obviously very different."

Barbi nodded in the general area of her work cubicle. "I can get you other samples."

Trent heard the prickly notes in her voice. He ignored them. "That won't be necessary." He sat back in his chair. "Do you have any idea why someone would want to impersonate you?"

Blood drained from Barbi's face as though she'd just realized the implications of someone logging into the reformatory, using her identity.

"No, I don't." Her voice was gossamer thin. "Am I in danger?"

"No, Barbi. I don't think so." Amber's tone was reassuring. "Someone used your identity as a matter of convenience. Maeve said the person pretending to be you didn't ask for any critical information. Have you told anyone outside of the department that you were assigned to Maeve's trial?"

Barbi looked at Trent. "Just my friends. This is a high-profile case. I was excited to be working on it. But none of my friends would go to the reformatory, not even to visit a relative."

"It's possible someone overheard you and your friends

speaking." Trent would trust Barbi's knowledge of her friends. He stood to signal the end of the meeting. "If you think of anything that would help us identify the person who impersonated you, please let us know."

Barbi pushed herself to her feet, moving her chair aside. "Yeah, I will. And you do the same."

Amber nodded. "Of course. Thank you, Barbi."

Barbi marched out of the office without responding.

"I'm sorry about Barbi's attitude." Trent crossed to his black faux leather executive chair.

"Her behavior's not your responsibility." Amber left the conference table to settle into one of the two visitor's chairs in front of Trent's desk. "I believe her."

"So do I." Trent dragged his hand over his hair. "The question is who met with Maeve and why did she pretend to be Barbi?"

"I'll ask Crys to get the security footage so we can review it. Maybe Barbi will recognize the person on camera."

"Sounds good." Then why did he feel so horrible? Trent scrutinized Amber. Her full rose lips were tight with stress. She seemed pale. But he couldn't ignore the unspoken question between them. Neither of them could. "Do you think there could be a connection between Barbi's imposter and the threats against you? Could those two things be connected?"

Amber gave him a haunted look. "I think we'd be foolish not to consider that."

He clenched his hands to keep from reaching for her. "Am, I promise to keep you safe." *Even at the cost of my own life.*

Chapter 9

The women's restroom door slammed open. Startled, Amber jerked toward the bang. She stood at the sink washing her hands Tuesday evening. Her heart stopped, then lodged in her throat. The thought that an assassin had somehow gotten past the security guards protecting the city attorney's office stole her breath.

Was it possible that someone could kill her in the restroom at her place of employment? Every muscle in her body tightened. Her blood froze. Her eyes stretched wide.

Then her mind registered Barbi, stomping toward her. Amber's relief made her knees weak. But then her eyes narrowed in bewilderment. What was the law clerk doing here?

Barbi stopped barely an arm's length away, glaring up at Amber in silence.

She turned back to the sink to finish washing her hands. "What's on your mind, Barbi?"

Amber sensed a girls-fight-in-the-high-school-bathroom vibe from the law clerk. She wasn't going to indulge the other woman. She didn't know what resentments had driven Barbi from the public defender's office. But the city attorney's office's restroom was not the venue in which to air them. Fortunately, they were the only ones in the room.

Barbi jabbed her right index finger toward Amber. "You deliberately tried to make me look bad in front of Trent to try to come between us."

Wow! From which prime-time TV drama had Barbi taken that absurd theory?

Barbi blocked Amber's access to the paper towel dispenser.

"Excuse me." She waited for Barbi to move before continuing. "No, I didn't."

"Yes, you did." Barbi's frown darkened.

Amber could feel the heat from the other woman's anger. She threw her paper towel in the wastebasket beside them. "I'm not playing this game with you, Bar—"

"This isn't a game." Barbi closed the distance between them. Amber could smell the chocolate on the other woman's breath. "You feel threatened by me so you're trying to destroy me professionally."

Barbi sounded like she was reading from some streaming channel drama script. It would be sad, if it weren't so concerning.

"I showed you the copy of the reformatory log with your name on it. Trent saw it, too. We now know the signature wasn't yours, but at the time, we didn't know someone had been impersonating you."

Barbi's eyes narrowed with venom. "Maybe the person impersonating me was you."

"No, it wasn't." Why hadn't Amber thought to ask Maeve for a description of the person who'd met with her?

Because she hadn't had a reason to suspect the person calling herself Barbi Hamlin hadn't been Barbi Hamlin. Now that she did, she'd already gotten a judge to issue a subpoena so Crys and Luke could get a copy of the footage from the reformatory's security camera taken during the date and time the imposter had signed in at the front desk.

Barbi crossed her arms under her chest. "We only have your word for it."

Amber wouldn't tell Barbi that she was getting the security camera footage to corroborate both of their claims. Someone close to the other woman had already used her identity to access the reformatory.

Barbi's perfume threatened to overpower Amber. The law clerk's round, porcelain cheeks were flushed with aggression. Her generous curves filled out the cheerful yellow coatdress. In her three-inch tan heels, Barbi was still a smidge shorter than Amber, who wore two-inch black pumps.

Amber tilted her head as she considered the law clerk. "Why are you convinced I'm the one who's trying to harm you?"

Barbi made a rude noise. "Oh, please. It's so obvious you still have a thing for Trent. I've seen the way you look at him as though butter wouldn't melt in your mouth. You stand so close to him it's as though you want to get into his clothes." The other woman rolled her eyes. "I've heard the two of you used to date. He dumped you more than a year ago, but you clearly still want him back. Well, he's never going back to you, *Amber*. You lost him and he's moved on."

"Moved on to you?" Amber spoke carefully, filtering any and all inflections from her voice.

"He's not interested in you, Amber." Barbi raised her voice. "Move on. Get over him. Have some self-respect."

That was rich, coming from someone who'd been told to stop harassing her supervisor or HR would reassign her.

There was a lot to unpack from Barbi's speech, some

truth and some misinformation. Thank goodness Trent had told her Barbi had a crush on him. If he hadn't, her thoughts would have flown to the wind when Amber started her tirade, and she wouldn't have been able to concentrate on the insights the other woman was sharing.

Amber checked her silver-and-gold Timex watch. Trent should be arriving soon. She thought it better not to mention that to Barbi. Hopefully, Trent would wait for her in her office, out of sight of his law clerk.

Time to speed this along. "You think I tried to make you look bad in front of Trent because I'm jealous of you?"

Barbi angled her chin aggressively. "Aren't you?"

No. "And you want me to leave Trent alone because you think I'm distracting him from you?"

"You are."

Amber held Barbi's hostile eyes. "Is that the reason you're threatening me?"

"What?" Shock shoved anger from Barbi's eyes. She took a stumbling step back. "I'm not threatening you."

Amber stepped forward. "Did you have one of your friends visit Maeve, pretending to be you so you could have an alibi?"

"I didn't do that. I don't need an alibi. I wasn't there."

Amber continued as though she hadn't heard Barbi. She was in full courtroom mode now. "Isn't it true that you planted the rumor Maeve was looking for a contract killer to deal with me? Were you hoping to scare me off the case and out of Trent's life?"

Barbi's jaw dropped. "That's ridiculous."

"Is it?" Amber tilted her head. "I don't know. I think it might be genius. Tell me, did you shoot at me that day at the courthouse parking lot or did you have one of your friends do it?"

Blood drained from Barbi's face. She backed toward the door. "You're making this up. You're making everything up!"

Amber replayed the words in her head. "I don't think I am, Barbi."

The law clerk clawed for the door behind her. Her eyes now filled with fear. "Stay away from me. And stay away from Trent!" Her last words were issued with defiance as she shoved her way out of the restroom.

Amber stared at the door as it closed behind Barbi. Was she onto something? Perhaps the threat against her didn't have anything to do with Maeve's case or Dragon & Kelp. Could the mastermind behind the rumors of Maeve hiring a hit man instead be motivated by jealousy?

It seemed most of Columbus, if not Franklin County, knew she and Trent used to be a couple. Did one of Trent's admirers feel threatened that they were back in each other's lives? It was a question worth asking. But how many secret admirers did he have? Amber pictured his clean, chiseled features; his long, lean physique; his charm and charisma.

She imagined the answer to that question was a lot.

"Are you going to tell me what's wrong?" Trent's quiet question made Amber wince.

They'd just disembarked from the elevator that had carried them to the lobby of the city attorney's building Tuesday evening. As she'd hoped, Amber had found Trent waiting for her after she'd returned from her confrontation with Barbi in the women's restroom. He'd accepted her apology for keeping him waiting without questioning her, only remarking that he was beginning to worry.

Amber had sensed the silence between them in the crowded elevator had felt uneasy, but she'd been at a loss as to how to break it. The admission, even to herself, seemed ridiculous. She was an experienced prosecutor. She should be able to figure out how to ask her ex-fiancé whether someone who had a crush on him might want her dead. She should, but she couldn't. That scenario hadn't been covered in her version of the Law School Admission Test prep book.

"There's nothing wrong. Everything's fine." Amber tacked on a casual smile, trying to buy herself time.

Trent scanned her features as he strode beside her. "That's your fake smile. Did you think I wouldn't remember it?"

Amber's smile winked away. "I'm trying to reassure you. I don't want you to worry about me."

She gave Trent a sour look as he moved to open the exit door. An early evening breeze, soft and warm, washed over her as she stepped onto the sidewalk. She hoped the casual glances she sent up, down and across the street belied her nervousness.

Were they being watched? Was anyone nearby? Was this whole thing just a hoax to put her on edge?

"I don't see that time ever coming." Trent handed the door off to the person behind him.

Amber frowned at him as they walked to the pedestrian crosswalk at the east corner of the block. Did his comment mean he didn't foresee a time when the threat would go away? Good grief, she hoped that wasn't true. Or was he implying something else?

Her mind skidded away from that possibility. "There is something I'd like to ask you." Her voice was hesitant and unsure.

The pedestrian light turned green. Trent glanced at her before stepping into the street. "What is it?"

She noticed he hadn't touched her, not once since he'd come to meet her in her office. That must be his concession to her stiffening against his palm after he'd made her angry last night. She regretted her reaction. She missed his touch.

Amber also realized Trent's eyes were continually scanning their surroundings. His concern eased some of the stress from her.

She took another breath. "I think you should—"

"Amber! Amber!" The male voice rose above the cacophony of automotive engines, footsteps and conversations.

Amber looked to her right as she stepped from the crosswalk to the sidewalk. Officer Paul Ciero and Officer Tawnia Dwyer smiled as they approached. Trent guided Amber out of the pedestrian traffic as they waited for Paul and Tawnia to join them.

This time, Amber's smile was natural. "Hi. It's good to see you both."

"Yeah." Paul's grin wavered as he noticed Trent beside her. He returned his attention to Amber, his smile firmly in place. "Twice in one week."

"I don't know if you know each other." Amber gestured toward Trent. "Trent Mitchell is a public defender. We're opposing counsel on Maeve Rhoades's trial." She swung her hand toward Paul and Tawnia. "Officer Paul Ciero and Officer Tawnia Dwyer. Paul and I have had a couple of trials together."

"It's nice to meet you, Paul. Tawnia and I know each other." Trent inclined his head. "How are you, Tawnia?"

"Good. Good. How 'bout you?" The female police officer beamed up at Trent in a way that triggered warning bells in Amber's head.

"I'm well. Thank you." Trent offered her a smile.

Amber considered his expression. Now whose smile was fake? Her eyes moved to Tawnia, seeing the attractive other woman in a new light.

Paul shifted his feet, returning his attention to Amber. "I—we—didn't mean to hold you up. I just wanted to see if you're okay. Let me know if you change your mind about my being your bodyguard until the threat is cleared. I really don't mind taking time off to help keep you safe."

Tawnia leaned forward, drawing attention to her. "I'd be happy to help, too."

Amber glanced at Trent beside her. She sensed his sudden stillness at Paul's and Tawnia's offers, particularly Paul's. She turned back to the officer. "Thank you very much but I think I'll be all right. I'm being careful."

Paul glanced at Trent again. "Okay. Good. I'm glad, but let me—let us—know if you change your mind. Tawnia and I would be happy to help you."

Amber shared a look between the two work partners. "Thank you, both."

Amber and Trent wished Paul and Tawnia a good evening and continued toward the parking garage. Amber glanced over her shoulder to see Paul and Tawnia waiting at the crosswalk. Paul caught her eye and waved. She smiled before looking away.

"What were you saying?" Trent prompted a return to their previous conversation. His palm was now light against the small of her back. "You think I should…what?"

Amber stepped into the parking garage elevator with Trent. Fortunately, they had the cab to themselves, affording them more privacy for this conversation.

She drew a breath to ease her tension. "I think you

should know Barbi came to see me this evening before you arrived to pick me up."

Trent seemed to stiffen with surprise. He shifted to face Amber. "She came to your office?"

"Actually, she cornered me in the restroom." Amber's tone was dry. It was a quick trip to the level on which Trent had parked his car. She stepped out of the elevator and started toward his silver SUV.

"I can't believe this." Trent's voice was so low. She wasn't certain he'd meant for her to hear him. His car chirped as he depressed his key fob, deactivating his alarm and unlocking the doors. Trent spoke louder. "Why did Barbi come to see you?"

Amber stopped beside the front passenger door. "She accused me of deliberately making her look bad as part of a campaign to win you back."

A look flashed in Trent's ebony eyes. Yearning? Longing? It was gone too quickly for Amber to be sure.

Trent took her briefcase and opened the passenger door for her. "Of course, you told Barbi she was mistaken." His voice was curiously devoid of inflection. "Did she drop the matter after that?"

"No, she didn't." Amber settled into the passenger seat.

Trent made a sound like he was blowing a breath through his teeth. He closed the door, set their briefcases in the back seat, then came around to sit behind the wheel. "Then how did you leave it?"

Amber sighed, shifting on her seat to face him. "I accused her of being behind the threats against me."

Trent's eyes widened. His lips parted in surprise. "You can't be serious."

"Someone shot me." She gestured toward her left shoulder, which was still sore from the bullet that had grazed her. "They want us to believe Maeve Rhoades is behind the threat, but she denies it. Barbi—or someone pretending to be Barbi—visited Maeve the same week the threat was made. What if the motive isn't the case? You were right. Quite a few people are aware of our past relationship. What if the motive is jealousy?"

"Someone who's jealous of you?" Trent's thick black eyebrows knitted as though he was struggling to follow her logic.

"Jealous of my being back in your life." Amber's cheeks heated. It sounded ridiculous when she said it aloud. This wasn't some made-for-TV drama. This was her life. She firmed her resolve. "I think we should consider the possibility that the reason someone's trying to scare me off the case is that they don't want us to be together."

Trent's expression became unreadable. "But we aren't together."

His words struck her like a gut punch. Had she flinched? She thought she may have.

Amber took a moment to catch her breath. "Barbi thinks we're getting back together."

Trent held her eyes in silence for several tense moments before putting his car in gear and reversing out of the parking space. The temperature in the vehicle was warm, too warm. And they were seated so close together, almost as though the SUV had shrunk while they'd been at work. Trent's scent surrounded her, seeming to wrap itself around her. She didn't want it to. It was a distraction she didn't need. Not now.

Amber waited until he'd navigated out of the garage and started the short drive back to his downtown condo building. "I don't mean to pry, but is there anyone else who might be interested in you besides Barbi?"

Trent brought his car to a stop at the traffic light. "I can't think of anyone, no."

Amber glanced at him from the corner of her eyes. He seemed to be deliberately avoiding looking at her. "What about Tawnia Dwyer? How do you know each other?"

The traffic light turned green. Trent moved his car forward. "We went out a few times—twice—when I returned to Columbus. The breakup was mutual."

Amber replayed Tawnia's expression as she'd greeted Trent in her mind. She questioned whether their breakup was mutual. The other woman had appeared almost enthralled to be near Trent again.

The idea of Trent dating someone else tore off a piece of her heart. She knew she wasn't in a position to feel this way, but she couldn't help it. She remembered how it felt to have the right to hold his hand, cup the side of his face, lay her head on his shoulder. Amber released a silent, trembling breath.

She gripped her bag as it sat on her lap. "Well, maybe other names will come to you. In the meantime, I'll discuss this new theory with Crys."

Trent's chuckle was soft, dry and devoid of humor. "I'm sorry, Am, but I'm not buying it. The idea that someone would be so infatuated with me that they'd threaten you seems absurd."

"I disagree. You can be very charming, Trent. You're handsome, intelligent, successful. I can picture you as the object of someone's obsession." *There was a time when you were my obsession.*

They'd arrived at Trent's condo building. He pulled into the garage. Neither of them spoke as he steered his car into his assigned parking space and turned off the engine.

Trent looked at her. "Your theory's worth looking into,

but I sincerely hope you're wrong. I would hate to be the reason someone's threatening your life."

"Don't ever think that." Amber put her hand on his shoulder and held his eyes. "You're not the reason I'm in danger. The person behind the threat is. I'm grateful for everything you're doing to help keep me safe."

Grateful to have you back in my life—although I know nothing can come of it.

"Luke and I questioned Roland Dragon this afternoon." Crys settled into the sofa beside Jade in Trent's living room Wednesday evening. "He said the morning you were shot, he was at an insurance association breakfast meeting. The organizers and five other attendees confirmed his alibi."

It was their second Sisters Dinner Night in Trent's condo. He'd joined them for the meal, which had been surprisingly enjoyable. It appeared she wasn't the only one who'd decided to let go of past mistakes and misunderstandings.

Amber heard the disappointment in Crys's voice. She was disappointed, too.

"Where was it?" She shifted to a more comfortable position in the armchair so she could better face her sisters. "Is there a chance he could have snuck out of the event without anyone noticing, then returned after the shooting?"

Crys was shaking her head before Amber had finished speaking. "The five people we spoke with were seated at the table with him. Luke and I spoke with them separately over the phone. They all said the same thing. Roland left the table twice before the presentation, once to take a call and the second time to use the bathroom before the program started. Both times, they claimed he was gone less than twenty minutes. One person said the call was less than ten minutes."

"Does anyone think his alibi matters?" Jade's tone was dry and angry. Her white polyester shell was similar to Crys's blouse but without the tiny purple rosebud pattern. She looked from Crys to Amber. "If he's the one who hired the assassins to kill Aunt Kenny, Vic, Carter Wainscott and Brock, then we know he has contacts who could be behind the attack against you."

A shiver rolled down Amber's spine. She wasn't the only one unsettled by this theory. She, Crys and Jade exchanged wide-eyed looks of fear and confusion.

"Thanks, J." Crys's frozen expression melted under her growing irritation. "That's a good and terrifying point."

Victor Hansen had been Crys's partner when she'd first made detective with the homicide division. He'd been murdered during what was meant to appear as a burglary gone wrong eight months after they'd started working together. Before his death, Vic had written a letter to Crys, confessing to having taken a bribe to destroy critical documents from her aunt's homicide case. Although, he hadn't destroyed the documents. He'd left them along with his written confession in a package to be delivered to Crys on the occasion of his death.

Working together, Luke and Crys had confirmed the connection between Kendra's and Vic's murders. They'd built a strong case, charging Sergeant Jasper Bright, Crys's former supervisor, and Special Agent in Charge Martina Monaco, Luke's former supervisor, with both Kendra's and Vic's murders. Jasper and Martina also were behind an attempt to have Crys fired from the police force under fabricated charges of ethics violations.

"No, no. J's right." Amber rubbed her forehead in a

fruitless effort to ease her burgeoning tension. This wasn't turning out to be their usual fun and relaxing night out together. "We have to consider all the possibilities, if I'm to remain safe."

Crys scowled. "You're definitely going to be safe."

Jade searched Amber's features. "Especially with Trent chauffeuring you around and letting you live in his condo until we nab whoever's behind this threat. How's that coming along?"

Amber glanced over her shoulder in the direction of Trent's study before scowling into Jade's inquisitive dark eyes. "Could we remain focused on the threat, please? Explain to me again what motive you think Roland Dragon would have to harm me."

Jade was silent for a breath. "All right. We'll circle back to the return of Trent Mitchell. I don't know what you or Crys think about Roland's motivation, but I believe he's behind every attempt to prevent us from investigating anything Dragon & Kelp related." She waved a hand toward Crys. "Jasper and Martina didn't concoct that ethics investigation on their own. Someone put them up to it. You're never going to convince me Roland Dragon wasn't behind that. And I'm positive he's the reason I was fired from *Capital Daily* because I was investigating the customer complaints against his company."

Amber sighed. "I wish you wouldn't say you were fired. *Capital Daily* laid you off."

Jade's features stiffened with a temper Amber had expected. "What's the difference?"

Crys handled that question. "You received a severance."

"Whatever." Jade rolled her eyes. "Point being Roland's already targeted Crys and me. It's your turn."

Amber still couldn't buy into Jade's theory. "He didn't

try to kill either of you, though. He interfered with your work, which I admit is bad enough. What would make him change his modus operandi now?"

Jade pursed her lips. "That part I haven't figured out yet. But I will."

"I'm sure." Amber sat back against the cushioned armchair.

"So am I." Crys stood to pace Trent's living room. "I'm really aggravated that the city wouldn't approve protective detail. Just because Maeve Rhoades denies our CI's claim that she's behind these threats doesn't mean the danger isn't work related."

"That's true." Jade's voice claimed Amber's attention. "And Officers Ciero and Dwyer would've made great protective details for you. They both have military training. They served in the same unit together."

"Have you been surfing the net again?" Crys tossed a smile over her shoulder at Jade as she wandered to another section of the room.

Jade shrugged. "I wanted to know who would've been protecting my sister."

"Thank you." Amber tried to smile. "I would've been glad to have had someone I know assigned to me for my security detail. It would have made the situation a lot less frightening."

"I'm sure." Jade gave her another close scrutiny. Amber wondered what her younger sister was searching for and whether she'd found it. "How are you doing, really?"

Amber spread her arms, crossing her right leg over her left. After work, she'd changed into dark gray slacks and a ruby short-sleeved cotton blouse. "As well as can be expected, I think. I'm having trouble sleeping. I'm flinching at shadows, and every time I change the bandage on my upper left arm, I feel anger, fear and sorrow."

Crys crossed to Amber's armchair and put her hand on her sister's shoulder. Her touch was warm and gentle. "Am, I'm so sorry."

A shadow moved over Jade's delicate, golden-brown features. "So am I. I hate that you're going through this. I feel like it's my fault."

Amber's brow tightened. "Your fault? Why would any of this be your fault?"

Jade shrugged restlessly. She stood, turning her back to her sisters as she roamed across the room. "It was my investigation into Dragon & Kelp that started—" she raised her arms "—all of this."

Crys's grip tightened on Amber's shoulder. "You're not responsible for other people's criminality."

"Crys is right." Amber struggled against her anger at the injustice of her sister blaming herself for something for which she wasn't responsible. "None of this is your fault. Your investigative report would have helped people. That's what all your reports did. They informed and helped the community. You have nothing to be sorry for."

Jade blew a heavy breath, still facing away from Crys and Amber. "We need a way of finding out whether Roland Dragon is behind the threats to Am."

"I may have another motive for the threats." Amber looked from Jade across the room beside Trent's entertainment center to Crys, standing on the other side of the room beside the picture window. "It's possible the person behind the danger is trying to scare me off the case because they don't want me to reconnect with Trent. The fact he and I were in a relationship more than a year ago is an open secret in the justice community."

"That's true." Crys walked back to the sofa. "A couple of cops and detectives have mentioned it to me since people found out you two were opposing counsel in this high-profile case."

Jade turned toward her from what Amber thought was a feigned interest in Trent's entertainment system. "So you think someone with a crush on Trent is trying to scare you away from him? Do you have any suspects?"

"At least one." Amber nodded. "Let me tell you about his law clerk, Barbi Hamlin."

Chapter 10

Trent's desk phone was ringing as he entered his office shortly before 8:00 a.m. Why should Friday be different from any other day? The smile that had lingered on his lips after leaving Amber at her office vanished. He crossed to his desk in two long strides, hoping to stop the call from rolling into his voicemail.

"Trent Mitchell." He circled his desk, standing his briefcase beneath it.

"Hey! Trent!" Alan Ma's enthusiasm sounded artificially enhanced. "How's it going?"

"Do you mean since the last time we saw each other?" Trent hadn't forgotten the way Alan had set him up to meet Roland Dragon.

"Oh, come on, Trent." His former colleague was stubbornly holding on to his fake good mood. Meanwhile, he was bringing down Trent's morning. "It's not like you to hold on to a grudge, man."

Trent shook his head in exasperation. "Alan, you put me in a compromising position with that stunt you pulled, inviting Roland Dragon to have dinner with us despite knowing I'm defending the woman accused of killing former members of his board of directors." He turned on his computer and waited for it to boot up. "You aren't so long

out of law school that you would've forgotten how bad
that would have made me look if the wrong people had
seen me with him."

"But the wrong people didn't." Alan's sigh was almost
exasperated. "So everything's cool. You should just chill."

"If I'm ever brought before the ethics board, I'll try
telling them to chill." Trent remembered now why he'd
never spent more time with Alan. It wasn't just their busy
schedules. Alan could be cavalier with the law. "Why are
you calling so early?"

He could really use another cup of coffee. The cup he'd
had with Amber before they left for work had been delicious, but it hadn't been enough.

"I wanted to catch you before you made other plans for
tonight." Incredibly, Alan added even more energy to his
voice. "Since dinner last week was a bust, why don't we
try for drinks tonight? It'll give us a chance to catch up.
You can tell me how things are at the public defender's
office, and I'll catch you up on the partners over here. It's
been whack."

Trent narrowed his eyes. Somewhere along the way of
their brief time together, he'd somehow given Alan the
impression he was as gullible as a fish.

He logged on to his computer. "Will Roland Dragon be
joining us again?"

"No, man. I promise. I learned my lesson the last time."
Alan sounded as though he was holding up at least one
arm in surrender. "I promise. Just you and me. Two old
colleagues catching up. How about it?"

"I'm afraid I already have other plans for tonight." It
wasn't a lie. He and Amber hadn't made actual plans, but
he'd much rather spend the evening with her than…do
anything else.

It was funny. In the past, he would've jumped at the opportunity to network with someone like Alan. He would have found a way to persuade Amber to join him or to understand if he was going to meet with Alan on his own. It was as Amber had said: Even when he wasn't working, he was working. He had been that focused on building a framework for a career in politics. But now, he was more interested in getting home to her.

"What about this weekend?" An edge of desperation had entered Alan's voice. "You've got to have at least some time this weekend to catch up. Breakfast? Brunch? Lunch? Dinner? Drinks? Name it. My treat."

Trent checked his emails. "Why are you so determined that we catch up? We weren't close when I worked at the firm. Why are you pretending we were?"

There was a pause on the other end of the phone, as though Alan was searching his mind for a response. "I'm trying to help you, Trent. Roland Dragon is one of the firm's biggest clients. I'm not even assigned to the partner who has his account, but he reached out to me. He asked me to put you in touch with him. He's interested in helping you get into local and maybe even national politics. This is a big opportunity for you."

Trent swung his chair away from his computer monitor, ignoring the emails that were demanding his attention. "And what would you get in return for arranging a meeting between me and Roland Dragon?"

Alan's chuckle was brief and dry. "I won't lie. Doing a favor for Roland Dragon will not hurt my career."

"No, I don't imagine it would." The situation Alan was describing turned Trent's stomach. He didn't know whether it was because Amber and her sisters were convinced Roland Dragon was corrupt or whether it was because Dragon was so determined to meet with him despite Trent's connection to Maeve Rhoades's case. "I'm sorry, Alan, but I won't be able to help put you in a position of having Roland Dragon owe you a favor."

"Do you know what having a connection with someone of his standing in the community could mean for your career?"

"And what it could do for yours."

"Have you even considered Roland's offer?"

"No, I haven't." Trent spun back to his computer and scanned his list of unread emails. If they were any indication of how his day would play out, perhaps he should go back to bed.

"Why not?"

Trent double-clicked on one of the messages to open it. "The more important question in my opinion is why would Roland Dragon be so interested in meeting me? He doesn't know me."

"That's why he wants to meet with you." Alan seemed impatient. "To get to know you and decide for himself whether he wants to support your political career. What's wrong with that? Can you blame him?"

"It's not about blaming him." Trent wrote a brief reply to the email he'd launched and hit Send. "I'm just not interested."

"But why not?" A light tapping in the background made Trent think Alan was drumming his fingers on his desk.

Because I don't want to be associated with someone rumored to have corrupt business practices. I don't want to work with someone who's constantly being sued, then files for chapter seven bankruptcy. Amber is suspicious of him and his company. Any and all of the previous reasons.

"It wouldn't be ethical for me to get involved with Roland Dragon." Trent launched another email message. He wondered whether Alan could hear the keyboard clicks. Probably.

"You've been seen cozying up to the prosecutor who's trying the case against Maeve Rhoades. How is that ethical?"

Why were people constantly bringing that up? Trent braced his left elbow on the arm of his chair and rubbed his eyes with the thumb and first two fingers of his left hand. "The judge and my client know Amber and I were once engaged. We don't discuss the case outside of business."

Another moment of silence as Alan seemed to try to regroup. "I thought you wanted to be in politics?"

Trent glanced at the time displayed in the lower-right corner of his computer monitor. They'd already been on this call for ten minutes. "I have to go, Alan. Maybe you and I can get together after this trial, but I'm not going to change my mind about meeting Roland Dragon."

Alan's sigh rolled down the satellite connection. "All right, buddy. But I think you're making a big mistake. It's your loss."

Trent said goodbye and disconnected the call. Alan couldn't be more wrong. His loss had come more than a year earlier. He hadn't yet found a way to convince Amber to give him a second chance, but he was confident forming an alliance with Roland Dragon wouldn't help his cause.

None of this was real.

Amber stood beside Trent in the nearly empty parking garage elevator Friday evening repeating that mantra in her mind. He'd come to pick her up after work, as had become their routine. They were on their way back to his condo, where she'd been staying for the past sixteen days.

During that time, they'd fallen into a routine. They'd make dinner and spend the evening together. In the morning, they'd have breakfast together before leaving for work. Together. Her mind knew this pattern was temporary. It was part of her personal security until the person threatening her life was apprehended. But her heart felt as though this was something else, something more.

Something real.

In her peripheral vision, Amber caught the quick side glances Trent was sending her during the ride up to the garage level on which he'd parked his car. He'd been tossing those looks her way almost since he'd picked her up from her office. Amber blocked a sigh. Trust him to be able to sense the tension pulling her nerves past the point of screaming. He'd always been able to read her moods. Except when it had mattered most.

Amber couldn't quite meet his eyes. "How was your day?" That was so lame.

The elevator stopped, opening onto the parking garage's third floor. Trent chose to park on one of the top floors because he thought it was safer. Amber wasn't convinced it made a difference. All the levels were crowded.

Trent held the door while she preceded him out of the conveyance. "It was fine. Thanks. How was yours?"

Amber walked beside him toward his silver SUV. "My day was fine also. Thank you for asking."

Trent's laughter was self-deprecating. "We can do better than this, Am."

"What do you mean?" Amber's clueless act was meant to buy herself time.

Trent called her on it. "You know what I mean. We were together for two years. For three months of that time, we were making plans to get married. We can do better than

'How was your day?' and 'Fine.' You can talk to me. Tell me what's on your mind."

Amber gave him a quick look. Confess that each day she found it harder to differentiate between their relationship now and what they had almost two years ago? That she was experiencing the phantom warmth of an engagement and possibly a wedding ring on her finger? No. Trent meant well, but he didn't understand what he was asking. She'd rather prevaricate than tell the truth.

"I just have—" Amber started as Trent wrapped his arm around her waist, drawing her closer to him and away from the car cruising behind them toward the parking garage exit.

The first pop had her dropping to her knees. Pulling Trent down beside her. Flashbacks of being shot in the Franklin County Common Pleas Court parking lot threatened to unravel her.

Amber's eyes stretched wide as the passenger side of the car behind her cracked. Had a bullet caused that? Was someone shooting at them?

Was that her scream?

The screaming stopped. The car raced away. The pops continued.

Around her, Amber heard other screams and shouts. Some nearby. Others sounding far away.

A muscled arm wrapped around her waist, squeezing the breath from her. Amber was pulled to her feet.

"Stay low. Stay close." Trent's voice was tight and hurried. He pushed her in front of him.

"What are you doing?" She didn't need a human shield. She didn't want another person taking a bullet for her, especially not Trent. He wasn't any part of this.

With his hand on the small of her back, he urged her forward. "Just run."

Amber ran, hugging the parked cars for cover. Everything was chaos. More screams. More running footsteps. More pops. Where were they coming from? Where should she run to?

Another bullet whizzed past her head and into the column in front of her.

"Left!" Trent used his body to push her to the opposite side of the parking level.

Amber dodged the fleeing cars. "The shooter's closer." She fumbled in her purse and freed her cell phone.

"And they're definitely aiming at you." Trent pulled her behind another column. This one was wide and cloaked in shadows. He pressed her between its gray concrete surface and his lean, muscled form. "We need a plan. What are you doing?"

"Texting Crys."

"Good plan." He took her briefcase, freeing her to use both hands to send the text.

Amber's fingers shook as she entered the message. 911. Shooter. Garage. She muted her phone and cupped the device to keep the light from giving away their location. She waited for Crys's response.

It came immediately. 10-4.

"She's on her way." Amber needed her now. She dropped her cell back into her purse.

Keep it together, Rashaad! Your life—and Trent's—depend on it.

"We can't stay here." Trent kept his voice low.

Amber wasn't confident her legs could move. She took back her briefcase. "Where?"

Three pops. Each sounded as though they struck the walls to their left. Amber's eyes widened as they locked with Trent's.

"We have to move." Trent's free hand took her arm. His eyes searched hers. "Trust me."

"Of course." Even her lips were shaking.

Trent seemed to relax slightly. "To your right. Stay low. Stick to the shadows."

He stepped away from her. Amber turned right. She felt Trent warm against her back. He was shielding her with his body. Amber squeezed her eyes shut and said a quick prayer for his safety. Staying low, sticking to the shadows, she moved away from the safety of the parking garage column.

Another pop. A long pause. Was the shooter searching for her? And then a pop.

Amber hunkered beside a red SUV. The shots and screams were muffled beneath her pounding heart and panting breath. The sound of shattering glass made her stomach muscles twist. She was still in the shadows. She was behind a half wall. But she'd never felt so exposed.

She was still in danger. And so was Trent. Why had she agreed to let him put his life at risk for her? Amber squeezed herself into the corner, making room for Trent.

"We have to get under the car." Trent shoved first his briefcase, then hers beneath the vehicle.

Amber stretched forward, sliding under the SUV in front of them. Trent followed her in. They squirmed around the cool gray cement surface, shifting among the dirt, cigarette butts, oil and mud until they lay lengthwise under the vehicle.

She became aware of the sudden deep and eerie silence

around them. What had happened to the other people in the parking structure? No one else had gotten off the elevator. No one had come off the stairs. No more cars had driven out of the garage. Were the other commuters hiding the way she and Trent were?

Crys, where are you?

"Breathe." Trent shifted closer to her. His advice sounded in her ear, making her shiver for a different reason.

Amber focused on his sandalwood-and-soap scent. A scraping noise commanded her attention. The sound of a shoe dragging over a cement surface. Amber bit her lips to keep from gasping aloud. It had to be the shooter. She sensed it was the shooter. Who else could it be?

The tread came closer. It was almost like a limp. But it was uneven, inconsistent. As though the limp wasn't real. Step-scrape. Step-scrape. Scrape. Step. From her vantage point beneath the full-size SUV, she saw the shoes, worn with baggy black pants—jeans?—coming closer. Step-scrape. Step-step-scrape. Black running shoes. They could belong to either a man or a woman. They were coming closer. Heading straight toward them with deliberate, measured steps.

Beside her, Amber felt Trent stiffen. What was he thinking? What was he planning to do? Amber reached out and gripped his suit jacket. There was no way she was going to allow him to put himself at even more risk.

Suddenly, the near silence shattered under the cacophony of police sirens speeding closer. It seemed like they were right outside. And from the volume, it sounded as though her sister had brought the entire police department.

The black running shoes froze for one precious second. Then they turned right, racing away. The limp was gone.

Amber's head dropped onto the briefcase in front of her. Her body was limp with relief. Her voice shook with it. "Thank you, Crys. Thank you so much."

Chapter 11

"**I** saw black running shoes." Amber felt drained.

It took all her determination to sit upright in the back of the EMT truck beside Trent. The vehicle had stopped in front of the parking garage Friday evening. It seemed to be serving as a barricade on this side of the structure while officers searched each level and collected evidence from the shooting.

A petite female medic with a gentle touch had tended to Amber and was now taking care of Trent. She was carefully cleaning and treating the cuts and bruises neither Trent nor Amber had felt while they were running for their lives. They were aware of them now. Nicks from cement shards disrupted by the nearby bullets. Scrapes from crawling under the car. Bruises from slamming into walls. The medic was using what appeared to be a mixture of warm water and mild soap.

Meanwhile, Crys and Luke stood in front of Amber and Trent, taking their statements. Together, Amber and Trent had recounted everything they remembered about the event, starting with Trent's picking up Amber from her office and ending with their hearing the police sirens and watching the black shoes running away.

"And black pants." Trent sounded as fatigued as Amber

felt. "They were baggy. From my position under the truck, I could only see them from the calves down. I couldn't tell if they were cut for a man or a woman. And I couldn't get an idea of the shoe size."

Amber's cell phone chimed, demanding her attention. She skimmed the text.

What's happening? I need an update.

"It's J again." Amber's thumbs flew over her phone screen. Still with Crys & Luke. Will call ASAP.

The petite female medic put her hand on Trent's arm, tossing him and Amber a friendly smile. "I'm all done. Glad you're both okay."

Amber's responding smile felt stiff. Physically, she may be fine. Mentally, she was definitely rattled. The medic collected her case and disappeared into the small crowd.

Now that their adrenaline had worn off, Amber saw lines of strain bracketing Trent's full lips. He looked pale. And angry, which was understandable. Someone had tried to kill them.

Amber stood from the back of the EMT truck, perhaps too quickly. She swayed on her feet.

Crys's arm shot out to catch her. Her elder sister's coffee-brown eyes seemed stricken and wounded. "I've got you."

Amber nodded. She squeezed her sister's elbow. "I know." As she held on to Crys, Amber's eyes wandered the scene. At least a dozen other people were giving statements to uniformed police officers. Some also were being treated for what looked to be minor wounds like hers and Trent's. "The pants were polyester."

"That's right." Trent stood beside her. "Shiny material. They looked like part of a uniform, maybe military."

A warm, soothing breeze brushed across her face as though trying to cajole her into easing the frown that creased her brow. She closed her eyes and filled her lungs with air. She drew in the scents of engine oil, foliage and Trent. She swayed closer to him, drawn by his body's warmth and sense of protection.

Her eyes popped open. "And the shooter walked with a limp. There was a distinctive gait pattern. But it was inconsistent almost as though they were faking it."

Trent's eyes brightened. "I remember. It was a drag-step, drag-step cadence." He mimicked the pattern with his hands.

"But it wasn't a prolonged drag." Amber held up one hand, palm out. "It was more of a slight favoring of one foot over the other. But as I said, it wasn't consistent."

Luke made notes in his writing pad. "We should still include it in our notes." He lifted his eyes, splitting a look between Trent and Amber. "Anything else?"

Amber shook her head, avoiding eye contact with the three people around her. Her voice was low. "He or she was targeting us and didn't care who they hurt along the way."

"They were targeting you." Trent's voice was rough, his eyes intense. He turned his attention to Crys and Luke. "The shooting stopped when I stood at her back. When we ran next to each other, they started up again."

Crys gasped, stepping forward to hug Trent. "Thank you for protecting my sister. I take back every bad thing I've ever said about you. If anything had happened to her, it would have destroyed me. And J."

Luke put his hand on Trent's shoulder. "Thank you. We'll never forget this."

Amber blinked. "You put yourself in so much danger for me. I don't know how I can ever thank you."

Trent held her eyes. "Stay alive."

Crys stepped back. She wiped her eyes with the back of her hands. "That just got more complicated. Obviously, Amber's stalker knows you've been driving her home. They probably also know you've been taking her to work."

Luke nodded. "They know your pattern, which means they probably also know she's staying at your place."

Amber's cell phone notification interrupted them again. "It's J."

In lobby of Trent's building.

Amber responded, Be there soon.

To be fair, she understood her sister's impatience. If their situations were reversed, Amber could admit she would react the same way. They all wanted answers. But Jade's texts were a distraction and, therefore, annoying. Very annoying.

"We need a new plan." Crys set her long, elegant hands on her slim hips. Amber could feel her mental wheels churning.

"We should start with finding a new place to park." Amber looked over her shoulder toward the city's parking garage. She couldn't suppress a shiver. "We have to get Trent's car, but after that, I don't think I'll be able to go back into that building, not for a while."

"You won't be the only one." Luke's voice was dry as he looked at the thinning crowd.

After giving their statements, commuters were starting to move away. Their reluctance to reenter the scene of the mass shooting was palpable. In many cases, officers were escorting grateful witnesses into the garage. Amber spotted Paul and Tawnia walking with a small group. Paul caught her eye, giving her a half smile. Amber nodded in return.

Trent gestured toward Amber, bringing her attention back to him. "Am should stay with me. She'll be safe at my condo. We have two security guards on shift twenty-four hours every day. We have a guard station at the main entrance. All other entrances are strictly key-card access only. And there are security cameras—"

Crys interrupted. "I agree, Trent. I've seen your building. If I didn't love my house, I'd move in there myself." She paused, letting her arms fall from her hips. "As much as I want to be the one to look after my sister, I know she's safe with you and I'm grateful."

Trent inclined his head, seeming to relax. "She is. Thank you."

"What I meant was we need a new plan for your commute." Crys looked from Amber to Trent and back. "For tonight, Luke and I will escort you home, make sure you're not followed. Starting tomorrow, I'll drive you both to and from work until we arrest this stalker."

Amber was shaking her head while Crys was still speaking. "We've been through this." Her patience was strained. "There's a reason J and I stopped carpooling with you, beyond the fact that J no longer works downtown. Your hours are inconsistent. You can't be worried about picking your sister up from work when you're on a case."

Crys jerked her thumb toward Luke beside her. "If I can't come, then Luke can pick you up."

Amber arched an eyebrow. "I'm sure Luke appreciates your volunteering him—"

"I don't mind." Luke shrugged.

Amber continued as though she hadn't heard him. "But the two of you are partnered on this stalker investigation, too, because it came out of the Maeve Rhoades case. His schedule isn't any more flexible than yours." She waved an impatient hand between them.

"What is with that shooter and parking places?" Amber wasn't trying to be funny. She wanted answers to her growing list of questions.

Crys frowned. "The courthouse parking lot. This parking garage. Both times they knew where you would be and when." She pinned Amber with a look. "Can you work from home for a while?"

Amber spread her arms. "You know I can't. I have too many cases in various stages of trial."

Luke pulled his cell phone from his front left pocket. "I have an idea. I know someone who works downtown and whose hours are about the same as yours." He tapped a couple of screens on his device. "Maybe we can work something out."

"Who?" Trent asked.

"Caleb. The *Capital Daily* offices aren't far from here."

Jade's nemesis. Amber exchanged a look with Crys. She shrugged. "Better the devil we know."

"Come on. I made us sandwiches."

Amber started at the feel of Trent's hand taking hers early Friday night. She hadn't heard him enter his living room. The TV sounded faintly behind her. She hadn't realized it was on. When had the room gotten so dark? It was as though her mind had been galaxies away as she'd stared blindly across the room at the dark fireplace from her position nestled in the corner of the sofa.

"I'm not hungry." Amber resisted Trent's pull.

Trent held fast to her hand. "Then keep me company while I eat. I made grilled cheese."

Her favorite. He had her attention. This time, she let him draw her from the sofa. "With smoked cheddar?"

"Of course." He led her into the kitchen. "And honey lemon tea."

Her comfort meal. That he'd not only remembered but had gone to the trouble to make it warmed her from the inside out. He'd chased out the cold fear that had been spreading from her heart to her toes since the first bullet had sped past her in the parking garage, almost three hours ago.

Had it been three hours? It felt like minutes.

"Thank you, Trent." She settled into the chair he held, then waited while he took the seat on the other side of the table.

"My pleasure, Am." His deep voice was soft with caring. His dark eyes were clouded with concern.

Under his watchful gaze, Amber bit into the grilled cheese sandwich. Warm smoked cheddar cheese exploded on her tongue. She tasted pepper, too. Trent had added extra seasoning the way she liked it. She briefly closed her eyes as precious memories and warm gratitude filled her. Little by little, her tension eased.

Seeming to relax as well, Trent guided their conversation into silly, throwaway subjects: which cheese was the second-best choice for grilled cheese sandwiches, the preference for hot or cold beverages to have with the sandwich, the lengthening daylight hours. These meaningless topics carried them to the kitchen cleanup.

Amber could almost forget the mind-rending debriefing Crys and Luke had put her and Trent through. And the barrage of questions and follow-up questions Jade had launched at them. Having to relive the terror in the parking garage over and over again had been almost as harrowing as the attack. Amber's heart was heavy. The one benefit of this experience—if anyone could refer to it as such—was that she could better empathize with victims of crime and their families. The fear—and to some extent, shame—was almost indescribable. How could she recover from this? The event had changed her forever.

Amber unclenched her teeth. "Thank you again for the grilled cheese sandwich and tea. It really helped."

"I thought you could use a hot meal. You've been through a lot today." Trent returned the pan he'd just dried to the cabinet beneath the kitchen counter.

"So have you." Amber turned off the faucet. "Please don't pretend you weren't also in danger."

"You're right." Trent straightened and closed the cabinet. "I was in danger, too. But you were the shooter's target. I saw that bullet go through the windshield of the car behind you barely a second after you stepped away. I almost fainted."

The image of Trent Mitchell collapsing under pressure was laughable. If he was trying to make her smile, he was on the right track. She could at least meet him halfway.

Her smile was faint and felt crooked. "You? You were impressive. I—I was a mess."

Trent caught her forearm as she stepped to move past him. His hand was large, warm and firm. "You were strong and amazing. You kept moving, which was *critical*. You did everything you could to stay safe, including crawling under a car without hesitation regardless of the damage to your beautiful suit."

Amber rolled her eyes. "A suit can be replaced. Your life can't be."

"*Our* lives." Trent let his arm fall back to his side. He watched as Amber crossed to the hand towel hanging from a hook beside the stove.

"I hate that you were in danger because of me." Amber's muscles felt tight. She dried her hands, then returned the towel to its hook. "I'm the reason people were at risk in that parking lot this evening. That shooter was after me and didn't care that innocent people, including you, were all around me. If—"

"When are you going to acknowledge that you aren't to blame for any of this?" Anger sharpened Trent's voice. It was like a blade slicing through the fog of her misery. "You didn't bring the shooter into the parking garage. The shooter chose that location."

"But if anyone other than me had gotten hurt—"

"It would have been the shooter's fault." Trent caught her shoulders, giving her a little shake. "Stop blaming yourself. We need to figure out how to do a better job of keeping you safe. Obviously, my plan was an epic fail. I almost got you killed."

Amber stiffened. She gave Trent a narrow-eyed stare. "It's okay for you to blame yourself needlessly but not for me?"

Trent's eyes locked onto hers. Their dark depths glinted, shining with an intensity that caused Amber's breath to lodge in her throat. "Whatever happens to you, happens to me."

His rough voice moved over her skin like an electric current. Without thinking, Amber stepped closer to him. Her eyes still holding his. She cupped the side of his lean, chiseled face with her palm. The warmth of his skin poured into her, rolling down her arm and across her breasts.

"I feel the same way." Her voice was thin, soft. Unrecognizable. "If any harm had come to you, it would have killed me."

Trent's eyes swept over her face, searching for an answer to a question that was still unclear to her.

"Amber." His ragged tone made her name a whole statement.

His breath caressed her lips before he lowered his mouth to hers. Amber's eyes drifted close. She shifted closer. Twining her arms around his broad, muscular shoulders, Amber pressed her body to his. Trent's arms wrapped around her waist. His hands held her close to him. So close. His warmth traveled into her breasts. It radiated throughout her torso and pooled in her gut. Every speck of fear that had burrowed into her system over the past almost three hours evaporated in his embrace. Amber felt a restlessness replacing it. Heat and longing were growing apace.

Trent's lips moved over hers, nibbling, caressing, coaxing her lips apart.

Amber moaned low in her throat. "Trent, let me taste you."

He opened his mouth at her command and welcomed her tongue inside. He tasted like lemon tea and sexy promises. Trent drew her tongue deeper into his mouth, stroking and teasing it. Amber moaned again, longer this time.

Trent broke their kiss and whispered against her throat. "I've missed holding you in my arms."

Amber slid her hands under his shirt. His skin was hot, smooth and firm under her fingertips. "Your body's so hot. You're making me crazy."

He lifted her off her feet and settled her onto the kitchen counter. Amber saw the heat in his eyes and melted. He stripped first his shirt, then hers and dropped them together to the floor. Oh, dear goodness. The man's torso looked like it had been sculpted by loving hands. Broad shoulders, firm pecs and tight abs. His biceps flexed as he drew her closer.

Trent looked at her. Amber's nipples tightened inside her cranberry lace demi-cup bra. Fires ignited in his eyes. They lit the dormant embers inside her. Amber throbbed. Trent lowered his head and kissed the top curves of her breasts.

Cupping his chin, Amber lifted Trent's head and pressed her lips to his. She wrapped her arms and legs around him and deepened their kiss. He tightened his arms around her. Dear heaven, she remembered this feeling. The feeling of being wanted, treasured, loved.

Loved?

Wait. What was happening right now? Amber dropped her legs. She let her hands slip from his shoulders to his rock-hard pecs. She broke their kiss.

Her body ached from that separation. "Trent. We need to stop."

Trent stilled. Amber could sense him clearing his thoughts. He leaned away from her. His eyes were cloudy and unfocused.

"Why?" He seemed to struggle with the word.

Amber swallowed. Oh, for the love of Pete. She wanted him so badly, she could taste him. "I don't want us to confuse the reason for what we're feeling right now." It was hard for her to say these things with him standing between her thighs. "We experienced a trauma today. I don't want us to confuse what we're feeling because of the attack in the parking garage with what we had in the past."

Trent searched her features, probed her eyes. Amber remained motionless under his scrutiny. He seemed to be trying to read her.

Finally, Trent stepped back from her thighs. "Of course. All right." Retrieving their shirts from the floor seemed to give him time to gather his thoughts. "I want to be clear, Am. I'm not confused." He returned her clothing. "I know what I feel, and I know what I want. I want you back in my life. If you need time to figure out how you feel about me, I understand. But my feelings for you will never change."

Amber watched Trent stride from the kitchen. She buried her face in her shirt and struggled to slow her heartbeat. She knew what she wanted as well. But after everything she'd been through, did she have the courage to go after it?

"What time should I pick you two up?" Caleb directed his question to Amber and Trent. He'd taken his usual seat on the left side of the sofa in Trent's living room late Saturday afternoon.

"You don't mind my joining you?" Trent's expression reflected the surprise in his voice.

He'd carried in dining room chairs for Luke and Crys while he'd taken the armchair beside the sofa. Luke was seated. The other chair waited empty while Crys roamed the room. Amber and Jade had joined Caleb on the sofa.

Amber's attention returned to Crys. Her sister wore a black cap-sleeve blouse with tiny yellow sunflower patterns and lightweight red slacks. Long strides carried her from Trent's picture window, which framed an aerial view of the Arena District, to his black-and-sterling-silver entertainment center, complete with a large flat-screen TV.

What was going on in that sharp mind of hers? Was she aware of the conversation around her?

Caleb's voice drew Amber's attention. "Of course not. We're all basically going to the same place. It's not a problem for me to drive both of you."

Jade's dark espresso eyes narrowed with her innate suspicion. "In exchange for what?"

Caleb shook his head. "In exchange for helping to keep them safe. If someone's in trouble and I can help, I'm not going to say no."

Luke looked at Jade. "He's proven that more than once."

Jade didn't say anything, but Amber sensed her sister wasn't buying it.

Amber gave Caleb a grateful smile. "Thank you. I appreciate your trouble. I'll split the gas with you."

"We both will." Trent inclined his head. "Thanks."

Caleb nodded. "So, it's settled."

They agreed on the time and place of their new routine, which would start Monday. Amber had reservations about bringing someone else into the danger that had become a big part of her life. She needed to find a way to repay Caleb and also Trent for their heroism.

Once Amber, Trent and Caleb had agreed to the details of their new strategy, Crys turned to face the room. It was as though she'd been waiting for them to complete their business before making them aware of the problem she'd been wrestling with.

Her coffee-brown eyes seemed to linger on Luke before moving on to Trent, Amber, Jade and Caleb. "Everything we're about to discuss stays in this room." She looked from Jade to Caleb. "This discussion is pure speculation and can only be used for background. Nothing else. It's not to be published, not yet."

Caleb sat forward. "Of course. I agree."

Jade nodded. "Always. I agree." She frowned at Caleb. "I'm curious. Why is *Capital Daily*'s executive editor assigned to cover the news? Aren't you busy enough managing the staff and the budget, neither of which are doing well?"

Caleb shrugged. His eyes moved over Jade's tense features. "My agreement with the paper was that I'd cover a couple of big stories each year, just to keep my hand in investigative reporting."

Amber could feel Jade bristling beside her. Her sister had been laid off from the newspaper—let go from a career she'd loved—allegedly due to budget cuts. The timing had coincided with Caleb being hired as the publication's first-ever executive editor. And now she'd learned part of the deal Caleb had made with the paper had been to cover the investigative journalism she'd loved so much.

Amber sighed a little inside. She understood her sister's resentment. But she maintained Caleb wasn't to blame. Jade's former boss, the late Brock Mann, and the newspaper's publishers were the reason for the staffing changes. Amber was confident Jade understood that. Caleb was just a target within her temper's reach. Amber felt sorry for the guy. It was obvious, at least to her and Crys, that Caleb had a crush on their sister.

Crys's expression softened as she looked at Jade. "Your podcast is great. You're doing a great job of focusing on Aunt K and her cold case. I appreciate you're not bringing Maeve Rhoades or the serial killings into your coverage."

Luke smiled. "Crys is right. You're really talented. Several agents at the bureau have subscribed to it."

Caleb raised his hand. "So have I."

"Thank you. I'm glad you're enjoying it." Jade's cheeks filled with a faint blush. "I wouldn't bring in Maeve's case without consulting you both first. Besides, this podcast is focused on Aunt Kenny's homicide investigation.

There doesn't appear to be a link with Maeve's case, at least not yet."

Crys glanced at Amber. "Let's review our theories of this stalking case."

Amber gave her sister a reassuring smile. "We know Maeve Rhoades denies any intention of plotting to kill me, despite what your colleagues' CI claims."

Luke shrugged his eyebrows. "The CI is sticking to her story, although now her handlers admit she hasn't always been reliable."

Caleb shook his head. "It would've been nice to know that up front."

Jade snorted. "I agree."

Amber ignored the startled look Caleb gave her younger sister. She focused on Crys, who'd started pacing again.

Crys spoke over her shoulder. "We also verified Roland Dragon's whereabouts for the time of the attack at the parking lot."

Luke stood, moving closer to Crys. "He has several credible witnesses who place him at an industry association breakfast meeting."

Jade interrupted. "But we agree it's possible he could've hired someone for the attack. He wouldn't have had to have been there himself. And he took a call during the breakfast meeting, which one could speculate could've been from the shooter."

Amber shifted to look at Jade. "As you said, that's pure speculation. We don't have solid evidence linking him to any of the murders, either Aunt Kendra's; Vic's; Brock Mann's; or Carter Wainscott's, the copycat murderer's victim."

Jade flipped a restless hand. "I know. I admitted I was speculating, but he's staying on my list."

Trent looked to Crys and Luke. "Have Martina Monaco or Jasper Bright changed their mind about the deal the city's offering?"

"No, they haven't." Luke crossed his arms. His pale blue long-sleeved T-shirt stretched across his broad shoulders. "They're both adamant that the murders—Kendra's, Vic's, Carter's and Brock's—weren't their idea, but they won't give up the name of the person who paid them."

Crys shook her head. "They're more afraid of whoever paid them to commit the murders than they are of going to prison and facing the people they were instrumental in putting into the same prisons they're going to."

"That's daunting." Caleb rested his elbows on his knees. "How powerful is the person who's pulling the strings?"

Jade arched an eyebrow. "As powerful as Roland Dragon maybe?"

"There's another theory about the stalker." Crys turned to Trent. "Someone who's interested in you may consider Amber competition for your affections."

Standing beside Crys, Luke shifted to face Trent also. "Sounds like a solid theory. Do you have any leads to share?"

Trent spread his arms. "As I told Am, the only person I can think of that could possibly fit that description is one of the law clerks in my office, Barbi Hamlin. I've told her that, regardless of my current relationship status, I'm not interested in having one with her."

Jade shifted on the sofa to face him. "Was that before or after she confronted my sister in the women's restroom of the city attorney's office?"

Trent's eyes leaped to Amber's. She shrugged. He knew she and her sisters didn't keep secrets from each other.

His attention returned to Jade. "It was before."

"And how did she take your rejection?" Caleb's dark eyes held a hint of sympathy. Trent wasn't sure if it was because of the situation with Barbi or at being the new focus of Jade's irritation.

"Not well." Trent sighed. "Other than Barbi, I'm not aware of anyone else being interested in me. And, candidly, I can't imagine Barbi shooting anyone, not even to scare someone off."

"It wouldn't have to be someone you met recently." Crys stepped closer to Trent as though willing him to come up with credible suspects. "It could have been an old relationship or an old acquaintance."

"That would've been three years ago." Trent stared at the honey-wood flooring, trying to access years-old memories. "Am and I dated for almost two years before our engagement. After our engagement, I returned to California for a year." Frustration pushed Trent to his feet. "If someone felt threatened by my relationship with Amber, wouldn't they have tried something three years ago?"

"Not necessarily." Amber shook her head. "Maybe they were working up the courage to approach you before you and I were assigned to Maeve's case."

Jade gave Amber a searching look. "Am, maybe you're the one with the secret admirer."

Amber's lips parted in surprise. "Me?"

"Don't act like it's a ridiculous idea." Jade waved her hand dismissively. "You're beautiful, intelligent, kind. Maybe the stalker's someone romantically interested in you."

Amber shook her head. "Then why would they be trying to kill me?"

"Because they're not thinking straight." Jade stood, seemingly excited by her new theory. "I think I'm on to something. Like you said to Trent. Perhaps the shooter is tired of you not noticing them and their infatuation has turned to resentment so they want to kill you. Or maybe they're thinking if they can't have you no one can."

Crys frowned. "Or maybe your stalker has a hero complex. By putting you in danger, they hope you'll run to them."

Every eye in the room turned to Trent.

Trent looked surprised and a little offended. "I'm not the shooter."

Amber shook her head again, expelling a disgusted sigh. "Of course you're not. You didn't even know there was a shooter until after Officer Blaze and I were shot."

"How do we know that?" Jade gave Trent a narrow-eyed stare. "We only have his word for that. Where were you—"

"J." Amber gestured toward the empty spot beside her on the sofa. "Please sit down."

Jade hesitated before returning to the sofa. She obviously wasn't ready to give up on Crys's hero-complex theory. Amber understood her sister's protective instincts. She would have felt the same way in Jade's position. Her eyes caught Trent's. She'd do anything to keep the people she loved safe—even from herself.

Chapter 12

Two more hours until he saw Amber again. Trent pulled his eyes away from the clock in the lower-right corner of his computer monitor late Monday afternoon. He was meeting Amber in her office, then Caleb would pick them up in front of the building.

It was only Monday, but the week already felt long. Knowing he'd be spending the rest of the day with Amber made it bearable. Another indication he had to convince her to give him another chance. Of course, he wished this time they were under more normal, safer circumstances. But Crys and Luke were hard at work searching for the person who was threatening Amber's life. He appreciated that they kept him updated with their investigation. Their information helped him protect Amber, which was the most important responsibility he—

"Excuse me, Trent." Barbi's voice carried in from the threshold of his office. "Do you have a few minutes for me?"

Trent swung his eyes to his doorway. Barbi sauntered into his office, pulling the door closed. That wasn't a good sign. Trent swallowed a sigh and hoped for the best. Barbi settled into one of the two gray visitor's chairs. The heavy cinnamon scent of her perfume wafted to him from across his desk. Her smile rang warning bells at the back of his brain.

He'd warned her that her continued harassment would get her transferred to another attorney. The ultimatum had seemed to have the desired effect. This morning, she'd been focused on her work, quieter, less demanding of his attention. Apparently, something had changed during the day.

Trent braced himself. "What can I do for you, Barbi?"

Barbi sat straighter in her chair, crossing her left leg over her right. "Well, you can start with rethinking your position on our personal relationship."

Tension gripped his neck and shoulders. "No, and since you won't respect my boundaries, you'll have to be reassigned to another attorney."

Barbi uncrossed her legs and leaned forward. "But, Trent—"

"No, Barbi." He held his right hand up, palm out. "I warned you." He lowered his hand. "If someone were harassing you at work, I'd make sure it stopped. I deserve the same respect."

Why did he have to keep having this conversation with the law clerk? She knew sexual harassment was against the law and a cause for dismissal. If their roles were reversed, he'd already be out of a job.

Barbi spread her arms. "Trent, I have so much more in common with you than Amber Rashaad does."

He wasn't going to humor her theories and arguments. They weren't the point. "Barbi—"

She interrupted him, waving a hand between them. "We're both defense attorneys. Amber's a prosecutor. What would you even have to talk about?"

Trent stood behind his desk. He'd had more than enough. "Leave my office, Barbi. Now."

"I'm just trying to get you to see the truth like my room-mate told me to." Still seated, Barbi stared up at him. Her silver blouse deepened the color of her grayish-green eyes. She'd paired the blouse with a red pencil-slim knee-length skirt. "My roommate is always encouraging me to stand up for myself, which is what I'm doing. She's always tell-ing me if you don't go after what you want, you'll never get it. She'd do anything for me."

Long, frustrated strides carried Trent to his door. "Enough, Barbi. You have to take me seriously when I tell you to back off."

"But we were meant for each other, Trent. We both have similar values, similar interests. I truly believe that. Please, Trent. I'm a better match for you than Amber is."

Trent unclenched his teeth. "This is where I work—"

Barbi stood. "Trent, I'm in love with you."

Trent froze with his hand wrapped around the door. He clenched his teeth and took a breath. For pity's sake. "I've told you I'm not in love with you. At all." He turned to hold her eyes. "And I never will be. I don't see you in that light."

Her chin trembled. "But you see Amber like that?"

"That's none of your business."

"She's wrong for you." Barbi clenched her hands at her sides. "She's broken up with you at least once before. What makes you think she's going to stay with you this time?"

Trent narrowed his eyes. "I'm not having this conver-sation with you."

He should have known Barbi would have learned the whole, sad story of his failed engagement with Amber. For some reason, she was determined to convince him to start dating her. Were his chances of reconciling with Amber as hopeless as Barbi's chances of a romantic relationship with him? He desperately hoped not.

Barbi crossed her arms and angled her head. "Why do men always want to be with women who are bad for them?"

He pulled open the door. "Leave. Now."

Barbi marched toward him. Catching Trent off guard, she shoved the door closed, grasped handfuls of his pale gray shirt and pulled him toward her.

Trent reared back. He pried her fingers free of his clothing and stepped away from her. "You've crossed the line, Barbi. You and I will never work together again. Get. Out. Now."

Choking back a sob, Barbi ran out of his office.

Furious, Trent exerted all his self-control to keep from slamming his door. Instead, he closed it with an almost silent click before returning to his desk. He briefly closed his eyes. He could imagine the horrible rumors that would start if any of his colleagues saw her dramatic exit.

Trent took a calming breath before returning to his desk. He had to call HR. Barbi needed to be reassigned. Now. Immediately.

His desk phone rang before he could take hold of his receiver. He answered it on the first ring. "Trent Mitchell."

"Mr. Mitchell, it's Roy Bivens with the DRC's deputy director's office." The male voice was brisk and professional.

Why was a representative of the Ohio Department of Rehabilitation & Corrections contacting him? "How can I help you, Mr. Bivens?"

"I regret to inform you that your client Maeve Rhoades is dead."

Trent straightened in surprise. Maeve was dead? His immediate reaction was regret that Maeve wouldn't have the trial she'd wanted. On the heels of that thought was concern for Amber. What were the odds that Maeve's death was connected to the threats against Amber?

Right now, he'd have to say that connection seemed very strong.

"The guards found Maeve in her cell. She was unresponsive." Luke loosened his brick-red tie and released the top two buttons of his pale gray shirt. He must have left his navy suit jacket in his car.

He was seated on one of the two chairs he and Trent had carried in from Trent's dining room Monday evening. They'd placed the chairs on the left end of the sofa. Crys had taken the second one.

Amber couldn't get past the surprise of Maeve's death. Trent had filled her and Caleb in on the news during the drive back to Trent's condo. He hadn't had much information to share. Apparently, neither had Crys and Luke. Roy Bivens had called them this afternoon as well. She'd considered the possibility Maeve would hire someone to kill her. It had never occurred to her that someone would kill Maeve.

It should have.

"I think I'm the only one playing catch-up." Jade wore casual black slacks and a black-and-white patterned blouse. "Was there anything suspicious about the scene? Were there indications of a struggle?"

Seated between Jade and Caleb, Amber felt bombarded by the investigative journalist vibes.

Jade had been the last to arrive at Trent's condo. Not surprising, considering the rush-hour traffic between downtown and her home on the northwest side. She'd ignored the space on the sofa between Amber and Caleb, and instead created a spot for herself beside the sofa's right arm, forcing Amber to slide over.

"No signs of a struggle." Crys paused as though reviewing her earlier call with Roy Bivens and Luke in her mind. "According to Roy, nothing about the scene raised any alarms. One of the guards found Maeve in her cell after lunch. It looked like she used her bed linens to hang herself."

Trent picked up the summary. "Roy said her death was being investigated but that it seems like she committed suicide."

To the casual observer, Trent seemed relaxed as he sat back in his armchair. He'd propped his left ankle on his right knee. But Amber sensed the tension around him like a force field. She was anxious, too. Something about Maeve's sudden death seemed…off.

Jade scanned the room, seeming to skip over Caleb. "Does anyone else have a hard time believing Maeve would commit suicide, especially before her trial?"

A chorus of yeses circled Amber. "Trent and I met with Maeve last Tuesday, a week ago. She'd been adamant that she wanted the trial to move forward. She was hoping to use it to expose Dragon & Kelp's corrupt business practices. It was part of the defense she'd wanted Trent to use."

Luke inclined his head toward Crys. "She told Crys and me the same thing when we questioned her about the threats against you."

Jade crossed her arms under her chest and pressed back against the sofa. "I wonder whether any of the prison guards are on Roland Dragon's payroll."

"We don't have proof that the guards were involved." Caleb leaned forward to catch Jade's attention. A plain bronze tie clip kept his emerald tie in place. Thin emerald lines striped his mint-green shirt.

Jade cocked her head. "Then what's your theory of the case, Poirot?"

Amber struggled with a smile at Jade's reference to Agatha Christie's famous fictional detective.

"Don't take her jabs personally." Crys waved a hand toward Jade. "Anger is her love language."

Amber gave Crys a wide-eyed look of warning. Knowing Jade's temper, Amber was surprised Crys would make such a revealing comment. They both knew she'd pay for her indiscretion at a time and place of Jade's choosing. Crys shrugged, her shoulders moving irreverently beneath her teal blouse. Images of large red and yellow tulips covered the cotton material.

"That's good to know." Caleb flashed a grin, breaking the silent exchange between Amber and Crys.

Jade's sharp cheekbones filled with an angry flush. She shifted toward Trent, putting her back to the rest of the room. "We have Roland Dragon's prior bad acts, which I know are not admissible in court."

"And we have the missing footage on the security camera," Crys muttered.

Amber's head snapped toward her. "What are you saying? That someone tampered with the camera?"

Crys exchanged a look with Luke. She seemed to take her boyfriend's almost imperceptible nod as agreement that she should share the information with the group.

"What I'm about to say does not leave this room." Crys waited for everyone to agree before continuing. "I'd asked Roy what the security camera footage showed. Maeve was found shortly after lunch and he was calling us at almost five. I was sure they'd had time to view the recording."

Luke picked up the narrative. "That's when he admitted there was almost eleven minutes missing from the video file."

Amber frowned at the hardwood flooring. "That sounds like enough time for someone to set the scene to look like suicide. But not enough time for the suspect to cover signs of a struggle. And why didn't anyone report hearing the attack?"

"Maybe Maeve was already unconscious." Jade shifted toward Crys. "Maybe someone tampered with her meal. Could you ask them to check for drugs in Maeve's system?"

Luke nodded. "That's a good idea."

Crys stood to pace the room. Amber had been waiting for her to do that.

Her older sister spoke over her shoulder. "We still need closure on the CI's claim that Maeve was trying to hire a hit man to hurt Am." She turned to face Amber. "Luke and I are meeting with the CI again in the morning."

Amber shivered. "I suppose we can't assume Maeve's death means I'm safe now."

Crys shook her head. "I'm afraid not." She turned to Trent. "If you don't mind, it would be best if Am stayed here a while longer."

Trent looked surprised. "Of course I don't mind." He addressed Amber. "Stay here for as long as you'd like."

Amber saw the heat in his eyes. She turned away. She wasn't ready to address it. She needed more time to find a consensus between what her mind was saying and the messages her body was sending. Although time seemed to be complicating their situation.

Caleb spread his arms, giving Amber a direction in which to shift her attention. "I'm happy to continue commuting with both of you. Same pickup and return times. And I promise not to reveal the information you've shared with me until you give me the okay."

Amber managed a smile. "Thank you, Cal. I appreciate that."

"So do I," Trent added. "With Maeve's death, we'll have to adjust our prep for a posthumous trial. I don't think it will delay the court date, though."

Amber ran through the necessary filings in her mind. "I hope not. The victims' families have been waiting for justice for their loved ones long enough." She shared a look between her sisters. "We know all too well how that feels."

Jade looked from Crys to Amber. "At the risk of sounding callous, what impact does Maeve's death have on our investigation into Aunt Kenny's homicide?"

Trent frowned. "It shouldn't have any effect. Maeve's case wasn't connected to your aunt's murder."

"Maybe not at first." Agitation seemed to propel Jade to her feet. "But Maeve's death changes things. It's not unreasonable to suspect Roland Dragon directed the murders of both Maeve and our aunt. Think about it." She spun on her heels to look at Trent. "He could've hired someone to pretend to be Barbi Hamlin so she could interview Maeve in an effort to find out what Maeve was planning to say during the trial. He knew if she got to trial, her testimony would damage his company. Again."

Amber frowned. "I hadn't thought about that."

Trent's eyes met hers. "Neither had I."

Caleb stood and approached Jade near Trent's fireplace. "But his threats couldn't scare Amber off the case. And he couldn't convince Trent to even meet with him to propose influencing Maeve's testimony."

Jade gave Caleb an approving nod. Amber wondered

if it hurt her. "So he resorted to yet another murder. First our aunt Kenny." She pointed to Crys. "Then your partner." She turned to Caleb. "Our editor and now Maeve. All of these murders are connected to Dragon & Kelp's corruption."

Trent's skepticism was palpable. "You think Roland bribed one of the prison guards to kill Maeve to keep her silent?"

"He's done it before." Amber's voice was dry. "Victor Hansen, Jasper Bright, Martina Monaco, Brock Mann. Circumstantial evidence points to Roland Dragon bribing all of them."

Trent glanced from Amber to Luke, Crys and Caleb before settling his attention on Jade. "What happened to your theory that the stalker was a secret admirer or ex-girlfriend?"

Jade snorted her derision. "That was just a momentary fad. My money's always been on Roland Dragon."

"This is all conjecture." Trent sat forward in his seat. "Victor Hansen didn't name anyone in his confession letter, right? And neither Jasper Bright nor Martina Monaco have taken the deal because they won't name the person or people who paid them, either. And Brock Mann is dead."

Amber's mind played images of the people who'd been connected with Dragon & Kelp LLC but were no longer alive: her aunt; three former members of the board of directors; Carter Wainscott, one of the company's lawyers; and now Maeve.

"Everything you've pointed out is true." Amber inclined her head toward Trent in consideration. "But we can't ignore these connections to Dragon & Kelp."

Trent raised his thick black eyebrows. "But even if the

connections to Dragon & Kelp are solid, that doesn't automatically mean Roland Dragon is involved."

Jade's tone was insistent. "It doesn't mean he's not."

Amber searched Trent's rugged features. "Why does the idea of Roland Dragon's involvement make you so uncomfortable?"

Trent shook his head. "I don't like the idea of accusing someone based solely on speculation. When you do that, you run the risk of making the evidence fit the person instead of following the evidence to the right suspect."

Crys returned to her seat. "You're right. I give you my word I won't do that."

Amber gave Trent a considering look. On the surface, his reasoning made sense and she was loath to think his defense of Roland went any further than that. But a little voice deep in the back of her mind asked whether there could be another reason Trent balked at their suspecting Roland's involvement in these murders. Could he be reconsidering Roland's tempting offer of financial support for his future political career?

"Good morning, Amber." The tentative voice coaxed Amber's attention from her computer to her office doorway.

It didn't take much cajoling. Between the attempts on her life, Maeve's suspicious death and her reawakening feelings for Trent, it was a struggle for her to concentrate. She jumped at the distraction.

Amber saved the file she was working on and spun her chair toward her doorway. Officer Paul Ciero stood in the threshold. She was momentarily taken off guard to find him in civilian clothes. His long-sleeved red cotton T-shirt hugged his muscled chest. He'd paired it with dark blue casual pants and black sneakers.

Her smile was natural. "I think this is the first time I've ever seen you in casual clothes."

He flashed his easy grin. "I took the day off."

"And yet you find yourself in the Columbus City Attorney's Office." She tilted her head. "I think you're doing this whole vacation thing wrong." Amber gestured toward her closest guest's chair. "Please come in."

"I didn't mean to interrupt you." Paul settled into the chair. "Well, actually, I did. Otherwise I wouldn't be here. What I meant was I'm sorry to interrupt you."

"It's not a problem, Paul. What brings you here?" Amber searched his earnest expression for a hint of what might have prompted his visit. His warm brown eyes were troubled. Lines of tension bracketed his mouth.

Paul cleared his throat. "I heard Maeve Rhoades died in prison yesterday."

The situation still didn't seem real. Perhaps that was because of all the unanswered questions surrounding Maeve's demise. Why would she have committed suicide if she was determined to go to trial? Why is there missing footage from the security camera closest to her cell? Had she hired a hit man? If not, why would someone want Amber to believe she had?

"Trent and I got the news late yesterday afternoon." She glanced back toward her computer. "We're preparing to hold a posthumous trial. I'm going to contact the victims' families later today to let them know."

Paul raised his eyebrows. "It's kind of you to let them know, which isn't surprising. You're a kind person."

Amber shook her head. "I think of it as part of the job.

Everyone who's grieving a deceased loved one deserves closure."

An image of her aunt Kendra settled in her mind. Kendra Chapel had been murdered one year, two months and five days earlier. She and her sisters were still searching for closure. Would they ever know who'd ordered her murder and why?

Not knowing the who and why of her aunt's attack was almost as painful as not having Aunt Kendra in her life. If she could help prevent the families of other victims of violent crimes from experiencing that same pain, she would. That was the reason she was going to personally contact the families of Maeve's alleged victims to let them know the trial was moving forward despite Maeve's untimely passing.

"Those victims' families are lucky to have you as an advocate." A glint of admiration brightened Paul's dark eyes. "But it must be a relief not to have Maeve threatening you anymore."

Amber tensed. She searched Paul's face. His open expression didn't give her cause to believe his statement was anything other than concern for her well-being. Still, it unsettled her.

She struggled not to reveal her dismay, either by her expression or her tone. "How did you know Maeve Rhoades was the suspect threatening me? We didn't divulge that information to anyone other than the people directly involved in her trial."

Amber didn't have time for subterfuge. She wasn't going to pretend not to know what Paul was talking about in an effort to maintain the trial's objectivity. She needed answers yesterday. And it seemed Paul had become an unexpected source of information. The only people who were supposed to know Maeve had been accused of trying to contract a killer were Trent and his supervisor, Amber and her supervisor, Crys, Luke, Barbi and the judge. Of course, they'd also told Jade and Caleb, but they'd been sworn to secrecy. And they'd both proven themselves to be trustworthy.

Paul's face darkened with a blush. His chuckle sounded nervous. "You know how the rumor mill is around here. Knowledge is like currency. Tawnia and I heard it on the grapevine, but don't worry. We haven't discussed it with anyone else, only with each other."

That was some comfort at least. Still, if they traced the source of the rumors, would it lead to whoever was trying to kill her? The idea was at least worth trying.

It was a struggle to manage her expectations of identifying the hitman now. "Do you remember who told you about Maeve or when you found out?"

Paul frowned as though gathering his thoughts. "Tawnia told me what Maeve had been accused of. I get most of my intel from her. She loves being in the know and thinks I should be, too. But I'm not as interested in gossip."

From the hesitation in his voice, Amber had her doubts that Paul was as opposed to hearing rumors as he claimed. "Do you remember when Tawnia told you? Was it before or after the shooting in the courthouse parking lot?"

Amber sensed Paul withdrawing as though her questions made him uncomfortable. Welcome to her world.

Paul frowned. "Why are you asking these questions? Tawnia doesn't have anything to do with this. She's not involved in any plots to have you killed."

Amber was shaking her head before he'd finished speaking. "I don't mean to imply that she's involved. But,

Paul, if you could help us trace the rumor, it might lead us to whoever is behind these threats."

Paul seemed unconvinced. "Maeve Rhoades was behind the threats. A CI overheard her asking about contract killers."

Amber sat back against her seat. He seemed to know a heck of a lot about a situation that was supposed to be confidential. "Actually, Paul, we're not convinced Maeve was trying to hire a contract killer. We think someone else was plotting to have me killed and was trying to set Maeve up to take the fall."

"Really?" Paul's surprise seemed genuine but how well did she know him?

"That's the reason the city didn't provide me with a security detail, remember? They didn't think the danger was work related."

Paul spread his hands. "They just told us the assignment had been canceled. We were never given a reason. Do you have any idea who made up the rumor about Maeve Rhoades?"

Amber shook her head. "That's what we're trying to find out. It would be helpful if you could ask Tawnia if she could remember who told her the rumor about Maeve, and whether she found out before or after the shooting at the courthouse parking lot."

"Sure. Sure, I'll ask her." Paul frowned at the floor. He seemed distracted.

"Paul, do you remember when Tawnia told you the rumor?"

He returned his attention to Amber. "It was after the shooting. I remember because Tawnia and I talked about how disappointed we were that we weren't going to be your security detail." He gestured toward her. "We were concerned about your safety, of course. But the assignment would have made a nice break from our regular patrol duties."

Amber's smile felt genuine this time. "I appreciate that. I was relieved when I learned you would've been my security."

"I should get back to it." Paul stood, circling the chair.

"Back to your vacation?" Amber tried teasing him. He still seemed very distracted.

Paul nodded. "That's right. I just wanted to see how you were doing."

Amber stood, too. "I appreciate your checking on me, Paul. Enjoy the rest of your vacation."

He nodded again, then gave her one last, lingering look before disappearing beyond her door. Amber stared at the threshold for a while. It hadn't been her imagination. Paul had come to her office for a purpose, but it hadn't been the one he'd claimed. Amber sank back into her seat. This situation was making her suspect everyone who wasn't related to her by blood. She buried her head in her hands. It would break her heart if Paul were somehow involved in this plot to have her killed.

Chapter 13

"Trent Mitchell." He'd been about to call Amber on his cell when the phone on his desk had announced a call. The identification screen read Unknown Caller. Never a good sign.

"Mr. Mitchell. May I call you Trent?" The voice was familiar; still, he wasn't going to take a chance in case he guessed wrong.

"With whom am I speaking?" Trent saved his computer file and focused on the call. Where had he heard that voice before?

A low chuckle rolled down the satellite connection. It had notes of power and privilege. "This is Roland, Trent. Roland Dragon. We were supposed to have drinks with your very good friend Alan Ma the other day."

Trent decided against correcting Roland's misperception of his relationship with Alan. "Mr. Dragon, as I explained that day, it's inappropriate for us to have any contact while Maeve Rhoades's trial is pending or during her trial."

Even after Maeve's trial, it was questionable whether he'd want to speak with Roland Dragon. The Rashaad sisters were not his greatest fans.

"Trent—"

"Mr. Mitchell." He needed the distance, not only to

counterbalance the appearance of impropriety but to help show Amber he was on her side and not Dragon & Kelp's.

Roland chuckled again. The sound was starting to grate on Trent's nerves. "All right, Mr. Mitchell. Although what's in a name?"

Trent wasn't in the mood for Shakespearean quips. He had a mountain of work to get through. More importantly, he wanted to speak with Amber to make sure she was okay. All right, who was he kidding? He needed to hear her voice. It was like a physical ache. He realized he'd taken Amber for granted the first time they were together. He'd learned his lesson and was hoping to prove to her he was worthy of a second chance so he could make things right.

"Mr. Dragon, I'm not jeopardizing my name and reputation by having conversations with you while I'm lead counsel on Maeve Rhoades's trial. Please don't call or—"

Roland Dragon interrupted. "I know Maeve is dead." His voice was flat, devoid of even the hint of humor he'd shown since the beginning of their call. "I read about it in the *Capital Daily*. Excellent newspaper. I think you know some people who work there or at least used to."

Trent narrowed his eyes. Was it his imagination or was that a subtle threat?

"Maeve's death doesn't negate the need for a trial." Trent's response was cool. "Her name still needs to be cleared or, if she's found guilty, convicted. The three victims and their families still need justice." He paused, more for effect than reflection. "Did you think if Maeve died, her trial would go away?"

During the brief but heavy pause, Trent heard the faint sound of a theme song and murmuring as though Roland was listening to a television or radio program. The clinking noise above those sounds brought to mind the image of Roland stirring a beverage, either coffee or perhaps tea.

"Trent—"

"Mr. Mitchell." He wasn't giving Roland any ground. He was standing firm for justice, for himself, and for Amber and her family.

"I will make my point, *Mr. Mitchell*." Roland sounded like he was smirking. "I know you have ambitions for political office. I've done my homework on you. I believe you're exactly the candidate my organization would want to support."

"Why?"

"Excuse me?"

"Why do you think I'm the right candidate for your organization?" Trent couldn't let Roland's comment go unchallenged.

"You're high profile, well-educated and well-connected."

Trent's eyebrows stretched toward his hairline. "You mean I look good on paper and my family's wealthy."

"That helps." Roland gave that irritating chuckle again. "My organization can provide for you not only the financial backing to fuel your campaign. We also can establish the infrastructure you'll need to get your message to the voters who matter."

Trent would need a shower after this conversation. "I'm not interested."

"Is that right? Well, we've come to a bit of an impasse. I can't take no for an answer."

Trent could tell. "Give it a try. I've heard practice makes perfect."

There was another brief but weighty pause. Was it part of Roland's pressure technique package?

"You surprise me, Mr. Mitchell. I'd think a man as well-educated and well-connected as you would at least take the time to consider my offer. I can be a great asset for you. Or, under other circumstances, an unfortunate obstacle."

Ah, there it was: the unmistakable, undeniable threat meant to scare him into compliance.

Or so Roland thought. Trent wasn't used to being underestimated. There was a first time for everything.

He checked his watch. They'd already been on the phone for almost fifteen minutes. That was fifteen minutes longer than he'd intended. Trent straightened in his chair. "And *I've* done my homework on *you*, Mr. Dragon. You're exactly the type of donor whose support I would *not* want. So there's no point in my considering your offer. I'm not going to change my mind."

"Really?" Roland's tone frosted over. Trent could feel the cold traveling down their phone connection. He'd angered the other man. Good. "You may have misunderstood me, Mr. Mitchell. My organization is intent on strengthening our footprint on the local, state and federal government levels. We take an interest in every political office. We'll take an interest in whatever position you intend to run for. We can either support you or your opponent. And make no mistake—our candidate will win."

"And all your candidates have to do in exchange is bend the knee to you."

Another pause. "My organization's interests would need to be considered in policy matters."

Trent's body burned with anger. That Roland Dragon thought his integrity could be bought and sold like a meal at a fast-food drive-through incensed Trent. He had to lecture himself not to take the other man's disregard personally. People like Roland Dragon viewed the world through a mirror that showed only their reflection. That's why they were convinced everyone had a price.

He forced his muscles to relax and his lungs to draw a breath. "I imagine that in this case, your organization's interests would be in ensuring Dragon & Kelp's internal policy determinations remain out of court records. Am I right?"

"You appear to have an impressive understanding of my organization's operating priorities."

Trent hesitated. If Amber and her sisters were correct, Roland was probably using a similar pressure tactic on Jasper Bright and Martina Monaco to keep them silent. They both had high-profile, experienced attorneys. He imagined even law enforcement officials on the take wouldn't be able to afford their hourly legal rates. Jasper and Martina must have a very wealthy and well-invested benefactor. Trent bet he was on the phone with that benefactor right now.

He pushed past his disgust of the other man. "If you want new legal representation for Maeve Rhoades, you'll have to make the proper requests through the Franklin County Public Defender's Office. Our contact form is on our website. But I'm sure the lawyers you're paying to represent Jasper Bright and Martina Monaco can help you with that."

Trent sensed Roland's surprise. He was certain it wasn't his imagination. Roland Dragon was paying Jasper's and Martina's legal fees, which meant in effect Roland's lawyers were counseling Jasper and Martina not to take the deal the Columbus City Attorney's Office was offering them.

Trent was repulsed. "As I said, my reputation and the trust the public puts in me are not something I take lightly. If I decide to campaign for an elected office, I'll be doing so without your support. And if I'm not elected, I'll be fine with that. There are so many other ways to serve my community."

"I see." Roland cleared his throat. "Is that your final answer? Because the decisions we make often affect others."

The urge to roar down the cell phone connection like a wild beast almost overwhelmed him. Almost. Instead, Trent thought of the Cold Case Team, who were fearlessly going after Roland Dragon in an effort to gain justice for Kendra Chapel. Individually, they were impressive. Together, they were proving to be formidable.

"More threats?" Trent allowed a smile to leak into his voice. "I'm not the one who should be afraid."

Trent ended the call before Roland could respond. He took a deep breath, then stood to leave his office. He needed to stretch his legs and calm down before he spoke with Amber. He owed her and her sisters an apology. They were right. Roland was involved in the corruption at Dragon & Kelp. But how far did the corruption go and how could they prove it?

"Don't the bathrooms in the Franklin County Public Defender's Office work?" Amber was caught off guard by a weird sense of déjà vu, watching Barbi glare at her from just inside the women's restroom on her floor of the Columbus City Attorney's Office late Tuesday afternoon.

Crys and Luke had verified that Barbi wasn't on the security tape the day someone had impersonated her. They'd removed her from the list of suspects for the attack against Amber. Yet here she was, seeming very stalkerish.

The fluorescent lighting bouncing off the white tiled walls made the small room seem bigger and brighter. It was easy to see the lines of tension carved into Barbi's round, pale face.

"You think this is some sort of joke?" Barbi's voice shook with anger. "You're playing with my life."

Her accusation stole Amber's breath. She struggled to keep her voice down. "*I'm* playing with *your* life?" She tore a paper towel from the dispenser and dried her hands. "What are you doing here? What do you want?"

In less than twenty minutes, Trent would arrive to escort her out of the building to where Caleb would be waiting to drive them home. Home. With Trent. The image was distracting. But not for long. Barbi's hostile countenance jarred her back to their bitter exchange.

"Don't pretend like you don't know." Barbi fisted her hands at her sides. Her pale cheeks flushed a deep red, clashing with her low-cut, powder-pink blouse. "This is all *your* fault."

Amber closed the gap between them and spread her arms. "What are you talking about?"

"You know what I'm talking about." Barbi glared up at her. Her eyes were dark with malevolence. "You want to hear me say it? You got your way, all right? Trent reassigned me."

He reassigned—oh. Good for him.

Amber's heart raced. She was furious on Trent's behalf. "Sexual harassment in the workplace is illegal and grounds for dismissal. As a law clerk, you should know that. You're lucky to still have a job."

The blood drained from Barbi's face. Her eyes widened with surprise. "I wasn't—"

"Yes, you were." Amber crossed her arms over her chest. "He warned you repeatedly. But you didn't listen, did you? Your reassignment is on you, not on Trent and certainly not on me. It's all your doing."

Barbi's soft features twisted into an angry, ugly mask again. "Liar! You told Trent to reassign me because you know he's attracted to me. You know I'm a threat to you, and you want me out of his life before he realizes I'm a better match for him than you."

"What?" Amber's head was spinning. She felt almost dazed by Barbi's irrational accusations. "You can't possibly believe any of that."

"It's all true and—"

The sound of a toilet flushing interrupted them. Amber had forgotten someone had entered the restroom earlier. She was mortified. The snick of the lock twisting in the metal door sounded like her reputation being torn to shreds. In an instant, the chilly room became uncomfortably warm. The day had already been stressful. And now her ugly argument with Barbi had a witness. Amber closed her eyes, fighting the urge to dig a hole in the floor with her bare hands and bury herself in it.

One of her colleagues exited a nearby stall. The tall, curvy blonde wore a modest navy skirt suit with a tan square-neck blouse. She gave them a look that was somewhat embarrassed and vaguely amused. "Sorry to interrupt but I couldn't wait any longer. I have to get my kids."

"No, of course." Amber cleared her throat. Her neck was stiff with shame. "I apologize for the disruption."

Her associate's smile looked more natural. She inclined her head as she stepped to the row of sinks. Her sensible navy pumps cracked against the dark gray tiled flooring. She quickly washed her hands, then sent Amber a sympathetic smile before striding out of the restroom.

Amber's stomach turned at the idea that a colleague

had heard her clash with Barbi. How long would it take for that story to circulate her department? The fact that Trent had been sexually harassed by one of his office's law clerks. The false accusation that Amber had pressured Trent into having her reassigned. Amber's skin burned with mortification.

She returned her attention to Barbi. The law clerk didn't seem ruffled that someone had overheard her ridiculous claims. It was as though the interruption had never happened. Was she used to airing her grievances to anyone who would listen? Who else knew about her obsession with Trent and her resentment against Amber?

"Only the judge, the public defender's office and my office were supposed to be aware of your connection to Maeve Rhoades's case. Did you tell anyone else?" Amber watched Barbi's expression closely to read her reaction.

"I've already answered that." Barbi sneered the words. "I told you and Trent that I mentioned it to a few friends. That's all. I don't typically go around discussing my cases with people. It's unethical."

"So is harassing coworkers but that didn't stop you." Amber's tone was dry. "Who are these friends?"

"No one I know would go near the reformatory."

"Are you saying it's a coincidence that someone impersonated you to visit Maeve in prison?"

"Why do you keep making me repeat myself?" Barbi planted her hands on her full hips in her dark gray slacks. "I told you my friends and I had nothing to do with that. I've never met with Maeve on my own. That wasn't even my signature on the visitor's log."

"And yet someone used your driver's license to sign in." Amber searched Barbi's pale, round face. It didn't seem like the young woman was lying but something wasn't adding up. "What's your connection to Roland Dragon?"

Barbi frowned. "Who?"

Her reaction brought Amber up short. Could the law clerk on Maeve Rhoades's defense team really not know who Roland Dragon was? "Roland Dragon is the principal partner of Dragon & Kelp, the life insurance company that denied Maeve's brother's beneficiary claim."

Barbi was shaking her head before Amber finished her explanation. "I don't know him. And stop trying to distract me. This is about you and me, not Maeve Rhoades or this Roland Dragon character."

"Yes, this is about you and me." Amber took a step closer to her adversary. "But it's also about Maeve and Roland. Someone's trying to kill me and putting the lives of people I love in danger." Her mind brought her an image of Trent. Her heart clutched again at the thought of him putting his life on the line for her. "And the motive and evidence keeps bringing us back to you."

"Me?" Barbi's right palm pressed against her chest as though hoping to keep her heart from leaping out. "That's crazy. Why would I want to kill you?"

"You said yourself you blame me for Trent not falling in love with you." Amber's eyes scanned Barbi's stunned features. "You think he'll magically become interested in you if I'm out of the way."

Barbi retreated. "That doesn't make any sense. If I were to kill you, I'd go to jail, then Trent will be lost to me forever."

Good point. But this time, Amber wasn't going to remove Barbi from her suspect list so easily. This was the second time the other woman had threatened her. And she was connected to Maeve Rhoades's case. She could have easily planted the story that Maeve was trying to contract with someone to kill Amber.

"Do you own a gun, Barbi?"

She gasped. "No! My roommate does but I don't. And if I were trying to kill you, why wouldn't I do it now?"

Amber shook her head. "Too many witnesses."

"Also, I'm not trying to kill you. I want you out of Trent's life and I'll get my way. But not by killing you." Barbi spun on her heels and slammed her way out of the room.

Amber almost believed the law clerk's innocence. But then, maybe Barbi was being used and wasn't aware of it.

"She threatened you?" Trent's voice was rough with anger.

Jade sprang to her feet. "We need to talk with her. Now."

"Hold on, Impulse." Amber referenced one of Jade's favorite DC Comics characters. "Barbi didn't threaten me. This time. At least not directly."

She intercepted her younger sister as Jade circled Trent's sofa Tuesday evening. Amber was so flustered by Jade's reaction, she couldn't tell whether she was making sense. Trent was once again hosting her, Crys, Jade, Luke and Caleb in his living room. They were discussing both the attacks against her and her Aunt Kendra's cold case.

Jade's delicate, golden-brown features tightened with temper. "She menaced you. We can't overlook that."

Trent gestured toward Jade. "She's right. At the very least, she needs to know she can't get away with that."

Crys stepped away from the tan-and-gray-stone fireplace and raised her arms, drawing Amber's, Trent's, Jade's, Luke's and Caleb's attention. "Let's take a breath. I'm angry, too, but we've already questioned Barbi in connection with the attacks against Amber. She has an alibi and there's nothing tying her to the attacks."

Jade crossed her arms over her red loose-fitting long-sleeved T-shirt. "Except that she's working on Maeve's case and someone impersonated her to visit Maeve in prison."

Crys spread her arms. "That makes her a person of interest, especially since she keeps threatening Am." Temper threaded her words. "But it's not enough to make her a suspect."

"She's still on my list." Jade returned to her seat on Amber's right.

"I think Crys is right." Amber spoke to end her sisters' impasse. "Which brings me to another theory—maybe someone's using Barbi to get to me."

Trent frowned. "Do you think Barbi's working with someone? Or do you think someone's setting her up to take the fall if something happens to you?"

"I don't know." Amber gave a restless shrug. "It could be either. It could be something else or nothing at all."

She stood to join Crys in pacing the wide, bright living room. Sunlight slipped through the eggshell venetian blinds hanging from the large picture windows and spilled over the honey-wood flooring.

Caleb's voice was pensive. "It's an interesting theory. Do you think Roland Dragon could be involved?"

Amber paused to face him. Before she'd gotten up to pace, she'd had her usual seat between Caleb and Jade on the sofa. Now that she was standing, the space between those two felt like the Continental Divide.

"I asked her what her connection was to Roland. She acted like she didn't know who he was."

"I don't think she was acting." Trent's words were dry.

He leaned forward on his armchair. "Barbi's not that great with details, regardless of their importance. She's more of a big-picture person. Her not remembering Roland Dragon's name is disappointing but not surprising."

Jade's voice was dripped with sarcasm. "Her obsession with you doesn't leave her time for those pesky details."

Trent sent Jade an amused look before turning his attention to the others in the room. "I got a call from Roland Dragon."

Amber's head snapped toward him. "What did he want?"

She barely heard her own question as the others in the room spoke over her and each other.

"That's interesting." Luke raised his thick black eyebrows.

Caleb shook his head. "Speak of the devil."

Crys stopped pacing. "When?"

Jade frowned. "Why?"

"He called me around lunchtime." Trent met and held Amber's eyes. "He was trying to persuade me to run for a political office and to accept his contributions to my campaign."

Amber felt as though the air had been sucked out of the room. She and Trent had ended their relationship in part because of his political ambitions. His drive to establish the groundwork for a campaign had consumed him. Amber had felt as though he didn't have room in his life for both her and his career aspirations. When she'd confronted him with her concerns, he hadn't denied them.

Was history threatening to repeat itself?

She filled her lungs with the cool air of the living room. "Are you considering running for an elected office?"

Still holding her eyes, Trent shook his head. "Not at this time."

Amber nodded. But he wasn't ruling it out for the future.

Jade sat forward. "Roland Dragon has never been a big supporter of political campaigns. Why is he getting into politics now—?"

Caleb shrugged. "We know he's driven by wealth and power."

Jade ignored him. "—and why is he determined to support you, unless it has something to do with Amber?"

"That occurred to me as well." Trent leaned back against his chair, propping his left ankle on his right knee. "He was adamant that he wanted to support my campaign, whatever office I chose to run for. When I told him I had no intention of getting involved with him or his organization, he threatened me."

"Threatened you how?" Luke's tone was sharp.

Trent pulled his attention from Amber and looked at the special agent. "He said whatever decision I make about whether to cooperate with him could have consequences for other people."

Crys's expression grew grim. "You think *other people* is a reference to Am?"

Amber couldn't suppress a shiver. She wrapped her arms around her waist as she looked at Trent. She almost gasped at the longing in his eyes.

Trent blinked and the expression was gone, almost as though she'd imagined it. Had she?

He turned his attention to Crys. "Roland didn't refer to Am specifically. But I'm sure he knows we were engaged. Alan would have told him."

Caleb looked from Amber to Trent. "Maybe Roland's pulling Barbi's strings behind the scenes."

"That doesn't track." Jade stood from the sofa and wandered across the room to the fireplace. "Roland Dragon uses hired guns to get rid of people: Victor Hansen, Brock Mann, Carter Wainscott." She paused. "Aunt Kenny. His manipulating a besotted law clerk is off-brand."

"You're right." Amber felt her brow tighten in a scowl. "If Barbi's being manipulated, it wouldn't be by Roland. That strategy would take too long, it's not reliable and he wouldn't have deniability."

"But something's spooked him." Jade turned away from the fireplace. "Why is he suddenly interested in politics?" She inclined her head toward Trent. "And why is he fixated on you?"

Chapter 14

"It's nice of Trent to let us use his condo for our Wednesday Sisters Dinner Night." Crys settled back against the sofa's far-right corner.

"Yes, it is." Amber was touched and grateful that Trent had arranged to get together with Luke and Caleb so she could spend a safe and relaxing evening with her sisters within the walls of his high-security condo building. She was curious as to where the guys were going and what they were doing, but she wasn't going to pry.

Jade curled into the sofa's opposite end. "Yeah. He's proven himself to be a real sweetheart through this entire ordeal."

Amber avoided the question in her younger sister's dark eyes. She wasn't ready to answer it yet. Instead she allowed the lingering scents of the oregano, cheese and tomato sauce from the pizza Crys and Jade had brought over for the dinner they'd just finished to distract her.

"Yes, he has." She wrapped her palms around the clear, cold glass that contained her sweet tea. "So have both of you, Luke and Caleb. I can't tell you how grateful I am. I couldn't ask for a better group of family and friends to go through this nightmare with."

"The danger's not over yet. Remember that." Crys's voice was low. Her dark eyes were intense.

Amber nodded. "And you're all still here with me. I'm really grateful."

"We love you." Jade shrugged a shoulder. "It's obvious Trent does, too."

Amber sighed, staring into her glass as though it could provide her with advice about her future. "He's admitted he wants us to get back together. He wants me to give us another chance."

"How do you feel?" Crys asked.

Amber lifted her head, deliberately avoiding her sisters' probing eyes. They saw everything. "I hate to admit it but he's getting to me all over again. The question is how much of what I'm feeling is real and how much of it is coming from this aberration?" She swung her hand around the living room to encompass her situation. "These are unusual circumstances. Someone's trying to harm me. Trent is providing me with a safe place to hide during this danger. Can I really trust my emotional judgment right now?"

"Good point." Crys crossed her right leg over her left. "You have to be careful making big decisions under these circumstances. You don't want to jump back into a relationship with Trent only to go through another breakup."

Jade sipped her iced tea. "Let's look at this from another angle, then. Are you still angry with him?"

Amber gave a helpless shrug. "How can I be? He's putting himself in danger for me every day. Willingly. He used his body to shield me from bullets." She turned her head away, blinking back tears.

"He's shown you *that* he loves you." Jade's soft voice broke the silence. "Does it still matter whether he can tell you *why* he loves you?"

Amber's chuckle was unsteady. "No, I guess not." She turned back to her sisters.

Jade flashed a wicked grin. "For the record, I'm not angry with Trent anymore. I stopped resenting him when he showed up at your door to see for himself whether you were okay after the shooting at the courthouse parking lot."

"That did it for me, too." Crys smiled. "He could've called—"

"Or texted." Jade gave a disparaging laugh.

"Right. Instead, he showed up. That meant a lot to me." Crys gestured toward Amber with her identical glass of sweet iced tea. "Not that we're trying to influence your decision."

Amber stood from the armchair and wandered toward the fireplace. "Of course, your opinions mean a lot to me. But despite everything going on, I've had a surprising amount of time to think about my feelings for Trent. I've been unfair to him. Yes, I was angry because I thought he'd taken me for granted. I've also been blaming him for something he had nothing to do with."

"What are you talking about?" Jade sounded understandably perplexed.

The cold, dark fireplace was a reflection of her anger toward herself. She fought an almost overwhelming feeling of self-disgust. "I haven't been completely honest with you about the night Aunt Kendra was murdered."

The sudden silence was oppressive. Oxygen seemed to drain from the room. Tension stretched across the spaces between them. Amber felt it like a band being pulled to its breaking point. There were too many secrets about their aunt's death and she'd been hiding one of the most painful ones.

"What is it, Am?" Crys asked. "You can tell us."

The kindness in Crys's voice made Amber feel worse. She closed her eyes, digging deep for the courage to tell her story.

"My part in Aunt Kendra's murder has been a burden on me all this time." Amber took a shaky breath. "Aunt Kendra and I had made plans to have dinner Friday, March twenty-first." For as long as she lived, she'd never forget the day her aunt died. "We were supposed to meet at six thirty. That would have given me plenty of time to wrap up for the day and get to the restaurant. Dinner was going to be my treat."

She smiled at the memory of the pride she felt at the idea of treating the aunt who'd often treated her to special meals and snacks when she was growing up.

Her sisters waited patiently for her to continue her recount. The tension in the room had not dissipated, though.

Amber continued. "When I got to the office that morning, someone mentioned Trent had left to start the yearlong assignment with the nonprofit organization based in California. The thought of him not being in Columbus anymore knocked me off-kilter. On the one hand, I was relieved I wouldn't have to worry about running into him every day. On the other hand, I missed him as though we were still together. That's when I told Aunt Kendra I couldn't keep our dinner appointment, that I got a last-minute case."

Amber turned away from the fireplace to face her sisters. They returned her regard with almost identical expressions of grief and pain. She didn't see or sense any condemnation.

"You were right, J." Amber sighed. "I didn't have to work late. I chose to stay in the office. The project wasn't even mine. I'd volunteered to help a colleague with research on her case."

Amber felt something tickle her cheek. She brushed at it and her fingers returned wet. She hadn't realized she was crying. Once she did, the tears flowed in earnest.

"I'm so sorry." She buried her face in her hands.

Two sets of arms wrapped around her. Warmth surrounded her. It offered her healing, if she wanted to accept it.

"Am, you were hurting." Crys's voice was choked with tears. "We understand that and so would Aunt K."

Amber's words were as broken as she felt. "If I hadn't been so selfish, Aunt Kendra would be alive today."

"Or you'd both be dead." Crys shook her head. "I thought we'd agreed to stop asking what-if. We'll drive ourselves crazy chasing answers that don't exist."

"Crys's right." Jade's voice was rough with irritation and grief. She stepped back from the group embrace and pinned Amber with her eyes. "We can't change the past, Am. We can't presume to know the outcome of every possible scenario." Jade turned to collect tissues from her knapsack. She kept one and offered the others to Amber and Crys. "We can only deal with the situation we're in now and get justice for Aunt Kenny. So let's focus on that."

"You're right." Amber used Jade's tissue to dry her eyes. "I just wish I hadn't used work to get over Trent. It created a distance between me and the two of you. I blamed Trent for that when it wasn't his fault."

"It's fine, Am." Crys followed Jade to the sofa. "We're making time for each other again. That's what matters."

Jade returned to her spot in the sofa's left corner. "It's time to forgive yourself. *You* aren't to blame for what happened to Aunt Kenny."

Crys gave a decisive nod. "Jasper Bright and Martina Monaco have confessed to Aunt K's and Vic Hansen's murders, and their trials have been scheduled."

Having shared her secret, Amber felt some of the weight lift from her shoulders. "Those trials will give Aunt Kendra the justice she deserves and give us the closure we need."

A shadow swept across Jade's features. Amber had the sense Jade wanted to say something but when she caught her younger sister's eye, Jade looked away. Amber let the moment pass. For now.

"Your cat doesn't eat in your house?" Trent leaned against the wall beside Caleb's kitchen pass-through Wednesday evening.

His host had hunkered down to set a food bowl beside the back door where a short-haired, black-and-gray-tiger-striped cat waited expectantly. It seemed insensitive for Caleb to make his cat eat outdoors. Beside him, Luke chuckled. Why was that funny?

Caleb stroked the cat's round head before straightening. He watched the animal eat for a second or two as though making sure the cat approved of the meal before returning inside.

"He's not my cat." Caleb locked the back door before turning to Trent. "And for some reason, he won't come inside. It's like he'd rather starve than enter my house."

Trent glanced at Luke. The other man shrugged, shaking his head as he crossed into the kitchen.

He returned his attention to Caleb. "Whose cat is he?"

"I don't know." Caleb washed his hands at the kitchen sink. "None of my neighbors have claimed him, although several said they've seen him around."

Luke pulled paper plates from one of the dark wood kitchen cupboards. "The cat surveilled all the other houses in this neighborhood and decided Cal would be an easy mark for free meals. He was right."

The Bureau of Criminal Investigations special agent's familiarity with Caleb's home was another indication of the two men's long friendship.

Trent's cell phone chimed. Amber had responded to his text asking if she was all right.

I'm fine. My sister has a gun. Please relax and try to have a good time.

Relax? Easier said than done. He'll relax when the person who was trying to kill her was behind bars.

Trent pocketed his cell phone and searched for something useful to do. Spotting the extra-large pizza box on the kitchen counter, he moved it into the dining room and set it on the table. Trent and Luke had picked up the pie on the drive over. That's when Luke had shared that he and Caleb had met in college. They'd been roommates all four years. After graduation, Luke had returned to Cleveland and Caleb had gone home to Chicago, but they'd kept in touch. The pair seemed to be the siblings neither had had.

Luke followed Trent with the plates and napkins. Caleb grabbed a six-pack of beer from his fridge.

Caleb's and Luke's accounts of their college years, and Trent's stories of growing up in California the youngest of four siblings, kept them entertained through dinner and made the kitchen cleanup go faster. Trent didn't remember the last time he'd laughed so much and so hard. Actually, yes, he did. It was before Amber had returned his engagement ring. They'd laughed together a lot. He'd

loved that about them. But they should have talked—
really talked—more.

After the meal, Caleb brought them into his family
room. He settled into the overstuffed burgundy vinyl re-
cliner closest to his kitchen. Luke took the matching re-
cliner across the room. Trent had the sofa to himself.

"This was a good idea, getting together while Jade, Crys
and Am are having their Sisters Dinner Night." Caleb put
the Chicago Bulls game on the TV.

Trent wasn't a fan, but it wasn't his house. His Los Angeles Lakers had the late game. He'd catch it later at home.
"You and Jade met at *Capital Daily*."

A cloud passed over Caleb's features before his easygo-
ing demeanor returned. "We were there together for about
two months before the layoffs. Losing her was a huge blow
to the paper. She's an exceptional investigative reporter."

Trent agreed. The Rashaad sisters were brilliant and
brave as well as beautiful, just like their aunt Kendra Chapel. Trent also heard what Caleb wasn't saying. Jade had
made a personal impression on him as well.

Luke spoke as though reading Trent's mind. "Cal would
never have taken the job as *Capital Daily*'s executive editor
if he'd known it would have led to people being laid off."

"But that doesn't matter to Jade." Trent returned his attention to the newspaperman. Poor guy.

"It's complicated." Caleb's coal-black eyes were unreadable. "Speaking of complicated, are you considering
going into politics?"

Trent smiled at Caleb's heavy-handed effort to shift the
attention from him. He understood the other man's need
to escape the subject. Dealing with a broken heart wasn't
easy. He knew this from experience. "Are you interview-
ing me right now?"

Caleb gave him an innocent grin. "No, I'd ask for permission first. Consider this more of a friendly heads-up. Roland Dragon's talking to the state's movers and shakers about the possibility of their backing you for a run for Congress."

Shock pushed Trent's thoughts from his mind. He glanced at Luke, who looked almost as surprised as he felt.

Trent frowned at Caleb. "Are you sure?"

Caleb gestured with his half-empty bottle of beer. "As sure as I can be based on my sources. I've been keeping track of Roland—who he's connected to and what he's doing—since his company's featured in the high-profile criminal cases *Cap Daily's* covering. The serial killer's victims worked for what is now Dragon & Kelp. And Jasper Bright and Martina Monaco confessed to killing Victor Hansen and Kendra Chapel to protect Roland's company. We have that on tape, thanks to Crys and Luke."

Luke drank more of his beer. "But we know they didn't decide to protect Dragon & Kelp on their own. I wish I knew a way to convince one or both of them to admit Roland hired them to kill Vic and Kendra so we could finally give Kendra Chapel the justice she deserves, and give Crys, Amber and Jade the closure they need."

"I knew Kendra." Trent brought to mind an image of Amber's vivacious aunt who looked so much like her. "She was an impressive woman as well as being the last connection Am, Crys and Jade had to their mother. I'm sure they won't rest until they know who paid Jasper and Martina to kill her and why."

"I agree." Caleb's voice was grim. "Roland Dragon is dangerous. That's why I'm doing as much research on him as I can. I don't understand why he's fixated on you, Trent.

I don't think it's because of your wealth—or at least not only because of your wealth."

Luke gave Trent a speculative look. "And why is he determined to back your political career even after you told him you're not interested?"

Trent spread his hands. "I wish I knew. I'm not thinking about getting into politics right now."

Luke cocked his head. "Is that because politics is the reason you and Am broke up?"

Trent arched an eyebrow at the special agent. "Crys told you? How long have you been waiting to ask me that?"

"It's been a while." Luke glanced at Caleb. "Inquiring minds have wanted to know. Crys is a special woman. I don't want to lose her."

The unspoken *Like you messed up with Amber* hung in the air.

Trent understood the other man's concerns. He looked at Caleb. "Are you looking for tips as well?"

Still holding his beer, Caleb raised both arms in surrender. "Whatever you're willing to share—off the record. I mean, we know the sisters are very different but any insights would be appreciated."

"Crys is impetuous." Luke looked from Caleb to Trent. "She wants to be in the middle of the action. Jade and Am don't seem to have that same need."

Caleb stared at the TV, but Trent knew he wasn't seeing the Bulls' aggressive offense. "I think you're right. Jade is more of a planner. When we worked together, she seemed to have multiple backup plans in case something went wrong with a source or story she was working on."

"And Am is a nurturer. She wants to make sure everyone's safe." Trent sighed, settling back against the sofa. "My greatest regret is that I took Amber's love for granted.

I didn't realize that's what I was doing at the time, but she's right. Just like anything else, relationships need time and attention to remain healthy and to grow." He lifted his half-full bottle in a mock toast. "Communication is the key, gentlemen. What you don't say will haunt you."

"What didn't you say?" Caleb shook his head in confusion. "You proposed to her, didn't you?"

Spoken like someone who didn't have a clue.

Trent gave the other man a pitying glance. "If I had it to do over again, I'd say a lot more."

Luke shrugged his eyebrows. "I can appreciate that. You have a second chance to say the things you wish you'd said the first time. Unfortunately, the opportunity presented itself because her life's in danger."

Trent closed his eyes briefly from the pain caused by those words. Even now, he was forcing himself not to text Amber just to check on her.

He pinched the bridge of his nose. "I know she's questioning what she feels for me right now. I can sense it. She's wondering whether she still cares for me or if she's just grateful for my protection. To be honest, I'm wondering the same thing."

"That's understandable. This is a high-stress situation." There was empathy in Luke's voice. "In a situation like this, emotions are stronger and even more confusing."

Trent swallowed to ease the pressure in his throat. "I wish so badly none of this had happened. I want this assassin caught yesterday. I want Am to be safe—even if in the end, she walks away from me again." An image of Amber filled his mind. Trent dropped his eyes to the floor. "But I don't know if I could survive that."

Chapter 15

"How could this have happened?" Shock and disappointment made Amber's head spin Thursday evening. She'd grabbed the first coherent question that leaped into her mind.

Seated on Trent's sofa between Jade and Caleb, she looked from Crys to Luke and back.

"We don't know that yet." Crys's voice was stiff with temper. Amber also detected her shared disappointment. "Here's what we do know—Jasper Bright was found dead in his cell around four p.m."

She and Luke sat on the matching chairs Luke and Trent had carried in from Trent's dining room.

Luke gave Crys a concerned look as he picked up the narrative. "At approximately the same time, Martina Monaco was found dead in her cell. Both deaths are suspicious. We're waiting for more information."

His eyes remained on Crys as she stood to pace the living room. Luke had loosened his magenta tie. His suit jacket was missing.

"Were these attacks somehow coordinated?" Amber crossed her right leg over her left. She leaned forward in her seat as though making sure she didn't miss what little information Crys and Luke had at this point.

Crys stared into Trent's dark fireplace. Her voice trembled with frustration. "The administration doesn't want to call them coordinated attacks, although it's obvious that's what they were."

"Let me guess." Jade's words were rough with anger and another emotion Amber couldn't identify. "Security cameras had been turned off, just like in Maeve Rhoades's suspicious death. And, just as with Maeve, no one heard or saw anything."

"That's right." Disgust hung around the edges of Luke's response.

Jade snorted. "Well, that's not suspicious much." She crossed her arms and pressed back against the sofa. Her long-sleeved black T-shirt was baggy on her small frame.

Amber exchanged a tense look with Trent. The regret in his eyes told her he understood the volatile mix of sorrow, anger and frustration twisting inside her. Crys had sounded tense when she'd called earlier to say she, Jade and Luke needed to speak with her and Trent in person. She'd never imagined her update would be that their last hope of bringing Roland Dragon to justice for their aunt's murder had been taken away.

"I can't believe this has happened." Amber clenched her fists on her right leg above her raspberry shorts. "When will they be able to give us the results of their investigation?"

"Not soon enough." Crys bit the words out. Her long, stiff strides carried her from the fireplace to the picture windows. The drapes were pulled open, allowing the fading sunlight to sweep into the condo.

Jade's eyes widened and her voice was strained as though she was struggling not to shout. "The women's prison has had two murders in three days and they're not going to expedite the investigation? Why are they acting as though there's nothing suspicious about this?"

Crys crossed her arms over her chest. Her long-sleeved pale blue blouse was dotted with large red rose petals. "They still believe Maeve committed suicide."

"Urgh." Jade exhaled. "What can they give us in the meantime? What did the security cameras record before the attacks? Who had Martina and Jasper spoken with before they were killed? Who visited them from the outside recently?"

"The prison administration is handling the investigation." Luke spoke with empathy. "They won't release any of that information yet."

Amber looked from Crys to Jade on her right. She felt her younger sister's fury gathering like a category four hurricane. She didn't know how to comfort Jade while she was struggling under the weight of her own temper.

"Then all we have now is speculation." Caleb spoke from Amber's left. His baby-blue tie picked up the matching stripes in his white dress shirt. "Do we agree a possible motive for the attack would be to keep Jasper and Martina from testifying against Roland Dragon?"

Jade blew an impatient breath. "Of course."

Trent was in his usual seat in his armchair. He'd changed into black jeans and a soft gray T-shirt. "But Jasper and Martina were refusing to take the deal."

Jade slid Trent a look. "Roland couldn't count on that."

"Since we're speculating, I agree with J." Amber rubbed her forehead. "Jasper's and Martina's trials were rapidly approaching, and Roland was probably getting increasingly nervous."

"True." Trent leaned toward her. "But when Roland

called me last week, I'd asked him whether he was paying Jasper's and Martina's lawyers—"

Caleb interrupted. "You did? Good move. What did he say?"

Trent shifted his attention to the newspaperman. "He didn't deny it although he didn't admit it, either." He shifted his attention back to Amber. "Having Jasper's and Martina's lawyers on his payroll is a good way for Roland to ensure they don't take the deal to testify against him."

Jade shrugged. "So is having Jasper and Martina killed."

"Fair." Caleb inclined his head. "But to Trent's point, are we sure no one else has a motive to kill Jasper or Martina?"

"Yes." Jade spoke with finality.

Her voice once again drew Amber's concern. Her younger sister stared fixedly at the honey-wood flooring. She was so still, as though her thoughts were miles away from them. What was Jade contemplating? Should they be concerned? Amber looked to Crys with the silent question. Crys shook her head and Amber let it go.

Her eyes swept the room. "How does this development impact our investigation into Aunt Kendra's murder?"

Trent, Luke and Caleb remained silent. It felt as though they were waiting for her, Crys and Jade to decide how to proceed in light of Jasper's and Martina's deaths.

Crys returned to her seat. "We have Jasper's confession to killing Vic and Aunt K on tape. He also implicated Martina on that same tape. That evidence can be used in court during their posthumous trials."

Trent balanced his left ankle on his right knee. "With that tape, we should get guilty verdicts on the murder charges against Jasper and Martina."

Jade frowned at Trent before she shifted to face Amber. "What about Roland?"

Amber saw the pain in Jade's eyes. She felt that same ache in her heart. Her need for Roland Dragon to be held accountable for her aunt's death was so strong it almost stole her breath.

"Without Jasper's and Martina's testimony, we don't have any evidence against Roland." Amber looked around the room. "This whole time, we've been talking as though it's a fact that Roland paid Jasper and Martina to commit murder, and bribed Vic to steal the case files on Aunt Kendra's homicide investigation, but we don't actually have any proof."

Jade threw an arm toward Crys. "What about Vic's letter to you? That's a lead."

Crys shook her head. Her voice was gentle, belying the anger in her eyes. "I'm sorry, J. But Vic didn't name anyone, remember?"

"That's right." Amber rested her hand on Jade's shoulder and felt her sister stiffen. "He referred to the people who'd paid him as very bad people who have connections in very high places." She'd never forget that foreboding phrase for as long as she lived.

"So that's it?" Temper seemed to propel Jade to her feet. "Roland Dragon gets to murder his way out of responsibility again?" Her eyes rested on Amber's before moving on to Caleb's, Luke's, Crys's and Trent's. She grabbed her knapsack from the floor and shrugged it onto her narrow shoulder. "No, I won't let him. I don't care what I have to do. He's not getting away with this any longer." Jade rushed out of Trent's living room.

Amber started to follow her. "J!"

"Am. No." Crys's voice stopped her. "As upset as she is

now, she won't hear us. And I don't blame her. I'm upset, too."

Amber heard Trent's front door open and close. "We're all upset. But she's too angry to drive safely."

Crys gave a faint smile. "I drove us here." She rose. "One more thing. The people we suspected might have a motive to take a hit out on you are either dead or have been cleared of suspicion. It's up to you, but I think you're safe to go back to your routine now."

Amber gasped. "Thank you. That's great news."

Wasn't it?

Amber thought she saw surprise and disappointment in Trent's expression before he masked it.

"I'm really happy for you, Am." He sounded sincere. Why wouldn't he be?

"I'll miss carpooling with both of you." Caleb grinned at her. "You must be relieved to have your life back, though."

"Yes, I am." Amber managed a smile. "I really appreciate your trouble. It was so generous of you."

Why wasn't she happier about Crys's pronouncement? She'd been stressed and frightened knowing someone was waiting for an opportunity to put a fatal bullet in her. She should be jumping for joy that her life was returning to normal. Instead, all she could think about was the fact that it was time to say goodbye to Trent. Again.

Or was it?

"It's late." Trent locked his front door Thursday evening before turning to Amber. "Why don't you spend another night here? I can help you move back to your place tomorrow." *Or the next day.*

He and Amber had just said good night to Crys, Luke and Caleb after Crys's announcement that the threat against Amber was most probably over because the suspects were either dead or alibied out.

"If you're sure you don't mind, I'd like to stay tonight." Amber waved a hand toward his front door. "I'm a little drained after our meeting."

"It was a lot." Trent walked beside Amber to the kitchen. He was relieved she'd given him a reprieve. He'd have one more night with her. One more night to convince her to give them another chance. "Jade's reaction surprised me. Do you think you should check on her later?"

Amber gave him a warm look over her shoulder as he stepped back to let her enter the kitchen first. "I think Crys is right. J needs a little time to work through her disappointment. And her grief. We've all be dealing with some guilt over Aunt Kendra's death."

"Guilt? What do you mean?" Trent took a seat at the small blond-wood kitchen table and watched Amber fill the silver teakettle with water from the faucet.

Amber hesitated. "My aunt had asked Crys and me to have dinner with her the night she was murdered. But we both canceled. Crys and I were shattered when we learned Aunt Kendra was killed at the time we were supposed to meet her."

Trent went cold. "Am, I'm so sorry."

"Thank you." Amber turned off the faucet and carried the kettle to the stove. "When we learned about the connection between Aunt Kendra's murder and J's investigation into Dragon & Kelp, J lost it. She reacted like she did this evening. She blamed herself."

Trent could imagine the emotional toll that would take on anyone, especially someone as empathetic as Jade. "I hope you realize now that Jasper and Martina are to blame."

Amber placed the kettle on the stove. With her back to him, she seemed to be putting a lot of care into setting the burner at the proper heat. "Intellectually, we know that. Emotionally, there are a lot of things I wish I'd done differently."

Trent watched Amber while they waited for the kettle to boil. His eyes moved over her tan, loose-fitting, long-sleeved T-shirt, tucked into her slim, raspberry slacks. Her tall, slender dancer's figure moved with mesmerizing grace as she stretched to reach the mugs, then turned to another cabinet to gather the honey and teabags.

This moment seemed so comfortable. Having her here felt so right. She practically glided around his kitchen with confidence and familiarity. She belonged here. With him. Did she sense it, too? His yearning was almost painful.

Trent shook free of her spell. "Can I ask what you wish you'd done differently?"

"There are so many things." The kettle boiled. Amber reached to turn off the burner. Her mass of wavy brown tresses swung behind her narrow shoulders.

"Tell me about one." The more she hesitated, the more curious Trent became.

Amber was silent as she prepared the tea. Was she picking an example to share with him or hoping ignoring his request would make him change the subject? If it was the latter, she was mistaken. He cared too much to let this go.

She brought the mugs to the small square kitchen table. She placed his tea in front of him and took the seat on the other side. "Let it steep a bit."

Trent wrapped his hands around the warm brown porcelain mug and watched Amber gather her thoughts. The steam carried the smoky, faintly floral scent of the black tea up to him.

"My aunt had called me a couple of days before she died." Amber's words were halting, picking up speed as she continued. "She asked if we could get together that Friday. There was a legal matter she wanted my advice on. Of course, I agreed. I told her I'd take her to dinner, my treat." She smiled as though the memory was a happy one.

Trent wanted to reach across the table and take Amber's hand. He resisted the urge. He didn't want to intrude on her memories, not the happy ones. He wanted to help her keep those alive.

He kept his hands on his mug. "Your aunt was proud of you."

Amber's eyes drifted back to him. "Thank you for saying that."

"It's the truth." He sipped his tea. It was perfect, like the woman who'd made it. "You were looking forward to having dinner with your aunt. What made you change your plans?"

Amber held his eyes. "You did."

Trent placed his mug on the table before he dropped it. "What? How?"

Amber stared into her mug as whiffs of steam floated up from it. "That Friday morning, I'd learned you had returned to California. I was overwhelmed with grief and regrets and second thoughts. The only thing I could think of doing to distance myself from all those feelings was bury myself in my work. I'd called my aunt that afternoon to ask her if we could reschedule." She paused and took a breath before continuing. Her voice slowed. "I lied and told her something had come up at work. She said she understood, but I sensed she was disappointed. If I'd only told her the truth instead of lying."

This time, Trent didn't suppress his need to touch

Amber. He didn't even try. Her hand was slender and cool under his palm. "Am. Don't. You're not responsible for your aunt's murder. Jasper Bright and Martina Monaco are."

Amber's throat worked. She turned her hand to hold his. "I know. I know. You're right." She drew a shallow breath before meeting his eyes again. "I'm so sorry, Trent. I never should have blamed you for my canceling dinner with my aunt. It was small of me to do that. I'm very sorry."

Trent offered her a smile, trying to lighten the moment. "Considering I didn't know you were doing that, I don't think any harm was done."

Amber's chuckle was unsteady. "No, I definitely didn't tell you. And I never told anyone else, either. I only blamed you in my head."

Trent's smile grew. "In that case, all is forgiven. Don't give it another thought."

Amber spoke on a sigh. "Thank you."

"Your aunt was a great woman. Crys has her energy. Jade has her sense of humor, and you have her elegance."

Amber's grin chased some of the sadness from her cocoa brown eyes. "I don't know which one is funnier, that you think Jade has a sense of humor or that I'm elegant. Crys definitely has a lot of energy."

Trent let his eyes soak in Amber's beauty, her golden-brown skin, thick wavy hair, high cheekbones and stubborn pointed chin.

Her winged eyebrows were set above long-lidded, expressive eyes. They clouded when she was sad, like now, and sparkled when she was happy. When she was angry, they shot sparks. He'd experienced a lot of those lately. But when she was feeling desirous, they melted. He missed those looks.

Her heart-shaped lips easily curved with amusement but would tighten in anger. He found them even more attractive when they were swollen from their kisses.

"You're absolutely elegant." He heard the huskiness in his voice. "And beautiful, inside and out."

The silence between them felt awkward, yet heavy with thoughts and feelings that perhaps neither wanted to express. Or was it only him?

Amber slipped her hand from his hold. "Thank you for listening to me. I didn't realize until recently how much my blaming you so unfairly was weighing on me. I feel better having told you and apologized."

"Of course." Trent's reply was automatic.

"And thank you for letting me stay another night. I don't think I could handle packing my things now, not after learning the only people who might be able to connect Roland Dragon to Aunt Kendra's murder are dead. I'm still having trouble wrapping my mind around it."

"Stay. Here." The words sprang from Trent's lips before he realized he was going to say them. "I could help you think about next steps."

Amber arched one of her elegant eyebrows. "I don't have to stay here for you and me to brainstorm next steps. You're part of our Cold Case Team now, if you want to be. You could meet with us at my place, or wherever we get together."

Trent was almost weak with relief. Amber still imagined him in her life. She wanted him to be a part of it. One hurdle cleared.

"I definitely want to help get justice for your aunt. Thank you for including me."

Amber tilted her head. "But?"

Trent shook his head with a chuckle. "You know me

well." He took a breath and met her eyes. "Am, I don't think you should leave yet. The shooter is still at large, and we don't have any idea who it is or what motive they have."

Her eyes softened, making his knees shake. "I appreciate your concern but Crys is right. Everyone who could have been responsible for these attacks is either dead—Maeve, Jasper and Martina—or has been cleared by police—Barbi and Roland. So now you can have your bed back and you no longer need to change in your home office."

Amber's smile didn't reach her eyes. Was it his wishful thinking or did she seem as unenthusiastic about moving out as he felt about her leaving?

"I've enjoyed having you here." Trent spread his hands. "Of course, I hate that you're in danger. But are we confident the threat no longer exists?"

Amber shrugged, helplessly. "We may never know who was behind those shootings or what they wanted. But I can't stay here forever."

"Why not?" Trent clenched his fists. "Am, I'm still in love with you. It would totally and completely destroy me if anything happened to you."

Amber blinked several times. She glanced down at the kitchen table, then around the room as though a response was hiding somewhere in the kitchen. "Trent, I can't deny I still have feelings for you. And that's part of the problem."

He frowned. "How is that a problem?"

"We've been playing house, Trent." Amber spread her arms to indicate his condo. "Getting ready for work, sharing breakfast, driving to and from the office, then sharing dinner. We've been acting like a couple."

Still confused, Trent shook his head. "What's wrong with that? I want us to be a couple."

"But this isn't real." Amber expelled a frustrated breath. "How much of what I'm feeling—what you're feeling—comes from our circumstances and how much of it is true?"

Impatient, Trent stood, circled the table and knelt on the cold white linoleum floor in front of her. He took her hand and held it against his chest.

"I wish you could feel what I'm feeling." His voice shook with emotion. He didn't care. "Everything that's in my heart. Then you would know that my love is very real. I didn't stop caring about you just because you ended our engagement. Where did you expect all that emotion to go?"

Her eyes shimmered with tears. Amber lowered her head to his. Trent leaned forward to meet her. Their lips joined and Trent felt his heart expand in his chest. Her taste was sweet. Her touch was warm. Her lavender fragrance filled his senses.

"You smell so good." His voice was rough. He buried his fingers in her thick, wavy hair.

"So do you," she whispered against his lips. "Like warmth and comfort."

Trent stood, bringing Amber with him. He needed to wrap his arms around her, feel her closer. Amber pressed into him. Her heart hammered against him—or was that his? He stroked his tongue against her lips, asking for entry. Amber opened her mouth and drew his tongue in. Each touch, each caress, each stroke of her tongue against his made his body burn hotter.

Amber slid her hands under his T-shirt, leaving a trail of fire against his skin. Trent moaned deep in his throat. Of their own accord, his hips press against hers. He needed to feel her. He needed to touch more of her. Skin to skin. He needed to feel her around him, to be with her in every way.

"I want you. To touch you." He pulled her T-shirt free of her pants.

Trent moved his arms over her back. Her skin was soft against his palms. Firm. Smooth. Warm. His body filled with need. He drew his hand up her torso and cupped the side of her breast. Its tender weight filled his palm.

Amber shivered against him. "Trent."

She made his name sound like a favorite old song.

Amber stood on her toes and pressed herself even tighter against him. Trent deepened their kiss as he caressed her breast. He stroked his thumb across her nipple.

Amber groaned. "Trent. I'm sorry. Wait. Please."

Trent closed his eyes. He forced himself to lower his hands to his sides and step back. "No, Am. I understand."

"I wish *I* did." She dragged a hand over her tousled tresses. "I don't think it's a good idea for me to get physical until I do understand. I'm sor—"

"No." Trent took another step back, coming up against the refrigerator. His eyes swept over her. Amber's lips were swollen. Her clothes were untidy. Her hair was disheveled. She was beautiful. "Please don't apologize. I get it. And... You're probably right."

"Okay. Well." Amber turned to leave. "Good night, Trent. I'll see you in the morning."

Trent called out to her. "Stay." He continued when she frowned at him. "Until Sunday. I'll help you move back to your home Sunday. I just don't want you to leave like this. And Sunday's the weekend. We can take our time getting you packed up and moving you back into your home."

Amber's kiss-swollen lips curved in a slight smile. "That sounds like a good plan. Thank you."

Trent didn't exhale until Amber left the room. He closed

his eyes with relief. He'd bought himself more time with
her. He had to make it count.

"Oh." Jade looked from Amber to Trent and back.
"You're still here. With The Ex." She stood beside Caleb on
the other side of Trent's front door late Saturday afternoon.

A twinkle brightened Trent's eyes. "Hello to you, too,
Jade. Hi, Cal." He pulled the door wider, silently inviting
the two in.

"Hey, Trent." Caleb nodded as he walked past Amber
and Trent. His long, lean body was clothed in a pale bronze
long-sleeved collared pullover, navy cargo pants and black
sneakers.

"The two of you came together?" Amber believed that
was much more noteworthy than her living arrangement.

Jade snorted. "We *arrived* together. There's a difference. We pulled into the visitor's parking lot at the same
time."

Caleb sent Amber a grin. "A happy coincidence—"

"That's not what I would call it." Jade adjusted her
black-and-gold knapsack on her right shoulder. "Crys and
Luke are on their way. Thanks for letting me interrupt your
weekend. When are you moving back home?"

Amber escorted them into Trent's living room. It was
comfortably warm. Late-afternoon sunlight spilled over
the honey-wood flooring. Could Caleb and her sister smell
the popcorn from Trent and her morning movie marathon
session? A cheesy, black-and-white sci-fi flick and a cute-
but-corny rom-com.

"Trent's taking me home Sunday. We're going to enjoy
the weekend in the meantime."

Jade nodded her approval, though Amber saw the teasing light in her espresso eyes. "Great idea. You can de-

compress from the tension of the past two-plus weeks." She smiled at Trent as she settled into her usual spot in the right corner of the sofa. She set her knapsack beside her feet. "Thanks again for taking care of my sister."

"Of course. It was my pleasure." Trent was just as handsome in jeans and Los Angeles Lakers long-sleeved T-shirt as he was in his business suits. His T-shirt was thick and soft. She could attest to that because she'd cuddled up against him while they watched movies.

Caleb sat next to Jade. Her sister shot the newspaper executive a chilly look before ignoring him. Amber gave Caleb kudos for his determination.

"I'll make tea." Although it would probably take more than herbal tea to break the ice between those two.

The doorbell rang, interrupting her.

Trent squeezed her shoulder. "I'll get it. Tea would be great. Thank you."

Amber didn't take long serving the drinks. While they enjoyed the beverage, the group updated each other on their jobs, sharing a few amusing anecdotes from an otherwise stressful week. With the exception of the three cases he was wrapping up with Crys—Maeve's serial murder trial, and Jasper's and Martina's murder-for-hire and bribery in public office trials—Luke had gone back to the Ohio Bureau of Criminal Investigations. His department had been assigned an interim special agent in charge until they found a permanent replacement for Martina. Likewise, Crys's department had a new lieutenant, who'd replaced Jasper.

At the newspaper, the publisher was filling in for their late editor, Brock Mann. A forensic review of the accounting system uncovered Brock's embezzlement. The newspaper was on its way to turning a profit again.

"Thank you for the tea, Am." Jade returned her mug and saucer to the serving tray. Like Crys and Amber, she'd had the orange-and-cinnamon tea. Amber had made black tea for Trent, Luke and Caleb. "And thanks to everyone for making time for this last-minute Cold Case Team meeting. I'm grateful."

"No problem, J. What's on your mind?" Crys's tone was empathetic. Still, she wasn't one for small talk. She sat beside Luke on the chairs they'd brought in from the dining room. Her lemon-yellow blouse was covered with images of violets.

Unfazed, Jade continued. "Recapping, Maeve wanted to use her trial to expose Dragon & Kelp's alleged corrupt business practices. With her murder, that probably won't be possible anymore."

"Maeve wanted to put Dragon & Kelp on trial." Trent linked his hands together, resting his forearms on his thighs. "But I don't know if we would have been able to get much if any of that information admitted. The prosecution would have questioned its relevance."

"Maybe. Maybe not." Amber shrugged her right shoulder. "In any event, we can't discuss the case. We may be trying Maeve posthumously but that doesn't mean we can lower our ethics."

Trent inclined his head. "You're right."

"That's my bad." Jade pressed a hand to her chest over her gray cotton blouse. "But two cases we can discuss are Jasper's and Martina's. Neither of you are involved in those."

Caleb folded his arms over his chest and shifted to face Jade. "Jasper and Martina insisted they didn't have anything to do with Roland Dragon."

"They're lying." Jade's eyes flashed with temper.

"I think we all agree on that." Amber sat on the sofa. It felt odd not being in her usual spot between Caleb and Jade. "At least we have their taped confession to killing both Aunt Kendra and Vic."

"That's not good enough." Jade stood to cross the living room. Her loose-fitting silver blouse seemed to float around her above her stretchy dark-blue jeans. She stopped beside the fireplace and faced the group. "Jasper and Martina didn't come up with the idea of murdering our aunt on their own. They didn't have a reason to want her dead. The only motive they had was a fat paycheck—or rather a wire transfer. I need to know who made that transfer and why. And I need that person—or persons—to be held accountable."

"So do we." Crys inclined her head toward Amber beside her.

"We all do." Trent's arm swept the room, encompassing the group. "Luke and Cal may not have met your aunt, but we all care about you and we care about justice."

Amber blinked back her tears. Trent's kind words warmed her, keeping the chill of her grief at bay. They also had the magical effect of taking some of the steam off Jade's temper.

She cleared her throat. "We need evidence that someone paid Jasper and Martina to commit those murders. Otherwise we don't have murder-for-hire. We only have murder and speculation."

"Am's right." Trent straightened in his chair. "We've been speculating about Roland Dragon. Speculation may be a helpful jumping-off point, but it could mislead us. It can obscure other suspects and possibilities."

Luke rubbed the back of his neck. "Let's take a second look at the evidence we collected from Jasper's and

Martina's homes. Maybe we overlooked something, or some paperwork might help us make a connection a second time around."

Jade's voice was strained. "Can we at least agree that Dragon & Kelp is involved in Aunt Kenny's murder?"

Luke shrugged. "The evidence connecting Dragon & Kelp to your aunt's homicide is also circumstantial. Why would they want to kill her?"

Jade paced in front of the fireplace. "Because she was helping me expose their corrupt business practices." She wrapped her arms around her waist and shivered as though the temperature in the warm room had dropped fifteen degrees.

Luke frowned. "Do we have proof they knew she was planning to expose them?"

Jade stopped pacing with her back to the room. "Her murder."

Amber exchanged a concerned look with Crys. They all wanted justice for Aunt Kendra, but there was something more behind Jade's urgency and determination. What was their sister hiding? And which one of them was willing to risk her ire by asking?

"I'm sorry, Jade." Luke spread his arms. "We need something more direct to link Dragon & Kelp to your aunt's homicide, like a letter or a canceled check, an entry in a calendar or other eyewitnesses."

"I know we're on the right track, though." Amber looked from Luke to Jade. "Dragon & Kelp had a lot to lose if any of their customer lawsuits moved forward. They also had a lot of loose ends to tie up—Aunt Kendra, Victor Hansen, Jasper Bright, Martina Monaco, Carter Wainscott, Maeve Rhoades."

"All of whom are dead now." Jade faced the room again.

"That can't be a coincidence," Caleb added.

Jade returned to the sofa. "One thing we agree on." She collected her knapsack and settled it on her shoulders. "So we need a letter, canceled check, diary entry or witness linking Roland Dragon to Aunt Kenny's murder. How about a signed confession?"

Caleb stood, following Jade from the room. "How're you going to get that?"

"I'll let you know once I figure it out." Jade spoke over her shoulder.

Amber hurried to catch up with them. She sensed Trent, Crys and Luke following her.

She tried and failed to shake off her irritation. "J, please don't do anything dangerous."

"Don't worry." Jade's voice carried back to her from the hallway. "You know me."

Amber closed her eyes briefly before turning to Trent. "That's why I'm worried."

Chapter 16

"You've been quiet. Are you worried about Jade?" Trent's voice was low, almost mesmerizing.

The end credits were rolling on the classic monster flick they'd watched Saturday night. The movie may have been scary when it was first released almost seventy years ago. It wasn't scary today, but it was still entertaining. It was one of the few films in their movie marathon that they'd both enjoyed.

Amber was cuddled close to Trent on the sofa bed. His arms were wrapped around her waist from behind, holding her loosely against him. Her head was on his chest. Her hand was just below his heart.

Trent was right. The mattress was pretty comfortable. And his body was warm and firm, and smelled so great. But she couldn't completely relax when her mind kept replaying Jade's dramatic exit from Trent's condo earlier in the day.

"My baby sister laughs in the face of danger." There was residual irritation in her tone. "J thinks she's invincible, which is a really infuriating trait she shares with Crys. But I keep reminding myself that she never goes into a project without a plan and usually at least two backup plans in case something goes wrong."

"Cal said he'd noticed the same thing about her when they worked together at the paper." Trent chuckled.

Amber heard the echo of it in his chest. It made her smile. "He seems to know my sister."

"He wants to know her better. Do you think she'll give him a chance?"

Amber shrugged, loving the feel of his chest against her shoulder. "I don't know. But Cal's persistent."

A comfortable silence settled over them. The only sounds were Trent's strong and steady heartbeat beneath her ear and the closing theme song from the movie as the credits continued to roll.

"If you aren't worried about J, then what's on your mind?" Trent's question sounded hesitant.

Amber gave a soft sigh. "I was thinking about tomorrow." She felt Trent's body tense beneath her palm. She continued, her voice low. "I know I need time and space so I can get clarity about my feelings for you. But candidly, I don't want to go."

"And I don't want you to go." Trent's words emerged on a sigh heavy with yearning.

Her heart and body melted at the sound. Trent shifted and Amber found herself half lying beneath him. She looked up into his dark eyes. They glinted with desire, bright and hot. A delicious longing rolled over her, leaving heat in its wake. The feeling was familiar and strange, and Amber could no longer deny herself the pleasure only Trent could give her.

If Amber rejected him again, it would break him. Trent had strained to keep his passion for her in check these past seventeen days. It had cost him in long, sleepless nights and frustratingly distracted days. But tonight, as he looked into her eyes, he saw the instant her desire rose to match his. His body sighed with relief.

Amber trembled in his arms, arching her body against his. Trent lowered his head to kiss her. Her taste was an elixir, breathing life into him. Her lips were full and sweet against his tongue. He drank from them, fueling his urgency. The music of their passion played in the breaths they shared. Amber sighed his name like a song against his lips. He buried his fingers in the heavy mass of her wavy hair. The tresses felt like silk between his fingers.

She moved closer. Her arms came around his shoulders. Her soft breasts were tight against his chest. Her welcome poured over him like a waterfall, washing away the sting of her rejection, a memory he prayed he could replace with the promise of their future.

Trent moved his palms over her body. He wanted to imprint the feel of her firm curves, long limbs and toned muscles. His skin hungered to have her against him again.

"I need to feel you." His hands traveled over her torso, stripping away her loose-fitting pullover and unfastening her bra.

"Yes," Amber sighed. "I want to feel you, too."

She mirrored his movements, her touch burning a path up and over his chest to remove his T-shirt. They rolled over the mattress, stripping articles of clothing and tossing them aside. A touch. A caress. A kiss. A nibble. Tokens of the deeper emotion that fed their desire.

Trent's eyes moved over Amber's golden-brown body as she lay on her side beside him. Full breasts, tight waist, flat stomach and long, toned legs.

"You're so beautiful." He sounded dazed to his ears. "Even more beautiful than in my dreams."

* * *

Amber's heart was beating hard and fast, as though it was trying to burst out of her chest. Her eyes moved over Trent. "Your body is a work of art."

His broad, sculpted chest was dusted with dark curls. It traveled down his six-pack abs, narrowing to a thin line that ended above his navel. His slim hips and long, muscular thighs and calves made her body ache.

Trent reached for her.

"Not yet." She evaded his embrace by rising up on her knees.

Amber pushed against his shoulders until he lay on his back. She straddled his thighs. The heat in his eyes emboldened her. Amber slid her body up and over his torso. She felt his desire flex against her abdomen.

"Amber." His groan urged her on.

"You did this." She cupped his face, then kissed him hard, letting him feel the strength of the hunger roiling inside her.

She pumped her hips against him. He hardened against her and her body sang. Trent's hands stroked down her back and came around her hips to touch her. Amber gasped, breaking their kiss. Trent gathered her to him and rolled over, balancing himself above her.

"Amber." He lowered his head and caressed her breast with his lips and tongue.

"Trent. Oh, my—" She moaned her pleasure. Arching into him.

"Let go, sweetheart." His words cast a spell over her.

His hands moved down her side, slipping between them to touch her. Amber gasped, pressing her head back against her pillow. She felt her desire pooling at the juncture between her thighs as Trent's fingers explored her. Each stroke and caress pushed her closer to the edge.

"Trent." Her voice was strained.

"Tell me what you need, baby. I'll do anything for you."

"Trent, I need you. In me."

"Now, sweetheart?"

"Yes. Please."

"Are you ready?"

Amber growled. "Don't play."

Trent's chuckle rumbled in his chest. He covered her mouth with his, then removed his hand from her legs. Amber felt a moment of disappointment before Trent joined with her. He was full and long and deep. Amber gasped her pleasure into his mouth. Trent swallowed the sound.

He ended their kiss and remained motionless a moment, letting her adjust to him before he slowly moved. Amber moved with him, an urgency building and building and building, gathering heat until she thought she would combust. Her hips pumped fast, holding him tighter, urging him on. Trent met her needs and added his own demands. They held each other close, moving in harmony, giving and taking pleasure. Her world narrowed to Trent, his touch, his taste, his scent.

Amber's hips strained up to him, matching his rhythm. And then Trent touched her again. Her body stiffened. Amber gasped as she felt herself racing to a crescendo.

"Trent!"

"Amber."

Trent's arms tightened around her. His hips pressed into hers as their passion exploded.

Amber felt Trent's eyes on her from his post at his bedroom doorway late Sunday morning. She must look as though she was packing in slow motion. Part of her so desperately didn't want to leave, but she knew if she stayed, another part of her would always wonder whether she was staying for the right reason. Who knew what those doubts would eventually do to their relationship.

She needed to step back. She needed time and space for these heightened emotions from this dangerous and traumatic experience to cool, so she could better understand what she was feeling and why. Earlier in the morning, she'd sent Crys and Jade a group text, letting them know Trent was taking her home. They wanted her to text them when she'd settled back in.

Amber zipped closed her second suitcase. She imagined the sound was similar to her heart tearing inside her chest.

She swallowed the large ball of emotion in her throat. "Thank you for understanding."

Trent stood with his shoulder propped against the threshold. He was almost too sexy—was that a thing?— in a copper long-sleeved jersey, black slacks and black casual shoes. "You want to be sure. I get it. I want that, too." He took both suitcases from her. "I guess I'll see you in court, Counselor."

Amber followed him to his front door, carrying her shoe bag and briefcase. "You'll see me before then. Remember, you agreed to let me cook dinner for you Friday night to thank you for letting me stay here for the past two-plus weeks."

"It's not a thank-you dinner. It's a date." Trent held the door open for her. "I keep telling you there's no need for you to thank me. You helped with the cleaning, even though I didn't want you to, and you split the grocery bill over my objections. My family doesn't even do that when they visit."

Amber couldn't resist the smile. "You wouldn't want them to."

At the lobby, Amber returned her visitor pass, which had allowed her access to Trent's security building and garage. The drive from his condo to her house on the north side of the city was quiet. They each seemed wrapped in their own thoughts. In the close confines of Trent's silver SUV, Amber's thoughts were overwhelmed by Trent's warmth, his scent and the way he'd made her feel last night.

She didn't regret the passion they'd shared. She'd wanted—needed—his touch. But the feelings he'd reawakened were making this parting more difficult, no matter how temporary it may be.

After thirty minutes that felt like an eternity, Trent pulled his vehicle into Amber's two-car driveway.

She leaned forward to view her home through the front windshield. Her eyes moved over the red-shingled roof and pale tan siding. Her lawn was a little high and the bushes needed to be cut back. "Everything looks normal. Then why do I feel anxious about going inside?"

She'd monitored her home security using the app on her cell phone. Jade and Caleb—separately—as well as Crys and Luke had checked on her house while she'd been with Trent. Crys also had requested additional patrols for her neighborhood. All those factors should give her confidence that her home was safe.

Trent pulled the key from the ignition. "Probably because of the circumstances that led to your leaving your home in the first place." He met her eyes. "But you're not going in alone, Am. I'll be right beside you."

Amber collected her shoe bag and briefcase from the back seat while Trent took her suitcases from the trunk. She let them inside. They checked her garage, the main level and the half basement before surveying the top floor. Amber didn't know whether Trent was humoring her or if he thought a thorough search of her home was necessary. Either way, she appreciated his efforts, and his carrying her suitcases upstairs.

"Thank you for bringing me home and for all your help with my luggage." She led him back to her main floor. "Can I offer you anything, tea, coffee?"

"I'm fine. Thank you." At the front door, Trent faced her. "Now that we've looked over your home, do you feel comfortable? I can stay, if you want me to."

Amber shook her head. "No, but thank you. I'll be fine. I'm glad you came back with me, but my staying here on my own is my first big step back to normalcy and reclaiming my life."

Trent nodded as though he understood but Amber couldn't miss the concern in his eyes. "Promise me you'll be careful. Be aware of your surroundings. Make sure all your doors and windows are always locked. Don't open the door if you don't know who's knocking."

His concern reminded Amber she wasn't alone. She drew strength from that knowledge.

"I promise." She couldn't look away from the caring in his eyes.

Trent closed the small distance between them and pressed his lips to hers. He wrapped his arms around her waist. Amber twined hers around his shoulders, drawing him closer to her. Trent moaned low in his throat. Amber's toes curled in her canvas shoes. She parted her lips for him. Their kiss was long, slow and deep. Too soon, Trent raised his head. He touched his cheek to hers.

"Lock up behind me." Trent whispered the words before stepping back.

Amber looked up at him. She pressed her lips together to keep from asking him to stay. She could still taste him on her tongue.

Trent stroked the side of her face, then he was gone.

Amber secured the locks. If it hurt this much to watch him leave, wasn't that a sign he was meant to stay?

Chapter 17

Trent entered the suite for the Franklin County Public
Defender's Office late Sunday morning. He didn't bother
turning on the main lights. The large windows that lined
the east and west walls provided more than enough sunlight to guide him to his office.

He was on autopilot after taking Amber home and driving away, one of the many difficult things he'd had to do
recently. Trent collapsed into his padded cloth desk chair.
He could deal with her moving out of his condo for now,
but not with her walking out of his life—again. He didn't
want to go through that heartache. This time would be so
much worse than the first. This experience had confirmed
he was better with Amber in his life. These seventeen days
had been stressful because the woman he loved was being
stalked and attacked. But they'd faced those dangers together—literally—and kept each other safe.

Trent turned on his computer before restlessness drove
him from his office to the employee break room. He
needed coffee. Making it would occupy his hands while
letting his thoughts wander. He replayed his conversation
with Amber from last night in his mind. Was there anything he could have said or done differently to convince
her to give him another chance?

His eyes strayed toward Barbi's cubicle a few yards from the break room. Trent had heard that she'd been complaining about having to move to a new area. Too bad. After her actions, she should be glad she still had a job, much less a desk in the office suite.

He noticed the picture on her desk beside her computer monitor. Something about the image drew him toward it. He picked up the framed photograph. In it, Barbi stood in what looked like a living room, mugging for the camera with someone else. Someone who looked a lot like her. Trent brought the picture closer. Her sister? He froze. He recognized the other woman. He knew her.

Tawnia Dwyer.

My roommate is always encouraging me to stand up for myself, which is what I'm doing. She's always telling me if you don't go after what you want, you'll never get it. She'd do anything for me. Trent's blood ran cold. Would Tawnia hurt Amber, thinking with Amber out of Trent's life, he'd fall in love with Barbi? That was a stretch, wasn't it?

Follow your instincts, Trent.

He dropped the picture on Barbi's chair and pulled his cell phone from the front right pocket of his black Dockers. Spinning on his heels, Trent jogged back to his office. He tapped Amber's number, but her cell sent him straight to voicemail.

He was sweating and shivering at the same time.

Trent hung up on Amber's voice mail and tried Jade.

The youngest Rashaad picked up on the first ring. "Sounds like you messed up again, buddy."

"Jade, where's Amber? I think I know who the stalker is."

Amber turned, jogging back toward her ruby-red sedan, which she'd parked in the lot beside the tennis courts near the entrance to the Park of Roses. Her driver's license and cell phone bounced around in one of the zippered pockets of her sapphire-blue windbreaker. She clutched her car and house keys in her right fist and used the back of her left hand to wipe the sweat from her eyes.

The park was packed with pedestrians. That wasn't surprising for a Sunday morning, especially with the unseasonably warm weather. During her run, she'd dodged birds, squirrels and exuberant dogs. She'd navigated past couples who hadn't noticed her, young parents who'd kept their toddlers close, and groups of friends, jogging, walking or cycling on the shared paths. She didn't mind the crowd. It made her feel safer with the remnants of fear caused by her stalker still clinging to the back of her mind. With so many people around her, Amber was able to lose herself in the park's sights, sounds and scents. Dogs barking, children laughing, birds singing, fresh-cut grass, spring buds and the nearby freshwater creek.

In the past, she'd do her longer runs at Griggs Reservoir Park. It was closer to her home, although not quite as nice. However, since that park had been the drop-off point for victims of what became known as the Griggs Reservoir Park serial killer, she'd found other parks in which to jog. It would be a while before she could relax and enjoy the reservoir again.

She'd run about thirty minutes—a little more than three miles—on the hilly, meandering route through the park before turning to jog back to her car. In the past, the aerobic workout had helped clear her mind and identify a strategy for addressing whatever issue she was facing. It had helped today as well. She'd found an answer to her question about what to do about Trent.

One final, long incline to go before finishing her run.

She was anxious to discuss her revelations with Trent. Amber leaned into the grade and shortened her stride to help her crest the hill. A brisk, chilled breeze rustled through the trees rimming the open field. It pulled several locks from Amber's ponytail. They blew across her face, temporarily blinding her. She tucked her hair behind her ear with her left hand just as she reached the plateau.

Amber caught her breath and lengthened her stride as she ran past the tennis courts. There was an older couple playing at one court and a doubles match at another. Amber smiled as the older woman—presumably the wife—at the first court shouted her victory before doing a little dance.

"Congratulations!" Amber waved as she called to the older woman.

The champion spun toward her voice, giving her an embarrassed smile. "Thank you, dear!" She waved back.

Amber grinned. "Nice moves!"

The older woman and her companion—her husband?—laughed.

Still chuckling, she slowed to a walk a few strides from her car. Pressing the key fob, she deactivated the locks and started to climb into the driver's seat.

"Excuse me." The gravelly voice drew her attention.

Then everything went dark.

Trent jumped out of Luke's navy-blue SUV as soon as the other man stopped his car in the Park of Roses parking lot near the tennis courts late Sunday morning. Crys, Jade, Luke and Caleb were with him.

"I don't understand." Jade clutched her cell phone as she turned, scanning the area. Her eyes were wide with fear. "The Find-A-Phone app shows that she's here. This is where she always parks when she comes here. We all park here."

"We know her phone's here." Caleb scanned the parking lot's concrete surface. "Let's look for it. Maybe she dropped it."

The idea Amber had disappeared without her phone rocked Trent back on his heels. They had to find her. Now.

A movement in the corner of his eye drew his attention. Crys was leading Luke toward the tennis courts. She looked to be on a mission. He followed them.

"Excuse me." Crys waved toward a group playing doubles tennis. Her voice was a command. "Have you seen this woman?" She pressed her phone and her badge against the fence between them.

The foursome stopped playing and approached Crys. Trent stopped beside Luke, who waited a step behind her.

One of the young men—tall, thin with a shock of curly red hair—gave Crys an uncertain look. "Isn't that you?"

Crys stared at him, expressionless. "She's my sister."

The curvy young blonde beside him pointed at the picture, nodding. "Yeah. She was here. Like five minutes ago. Ten minutes ago. Jogger. She was talking to them."

Trent looked over his shoulder in the direction she was pointing. An older couple, walking arm in arm, strolled past him.

He brought an older image of Amber onto his phone as he hurried toward them. "Pardon me. I'm sorry to interrupt you."

The man stopped, giving Trent a curious look. His attention moved past him toward Crys and Luke before returning to Trent. "Can I help you?" He spoke with a deep, authoritative voice that would have demanded attention in a courtroom.

Trent held up his cell phone. "Do you remember seeing this woman earlier this morning?"

The other man leaned closer, studying the image on Trent's phone. He glanced up. His dark eyes were suspicious. "Who are you?"

Crys stepped forward to show the cautious witness her badge. "I'm her sister, Detective Crys Rashaad." She gestured first to Luke, then Trent. "This is Special Agent Luke Gilchrist, and my sister's friend, Trent Mitchell. It's urgent that we find my sister. Please. Have you seen her?"

The older woman smiled. "I see the family resemblance. Yes, we saw her about ten minutes ago. She was running past the tennis courts just as I beat my husband in our final match." She tossed her spouse a cheeky grin. "She was a doll. She was running toward the parking lot." She pointed toward the lot from which the trio had just left.

"Was she with anyone?" Luke's voice was urgent.

The married couple exchanged concerned frowns before the man spoke. "No, she was alone when we saw her."

"Is she in danger?" Concern laced the woman's words.

"I'm afraid so." Crys's expression was grim. "Is there anything else you can tell us about your exchange? Did you see anyone nearby?"

"No." The husband shook his head, frowning. "I'm so sorry."

"I didn't notice anyone around, either." The wife looked around the park as though trying to nudge her memory. "But then I wasn't paying much attention. Your sister saw my victory dance. She called, 'Congratulations. Nice moves.' Then she waved. She never even stopped jogging."

"Crys!" Jade's shout claimed Trent's attention.

He turned to see Jade and Caleb running toward them. Trent recognized the cherry-red phone she held aloft. It was Amber's. Trent's stomach dropped. This wasn't a good sign. Amber wouldn't have left her phone behind. She would have heard it drop and stopped to pick it up.

Where was she? How was she? They'd already lost at least ten minutes in tracking her.

You fool! Why had you left her alone?

Crys murmured a thank-you to the older couple before turning away. "I'm calling this in." She spoke as she tapped her cell phone screen, then put the device to her ear. "This is Detective Rashaad. I need an APB on a red 2019 Toyota Camry. Urgh. What's her plate?"

"HQN0314," Jade said.

Crys looked at her in amazement. "How do you remember that?"

"How do you not?" Jade hurried back to Luke's car.

Trent kept pace beside her.

Crys repeated Amber's license plate number into the phone before disconnecting the call. "Tell us again why you think Tawnia Dwyer's the stalker."

They didn't have time for him to repeat everything he'd said. Trent forced him to breathe and remain calm as he climbed into the back of Luke's SUV. He couldn't help Amber if he lost his self-control.

"Tawnia is Barbi's roommate." His tone was clipped, impatient. He didn't care. He'd already gone over this. "She'd said Tawnia encourages her to go after what she wants, including me, and that Tawnia would do anything for her."

Jade leaned forward, catching his attention. Her eyes were wide and dark with fear. "You think Tawnia would kill Am for Barbi?"

"Is that any stranger than Barbi killing Am herself?" Trent's hands were fisted against the cushioned seat on either side of him. He didn't want to add to the tension bearing down on them inside the SUV but denial wouldn't save Amber.

"No." Jade pressed back against her seat.

"We need to speak with Barbi. I have her number." Trent leaned forward to better see Crys. His frustration spiked when he realized she was making another call. They needed to get moving. Now. Every minute in this vehicle was another minute Amber was in danger.

Crys spoke into her cell phone. "Dispatch, is Officer Tawnia Dwyer on duty?" She paused for the longest seconds of Trent's life. "Thank you." She ended the call as she looked at him over her shoulder. "Tawnia's not at work. Call Barbi. Let her know we're coming to see her."

Trent had connected the call before Crys finished speaking. "Barbi, I need to see you. What's your address?"

"What's going on?" Barbi stood framed in her doorway. Her eyes were wide as they moved from Trent to Crys, Luke, Jade and Caleb.

Jade stepped forward. "Your roommate's trying to kill my sister."

Crys caught Jade's arm. "Ms. Hamlin, I'm Detective Rashaad. This is Special Agent Gilchrist. My sister Jade and our friend Caleb."

Barbi's eyes widened with surprise. "You're Amber Rashaad's sisters."

Luke's voice was devoid of inflection. "Ms. Hamlin, we need to speak with your roommate, Tawnia Dwyer. Could you tell us where she is, please?"

Barbi frowned her confusion. She glanced at Trent before answering. "Tawnia's at work. She picked up an extra shift."

Crys shook her head. "No, she's not." The patience in her voice was fraying around the edges. "I called the dispatcher."

Trent struggled to remain calm and focused. "Barbi, do you have any idea where Tawnia would go if she wanted to…be alone. What are some of her favorite, out-of-the-way locations?" *Where had she gone* with Amber?

Barbi straightened. Her eyes blazed with anger. Her cheeks flushed with temper. "What is this about? What do you want with Tawnia?"

Trent sighed. "Barbi, we think Tawnia's the one who's been trying to harm Amber. Now Amber's missing. We need to find her. Please. Do you have any idea where Tawnia would take Amber if she's the one who has her?"

Barbi's face paled. Her eyes darted around. "No. That can't be true." But her voice lacked certainty.

Trent sensed her making the same connections he'd made upon seeing the photo of Tawnia with Barbi. The imposter's clothing wasn't just like Barbi's. They were Barbi's. Her missing driver's license. The information the imposter had known about the case had been given to Tawnia in confidence by Barbi.

"Where is she?" Jade growled. "Where's my sister?"

"I don't know." Barbi looked at Trent in horror. "I'm so sorry. I never—"

Crys's radio crackled on her hip. A staticky female voice came over the speaker. "2019 red Camry plate HQN0314 spotted south on state route 33 in Grove City."

No one stopped to think. They raced back to Luke's SUV, intent on following the radio's report of the location of Amber's car.

Trent was keenly aware that, depending on where Amber's car was in Grove City, they could be as much as thirty minutes behind.

A lot could happen in half an hour.

Why was it so cold? Why am I so cold?

Amber slowly, reluctantly drifted out of sleep. But she didn't feel like she'd been sleeping. It was more like she'd passed out.

And why does my head hurt so much? It was killing her.

She forced her eyes open. Her mind was sluggish. Was that her steering wheel? Had she fallen asleep in her car?

Where am I? And why am I so cold? And wet?

Amber looked past the steering wheel. Her eyes stretched wide. Her breath trapped in her throat. Water was rushing up her calves. Her mind was screaming.

What? How? Why?

She jerked upright, battling panic. Panic was winning.

She spun her head toward her driver's side window. Blinding pain flashed behind her eyes. Amber blinked and refocused. Water was rising outside her car. It was already halfway up her window. Inside, the water was to her knees. Her feet were going numb.

Amber pressed the lock release. She ignored the pounding in her head and slammed her shoulder against the door. It didn't move.

What now!?!?

Amber heard a local broadcast reporter's voice in her head. It was from the segment he did every spring on water rescue in case the viewers were trapped in their cars during a flash flood.

Seat belt. Window. Out.

Her fingers fumbled with the seat belt fastener.

Work. Work. Please work.

The seat belt snapped free. Relief almost made her weak. No time. The water was on her lap.

Amber wriggled around to face her seat. She pressed in the levers to pull out her headrest.

Seat belt. Window. Out.

Her muscles were shaking harder. It was so cold and she was so scared. The water was to her waist now.

With trembling hands, she turned the headrest so the metal spokes faced the window. She angled them toward the lower-right corner of the window opposite the driver's side mirror. Taking a deep breath, she slammed the headrest's spokes into the window with all her might. The window shattered. Tears of relief mingled with the water rushing through the shattered glass. The force of the water almost swept away the headrest. Almost.

Grasping the headrest firmly in both hands, Amber cleared away the glass shards around the window as best she could. The water was around her neck. Lifting her chin, she filled her lungs with air before ducking into the cold water and pulling herself free of the car. Kicking strongly, she propelled herself toward the surface.

"Amber!"

"Trent?" Amber turned toward the sound of his voice.

She was shaking so hard from fear and cold, his name emerged in three syllables. She turned to find him swimming toward her. It was as though the river had produced him when she needed him most.

"Amber. My God." He grabbed her shoulders and pulled her to him. He held her so tight. "Come on." His voice was soft against her ear. "I'll be right beside you."

Amber wasn't a strong swimmer. The numbness in her fingers and toes wasn't helping, and neither were her shaking limbs. She allowed anger to fuel her strokes.

She could see Jade waiting at the shore. Her younger sister looked on the verge of tears. Amber knew if she didn't hurry, Jade would jump into the river and drown her in her effort to rescue her.

"Am!" Jade's voice reached her from what felt like miles away but was just a few more yards. "You're almost here. Hold on just a little longer. You've got this."

As soon as he could stand, Trent helped her to her feet. Jade waded into the water to join them on Amber's other side. Together, they half carried her to shore where Amber collapsed, rolling onto her back.

"Who did this to me?" Her voice was thin and unsteady.

"Tawnia Dwyer." Trent bit the officer's name off. "She was your stalker."

"What?" Amber's eyes popped open in shock. "Why?"

Jade took off her navy-and-cream hooded jacket. Kneeling beside Amber, she covered her with it. "She thought with you out of the way, Trent would turn to Barbi."

Amber rolled her head to meet her sister's eyes. The thin spring jacket helped warm her. "Did she tell you that?"

"No." Trent sat beside her on the muddy ground. His eyes moved over her as though searching for injuries. "Tawnia's not talking."

Jade jerked her head over her shoulder. "Crys and Luke caught Tawnia. Trent and I came for you."

With a gentle touch, Trent brushed her hairline. Amber sucked in her breath. The pain surprised her. He withdrew his hand. There was blood on his fingertips. "We need to get you to the EMTs. They should be here by now."

The blood caught her by surprise. She'd thought it was just a headache. Amber gingerly rose to a sitting position. Trent helped her to her feet. She resisted his attempt to lift her into his arms.

"I can walk, with your help." Amber turned as Jade helped her into the jacket. "I want to speak with Tawnia, and I don't want her to see me being carried."

Trent offered her his arm. "Are you sure you want to confront her now?"

"I would." Jade's voice was rough with anger.

Amber took Trent's arm, allowing him to help her up the steep incline. A short distance from them, she saw tire tracks leading down the hill and into the river. Her car's tire tracks. Amber stumbled on the mud. Jade caught her waist from behind, steadying her. She crested the incline with Trent at her side and Jade hovering behind her.

"Am!"

Amber turned to find Crys sprinting toward her. Luke and Caleb jogged after her. Amber braced herself for Crys's arrival. Her older sister grabbed her and squeezed the breath from her lungs.

Luke rested his hand on her arm. "I'm so glad you're safe."

"So am I." Crys's words were choked.

Caleb sighed. "Me, too."

"Easy. Easy. Head injury." Amber panted through the pain.

Crys stepped back, still holding on to her upper arms. Her expression was stricken. "Oh, no." Her eyes were fixed on Amber's hairline. "Let's get you to the EMTs."

Amber turned toward the assembly of police cruisers and the emergency medical van. "First, I want to speak with Tawnia."

Crys searched her face. Seeming to find whatever it was she'd been looking for, she nodded. "All right."

She led Amber to the cruiser in which they were holding Tawnia. Luke, Trent, Jade and Caleb followed them.

Crys nodded toward one of the uniformed officers. "Open the door, please."

The officer pulled the door wide. Tawnia looked up. Her eyes landed on Amber. Shock parted her thin pink lips. Hate hardened her eyes before she masked it. But Amber had seen the ugly expression. Any doubt she had that this woman who'd feigned a cordial relationship with her had been plotting her murder was wiped away.

"Why?" Amber's fists tightened around the edges of Jade's coat, pulling it closer around her. "Why did you try to kill me?"

Tawnia raised her eyebrows and shook her head. "I don't know what you're talking about."

Amber looked over Tawnia's gray oversize, heavy-weight hoodie and baggy gray sweatpants. "I'll see you in court."

Tawnia's satisfied expression faded. Amber acknowledged the moment the police officer realized what was most probably facing her: imprisonment with the inmates she'd helped put in there.

Straightening her shoulders, Amber stepped back. The officer shut the door on Tawnia's frozen expression.

Crys put her hand on Amber's shoulder. "She had your car keys. She claimed she'd found them and was bringing them to the police station, but it links her to your disappearance."

Luke nodded. "I believe we'll also be able to match the bullets recovered from the courthouse parking lot and the parking garage to her gun."

Amber turned away from the police cruiser. She looked at the people standing around her: Crys, Jade, Trent, Caleb and Luke. They'd been by her side, protecting her, comforting her, reassuring her from the beginning. And then when the worst had happened, when the stalker had kidnapped her, they'd found her. They'd rushed to her rescue, taken the suspect into custody and smothered her with their love.

She wiped her tears away. "I don't know how you found me." Her voice was choked with emotion. "But I'm so grateful you did."

They circled her, putting their arms around her and each other as Amber's emotion overwhelmed her. The EMTs would need to wait a little longer.

The window wouldn't break. No matter how hard she hit it with the spokes from the headrest, it wouldn't even crack. The water was rising. It was at her throat. It rose so fast. And it was cold. So cold. She was trapped. She was alone. She was helpless. She was going to die. There was nothing she could do...

"Am, sweetheart, wake up. Please wake up. I'm here. I'm with you." Trent's baritone was soft but unsteady against her ear. His arms—strong, competent and caring—were wrapped around her waist. His body was warm and real against hers.

Embarrassed, Amber pulled away, putting distance between them in the bed. "I'm sorry. I—"

"Don't apologize." His voice was low but firm. "Another nightmare?"

"Yes." Amber rolled onto her back and covered her eyes with her left forearm.

"Do you want to talk about it?" The mattress dipped as Trent shifted onto his side to face her.

"It's always the same." Amber was weak and shaky. She fought against the remnants of the nightmare as they tried to pull her back in.

Slow, deep breaths.

She was taking the week off. She had almost a hundred hours of sick time. When she'd called her boss Monday morning to explain everything that had happened Sunday, she'd told Amber to take at least forty of those hours. Amber hadn't argued.

Neither had she argued when Trent had brought her back from the hospital Sunday evening and stayed. Amber didn't know whether he was using sick time or vacation days. She was just glad he was here.

Trent pressed. "It still might help to talk about it, get it out of your system."

"I don't want to talk about that." Amber took a deep breath, then exhaled. "I was wrong about us." She sensed him stiffen beside her.

"In what way?"

A lot had happened in the two days since Tawnia Dwyer had tried to kill her. Barbi Hamlin had moved back home to Kentucky. She'd been horrified to learn her best friend was capable of murder. Paul Ciero also had been shaken by his partner's arrest. He'd sent his regrets for what had happened via her boss. His guilt made her feel worse. But one thing at a time.

Amber lowered her arm and turned her head to face Trent. He deserved to have her look him in the eye. "I thought you weren't relationship material. That you'd always put your work, your career, first. I couldn't have been more wrong. You put yourself in danger to help keep me safe. Even now, you're taking time off to help me cope with all this. I'm so sorry I misjudged you."

Trent took her right hand and kissed the back of her fingers. "You didn't misjudge me. I'm ashamed to admit the man I was when I proposed to you did put his career first. I can't honestly say the old Trent would be here with you like this. He didn't deserve you, Am."

His comment made her chuckle. She really needed that smile. It pushed the nightmare a little further away.

"The old Trent wasn't so bad." Amber turned onto her side to face him. The moonlight sneaking through the curtains covering her windows highlighted his sharp cheekbones and squared chin. "After all, he's the man I fell in love with. Great dancer."

His even, white teeth flashed in a brief smile. "Maybe we could see whether the new Trent has some moves."

"Oh? I'd like that." The nightmare faded more. The tension in her shoulders disappeared.

Trent stroked her left cheek with the back of his right hand, then let his arm drop back to the mattress. "The truth is, Am, you were right to end our engagement. Losing you made me take a hard look at myself. I took you for granted. I gave you the words, but I didn't back those words with action. I told you I loved you, but I didn't show you."

"Words without action are harder to believe."

"I understand that now. It took your leaving for me to realize how much I need you in my life. How much I love you." Trent's tension was like a presence between them. "Amber, do you think you can give us another chance? Could you let me show you this time how much I love you?"

Amber swallowed the lump of emotion in her throat. "You already have, Trent. I believe in your love." She shifted closer to him. "And I love you so very much. I want nothing more than another chance with you."

Amber leaned in to kiss him. Trent's arms wrapped around her, and he pulled her on top of him. Trent deepened their kiss, stroking her lips with his tongue before slipping it into her mouth. She opened to welcome him. Amber's toes curled. Her eyes drifted shut. She sighed. They'd been through the fire, and they'd emerged stronger—and together.

* * * * *

Get up to 4 Free Books!

**We'll send you 2 free books from each series you try
PLUS a free Mystery Gift.**

FREE Value Over **$25**

Both the **Harlequin Intrigue**® and **Harlequin**® **Romantic Suspense** series feature compelling novels filled with heart-racing action-packed romance that will keep you on the edge of your seat.

YES! Please send me 2 FREE novels from the Harlequin Intrigue or Harlequin Romantic Suspense series and my FREE gift (gift is worth about $10 retail). I may cancel anytime by emailing ReaderServiceInfo@Harlequin.com or by calling 1-800-873-8635.If I don't cancel, I will receive 6 brand-new Harlequin Intrigue Larger-Print books every month and be billed just $7.19 each in the U.S. or $7.99 each in Canada, or 4 brand-new Harlequin Romantic Suspense books every month and be billed just $6.39 each in the U.S. or $7.19 each in Canada, a savings of 20% off the cover price. It's quite a bargain! Shipping and handling is just 75¢ per book in the U.S. and $1.75 per book in Canada.* I understand that accepting the free books and gift places me under no obligation to buy anything—they are mine to keep for free no matter what I decide.

Choose one: ☐ **Harlequin Intrigue Larger-Print** (199/399 BPA G3CD) ☐ **Harlequin Romantic Suspense** (240/340 BPA G3CD) ☐ **Or Try Both!** (199/399 & 240/340 BPA G3CE)

Name (please print)

Address   Apt. #

City   State/Province   Zip/Postal Code

Email: Please check this box ☐ if you would like to receive newsletters and promotional emails from Harlequin Enterprises ULC and its affiliates. You can unsubscribe anytime.

> **Mail to the Harlequin Reader Service:**
> **IN U.S.A.:** P.O. Box 1341, Buffalo, NY 14240-8531
> **IN CANADA:** P.O. Box 603, Fort Erie, Ontario L2A 5X3

Want to explore our other series or interested in ebooks? Visit **www.ReaderService.com** or call 1-800-873-8635.

---

*Terms and prices subject to change without notice. Prices do not include sales taxes, which will be charged (if applicable) based on your state or country of residence. Canadian residents will be charged applicable taxes. Offer not valid in Quebec. This offer is limited to one order per household. Books received may not be as shown. Not valid for current subscribers to the Harlequin Intrigue or Harlequin Romantic Suspense series. All orders subject to approval. Credit or debit balances in a customer's account(s) may be offset by any other outstanding balance owed by or to the customer. Please allow 4 to 6 weeks for delivery. Offer available while quantities last.

Your Privacy — Your information is being collected by Harlequin Enterprises ULC, operating as Harlequin Reader Service. For a complete summary of the information we collect, how we use this information and to whom it is disclosed, please visit our privacy notice located at https://corporate.harlequin.com/privacy-notice. Notice to California Residents—Under California law, you have specific rights to control and access your data. For more information on these rights and how to exercise them, visit https://corporate.harlequin.com/california-privacy. For additional information for residents of other U.S. states that provide their residents with certain rights with respect to personal data, visit https://corporate.harlequin.com/other-state-residents-privacy-rights.

HIHRS2603